Praise for
DISHONOR THY FATHER

"*Dishonor Thy Father* is an intricate murder mystery with edge of your seat suspense. It abounds with twists and turns, leading to a stunning final reveal! A real page turner – you'll want to finish it all in one sitting!" –Paul Bernbaum, Writer/Producer, *Hollywoodland,* starring Ben Affleck, Adrien Brody and Diane Lane; *Next,* starring Nicolas Cage and Julianne Moore

"What do you get when you add a driven neurotic cop to a stunning ice-princess surgeon with a mix of murder, mayhem, and lust? A heck of a thrilling read!" –Robert Lloyd Lewis, Producer, *Dexter; Kidding,* starring Jim Carrey; *Goliath,* starring Billy Bob Thornton

"From beginning to end, *Dishonor Thy Father* is an intuitive and riveting novel that will challenge and strengthen readers. Robinson & Richards' murder-mystery explores sexism, racism, and bigotry through a fresh lens that probes far beyond simple themes and played out storylines that readers will struggle to put down." –Jessica Tingling, *San Francisco Book Review*

"A persistently suspenseful crime drama... cleverly composed... provocative commentary on how the past can haunt one's present." –*Kirkus Reviews*

"This dramatic, fast-paced novel tells a dangerous tale like real ones that take place in Iran, Turkey and even sunny Southern California. The female characters are well-educated and dimensional, and an obsessed LA detective is on the case—here they all are, in living, cinematic color!" **–Phyllis Chesler, Author,** ***Women and Madness*** **and** ***An American Bride in Kabul***

"My heart beat a little faster when I read *Dishonor Thy Father,* because I have been to Iran and was mesmerized by the vigor, intelligence, passion, and sensitivity of the Iranian people. And so, it was with great interest that I began to read the story of an Iranian girl, and what happens to her when she comes to Los Angeles. It's a thrilling ride through anti-immigrant sentiment, family honor, love, lust, personal identity, and everything else you want from a murder mystery that takes you deep into another culture." **–Judith Fein, Award-winning Author of** ***Life is a Trip: The Transformative Magic of Travel*** **and** ***The Spoon from Minkowitz***

"An electrifying procedural graced by bold writing." **–Marvin J. Wolf, Author of the** ***Rabbi Ben Mystery Series***

"This story could have been ripped from the headlines. So relevant to what's going on today! I've written my share of thrillers in my time, but none as tightly wound as this one. The characters and plot just fly off the page. Can't wait to see the movie!" **–Bill Taub, Writer/Producer,** ***Friday the 13th-The Series; Dark Shadows; Relic Hunter,*** **Instructor, UCLA Extension**

"A taut, exciting thriller that explores a timely theme, shocking to many." **–James Rossner, Retired FBI Analyst**

"Here is a detective story with a surprising international backdrop. As a world traveler and a native Angeleno, I've experienced the places described in this novel, and know that hidden exotic lurks beneath the surface of every big city. *Dishonor Thy Father* is a fast-paced, twisting trip through a contemporary Los Angeles that Raymond Chandler could've never imagined." **–Paul Ross, Award-winning International Photographer and Travel Writer**

"Murder – racially motivated, anti-feminist, professional jealousy, or family vendetta? The Iranian-American women in this mystery-thriller must confront hate from all directions. Tense and engrossing!" **–Gerald Everett Jones, Author of *Clifford's Spiral* and *Preacher Finds a Corpse***

"Though this story is fictional, thousands of women across the globe are real life victims of honor violence and honor killing every year. Hopefully *Dishonor Thy Father* will help shed some light on this atrocity that is rarely addressed." **–Yasmine Mohammed Ex-Muslim, Human Rights Activist, Author of *Unveiled,* Founder of Free Hearts, Free Minds**

"*Dishonor Thy Father* is a great read. It's a fascinating thriller with romance that takes the reader on a journey across cultures and continents." **–Carole Isenberg, Associate Producer, *The Color Purple***

"A unique and relevant mystery that brings together different worlds in a fresh way. It's cleverly crafted with sexy characters and a thought-provoking premise. *Dishonor Thy Father* has the same kind of exciting dynamic and intense passion as the classic films "Sea of Love" and "Basic Instinct," but with a contemporary feel that's incredibly indicative of today's world." **–Fern Field Brooks, Author,** *Letters to My Husband,* **Producer,** *Monk* **and** *Counterstrike*

"...a rousing mystery that will keep readers guessing...well rounded characters and thought-provoking plot twists...an unforgettable narrative saturated with romance, mystery, perseverance, and commitment...earns five stars for its originality and command of language..." *–Manhattan Book Review*

"…The authors offer jaw-dropping twists until the end. Tami Hoag fans will be pleased." *–Publishers Weekly*

DISHONOR *Thy* FATHER

A Novel

Mike Robinson
&
M.J. Richards

POTPOURRI BOOKS
Los Angeles, California

DISHONOR THY FATHER
Copyright © 2020 by Mike Robinson & M.J. Richards

Published by Potpourri Books, Los Angeles, California
Trade Paperback ISBN: 978-0-9985104-2-2
eBook ISBN: 978-0-9985104-3-9
Kindle ASIN: B08C6Z9FRF

Library of Congress Control Number: 2020911137

Cover Design by Opeyemi Ikuborije
Formatting by Polgarus Studio

www.potpourribooks.com

CHAPTER ONE
Karaj, Iran
1999

AT FIFTEEN, SHE FELT for the first time what she thought might be her soul.

For over a decade she had been in control of herself. There were others, of course, like her father, or Allah, who dictated much of her life, her fate. She was still a child, after all, still malleable, still shaped and imprinted by many hands. And she knew that, even as an adult, such external designs upon her would persist.

But there were places no one else could touch, a refuge of curiosities, imaginings, passions and opinions dwelling pristine within her. She did not know if these things constituted her soul, but they were her solace and, wherever or whenever possible, her guidance. Retreating to them afforded peace.

And then Hassan had smiled at her and she knew something greater. Much of her old self had scattered, been shoved aside and disarrayed. A new, lively spirit had taken her. Her voice stuttered. She shot glances she shouldn't have, tempting herself. Her mind filled with images alternately wonderful and repulsive.

Together they stood in an alleyway, one thankfully not in her neighborhood. Hassan held the bulge of blue plastic wrap out to her.

"I brought some tahchin," he said, unfolding the plastic. The rice cake, golden crust over lamb chunks dusted with saffron, looked delicious. "Mother made it."

Mother, she thought. Like "our" mother. She glanced around. She and Hassan had to act like siblings. The danger, of course, was being spotted by someone who recognized them. So far, only her friend Mahsheed knew about them, the best person *to* know. But even though she trusted Mahsheed, the threat of reveal was always an imminent possibility.

Behind a nearby corner she saw a hazy figure, half-covered in stone. As soon as her eyes drifted to it, the figure retreated. She wondered if they were being watched. Who was it? Someone from school? One of Hassan's friends? Or just her imagination?

Hassan studied her. He clasped her hand. "No one sees us," he said, reassuringly.

Except Allah, she thought. She had dwelled so much on imagining her family's reaction, yet she'd thought little on what it meant for her spirit. But Allah was just and Allah was right, and because this felt right, it had to at some level be of Allah. Besides, His eyes were everywhere—if she had done wrong, what would stop Him from punishing her where she stood? From taking Hassan away from her?

She studied Hassan's face. So much intensity there: the charcoal-streaked eyebrows, the dark pupils, his sharp nose; elegant smile. His face was a volatile mix of thought, dreams, and experience, though at sixteen, most of it was still dreams. She suddenly felt invulnerable, like there was nothing to fear next to his strength.

She picked at the tahchin. Hassan allowed her most of it, relishing her enjoyment. As she chewed, she recognized his desire, and her eyes strayed from his. Guilt hardened her, made her feel more conspicuous.

"I should go," she said.

"Not yet... please," he answered.

He brought his face forward. Close to her. Closer than it had ever been before. He moved his lips to hers. Softly, he kissed her.

It lasted only a moment, but in that moment, she glimpsed an electrifying infinity. The kiss so soft, tender, left a cool burn on her lips. She gazed at him. Joy spread through her.

It was a feeling she wanted again, and forever.

She moved her face closer to Hassan's. She couldn't initiate it, but she wanted it. The tender touch of his wondrous boyish lips—no, his wondrous *manly* lips, on hers.

A quiet thrum of energy between them, unspoken, strangely calming. By his eyes, Hassan reassured her it was fine and that it was right.

But when he leaned in to kiss her once more, she pulled back. "No, I have to go."

He stared at her.

"For now," she said. "Until next time."

He wanted to understand. He did understand, but she sensed the lively new spirit that had rustled to life inside her, disrupting everything she knew, had also rustled to life in him, and that it was more difficult for him to control.

Hassan clasped her arms, gentle but firm.

"Do not be afraid," he said. "We will be together."

They stared at one another, eyes afloat beyond this world. She craved a release.

Not here, she thought.

Then, with further dismay, *Not ever*.

The back door of a nearby bakery opened. She wrenched away and moved off down the alleyway beneath the spindly canopy of telephone wires. She did not look back, only lowered her head and tightened the hijab around her scalp. Her mother had placed it on her when she was nine years of age, while she sat in the small green rocking chair her grandfather had made for her. Her father had watched. They had explained how she was going to become a woman and that interaction with any boys, any men, outside of the family was forbidden. Until marriage.

On her return, her friend Mahsheed was looking at her, face alight with questions she dared not voice.

"I'm not going to do this for you much longer," said Mahsheed. She was uncharacteristically strict, but it was understandable. Surely Mahsheed was jealous.

She said little in reply and they continued their afternoon together, taking pictures with her new camera, a secret gift from Hassan. After school, the girls took it to the back of an abandoned house, covertly capturing each other's smiles.

The afternoon dimmed. It was getting late and all she could think about was Hassan. At some point, she went walking aimlessly down the sidewalk, unmindful of other people or where she was going.

Behind her, Mahsheed spoke, but it took two calls to get her attention.

"Turn around," Mahsheed said.

She did. The camera went off, snapping her in mid-smile. She kept her stance, waiting for another picture, but Mahsheed just stood there and looked at her over the camera.

"I'm not a match for you," Mahsheed said, her voice small, hesitant. "Especially not when you smile."

"Stop that," she said. "You should stop saying that."

"And now, your smile seems more happy than usual... somehow."

The yellow chaos of the sun fell on a window, and the glare hit her eyes. Quickly she dropped her head, as if physically struck.

"I'd better get home," she said. "It's almost time for prayer."

Mahsheed held up the camera at her. "One more."

When she arrived home, darkness had fallen. Her mother was sitting in the kitchen, her back straight, face stern, fingers tumbling over soft bread dough. Standing beside her was her father, looking deflated. He turned to her, his eyes cement.

"What were you doing?" her father said. "Where were you?"

She looked at her mother, who wordlessly advised her to answer fast and honestly.

A noise behind her. Shaheen's boyish head was peeking out from the entrance to the kitchen, his small fingers curled tight around the edge of the wall, nostrils wide with heavy breath. His eyes were serious, but his lips flirted with a mocking sibling smile.

"Shaheen," said her mother. "This does not concern you."

Shaheen disappeared, though she still felt his presence. He could hear everything. He was remarkably sneaky for a young boy.

Her father just looked at her, his inquiry renewed constantly in the air between them.

"I was with Mahsheed," she said. "We were at the library, studying."

She wasn't sure why she twisted the story this way—she *had* been with Mahsheed, after all. Yet she could not say she was out in the streets, because anything could happen out in the streets and her father was not stupid and he could imagine. Of what he knew, she couldn't be sure, not in this case, but perhaps she had failed somehow in her meetings with Hassan, brief as they were. Perhaps she had inadvertently insulted Hassan, and he or his uncle had told her father of her behavior? Or perhaps Mahsheed had said something…

Or someone was watching, as she'd felt. Perhaps another classmate who saw them and…

And told?

"You were at the library?" her father echoed.

She nodded. In the broad wasteland of that face before her, she glimpsed what might've been her father's soul, which, perhaps trapped between love and duty, seemed to plead with her, plead that in fact she had the control here, that she could save the honor of him, herself, their family.

Do not do this, she thought.

But she had.

After night prayer, she went to her room and closed the door. Mother and father were beginning to argue, their voices subdued initially, but rising. She could have listened more closely had she wanted to. But she knew what was happening. They were talking about her. They were ready to reshape her life in a drastic way. Why would she lie to them?

What had she done?

In seeing herself in the dresser mirror, she stopped, looked closer. Hijab removed, her velvet-black hair shimmered down her shoulders, framing her light face—*too* light, she thought. She fixated on her little creases and blemishes.

Mahsheed is wrong. I am ugly.

The memory of Hassan's kiss touched her like a breeze. A small grin formed.

No. Hassan doesn't think so. He likes how I look. He thinks I am pretty.

She brushed her fingertips lightly over her lips. *I wonder what I would look like with lipstick*, she thought. She pictured them pink, then bright red, then looked at her reflection blushing back to her. She shook her head.

She shut off the light, got into bed and lay on her side, staring at the small green rocking chair next to her dresser, the one from her grandfather. It had been there since she was seven years old.

I once fit in that chair, she thought. *I once fit so well.* The child fit so well. But no longer. Things made so much sense then. No longer. More is expected. Less is expected.

Amid her parents' garbled voices, amid the stampede of her thoughts and between the many pictures splayed and shuffled across her mind, she was able to find a spot of peace and rest. It was a shallow sleep.

Had it been deeper, however, she might not have moved in time.

She awoke to the door clicking open. Against the faint light from the front room moved a shadow of generous stature. Her father. He seemed to be stepping back and forth, shifting indecisively at the entrance. His stare was a physical thing on her.

"You are awake," he said.

No you're not. You're asleep. Sleeping.

Her breathing increased. Surely he could hear it as he walked in. With help from the pale moonlight beyond the curtain, her eyes adjusted quickly to the darkness and so, eyelids partially drawn, she followed his path, which ended close to the left side of her bed. Deep shadow pockmarked her father's face, his cavernous features skull-like.

He moved closer toward the window, where moonlight flashed briefly on the long strip of metal jutting from his hand.

"You were not at the library," he said, a detectable crack in his voice. "You were with a boy. You shamed your family. You betrayed Allah."

She took in a heavy breath, as if to recapture the wind those words had taken from her.

Then, he lunged.

She moved.

The first strike found her left breast, though it was a glancing blow. The blade opened a small, bloody gash that shot a fiery bolt of pain across her body, shocking her almost into submission. She scrambled from the sheets, fell briefly to the floor. The dark tide of her father crashed toward her and she grabbed the leg of her small rocking chair and hurled it his way and it struck him. A cracking noise. He stumbled.

Guilt, terrible guilt, exploded in her chest. She wanted to cry and embrace her father, but she had to get away and so she kept on, bounding from her room, through the house, toward the door.

Her attack had given her the delay she needed, yet he roared for her still. He would be close behind. As she ran into the streets, she heard the stirring of the rest of her family, questioning voices, shouts. Above them all, her father yelled her name in a pervasive, hammering tone, a tone that would haunt those walls forever, a tone that made her realize, like a needle in her brain, that she would never see her home again. She would never see Hassan again.

You should stop. This is your family. Your family.

No. No. I cannot—

She kept to the alleyways and dark streets, avoiding the light of the streetlamps, the milling marketplaces or cafes still open. The angle of the moon cut the city of Karaj into irregular shadow shapes, midnight geometry stretched across the buildings. There were other people, other voices, other eyes and other souls, but in that moment they were not real to her. They were apparitions, placed here in this empty maze where only she and her father dwelt, caught in a febrile dream.

Somewhere behind her, he continued shouting for her.

Her throat closed and the heat filled her. The streets were a labyrinthine smear. She was going to pass out—she was going to faint right here in the open. She would be found and delivered.

I'm the farthest I've been from home in so long.

Her rational mind made sporadic appearances, wondering,

gratefully, how she could have so deftly evaded her father. No one had wanted to get involved; even if they had tried, they'd have been unsuccessful. She felt protected, guided by forces larger than she, yet were they? Was it not just her, allowing her soul to guide her, to get away from things that were wrong?

Things like her father.

Her family.

"Allah forgive me," she muttered.

In a desolate alley, she found a small recess with steps leading toward a rusted, locked door. She gathered an old ripped blanket from a nearby trash bin and shifted two crates in front of the recess, where she lay covered on the first rung, holding her bleeding breast, pressing it occasionally for a kind of masochistic gratification.

She looked at the stars, the small outcrop of cosmic gleam she could see, and wondered who else in the world might also be in such pain, and wondered too if they might be looking at the same stars.

Then, for a long while, she cried.

CHAPTER TWO
Los Angeles, California
Present Day

YOU NEVER THOUGHT YOU'D grow this… accustomed, did you?

The patient lay there, the vulnerable nucleus of the room. Dr. Tara White kept a vigilant eye on the bulbous vitals enlarged on the monitor, as the laparoscopic instruments deftly plumbed them.

Across the operating table, she met eyes with Dr. Marika Javid, who, Tara knew, understood her thoughts too well. Though neither would admit it, the growing sense of routine was undeniable. The anxious high of her residency years had given way to a low, habitual ebb. Her surgical career had progressed quickly. She was focused. Meticulous. All this was good, of course, but Tara couldn't help wondering if along the way she'd traded some intangible benefits of fresh nerves and zeal for colder efficacy.

The nephrectomy went faster than expected, the entire pink mass of cancer-chewed kidney removed. The incision was small and so was sutured quick, and the patient—a man in his forties by the name of Gardner—was gingerly wheeled from the room while Tara and Marika tended to the equipment and cleaned up.

"You're handling the family, right?" Marika said, in an almost childishly pleading tone.

Tara nodded. She washed her hands, then headed out of the

operating room toward the double doors through which so much devastation, and hope, had been born.

Emerging in the lobby, she removed her surgical mask.

Gardner's family turned to her. Some stood, others remained sitting, hands clasped. In Tara's sharp blue eyes—stronger reflectors of her thoughts than she would've liked—they saw the neutral expression, and relinquished a collective breath.

"We removed the entire kidney," she said. "Invasion was minimal. He's just coming out from the anesthesia. You'll be able to see him within the next half hour or so."

Gardner's wife, a portly, watery-eyed woman, approached her. Behind her stood an elderly couple, a middle-aged man, and a college-aged boy.

"He's going to be fine?" Mrs. Gardner said.

"The margins are clear," Tara said. "And as we discussed before, it hasn't spread. The other kidney will take over its duties and function fine. Now, in the incision, we had to sever some nerve tissue, so he'll experience numbness in the area. There might also be some discomfort in breathing or coughing, but we'll work on giving him some breathing exercises to do to minimize this. There are also medications he can take, or therapies he can undergo."

"Thank you, Dr. White."

Tara fielded a few more questions. The college-aged boy stepped forward, hands in his pockets. He was pale, and trying to appear casual.

"What's going on outside?" he said.

Tara snapped a glance at him. "What? The protestors?"

"Yeah. They're complaining about foreign doctors."

"Brian—" said Mrs. Gardner, holding a tissue to her face.

Tara shook her head and waved her arms, gesturing to let it go. Inwardly, she didn't. Why was this boy asking about that when his father (or uncle, she wasn't sure), had just gotten significant surgery? Tara thought it callous, but figured it was a distraction tactic, a minor "macho" coping mechanism.

After receiving more thanks, Tara went to change from her scrubs, then returned to her office, once shared with Marika, where she saw her colleague gathering some of the final items to transport to her new office as the freshly-minted Chief of Surgical Oncology.

Marika looked at her with a mildly dramatic smile, like a teenager awaiting the verdict of whether or not someone likes her. Tara felt a twinge.

Goddamn these politics, she thought. *Goddamn these people.*

Yet the sad truth was that, even before the political ruckus, it had been understood on a wordless level that it was best Tara interface with the families. Whether something innate in her character, or the quietly—and shamefully—considered fact of her blonde hair and blue eyes versus Marika's more "exotic" descent, one couldn't be sure.

"Go okay?" Marika said.

"It did." Tara looped a strand of hair around her ear. "Want to get lunch?"

Marika's gaze dropped, surveying the boxes and loose papers remaining. She scratched the back of her neck, over and over. Her excitement for the new job, Tara observed, had taken a backseat to the sustained annoyance of logistical labor.

"Sure," Marika said. "Would you mind helping me carry the last of this stuff?"

After transferring the items to the new office, they walked in silence to the elevator and took it down three floors. They spilled into a long airy corridor, the westward side of which held long adjacent windows offering a panoramic view of Los Angeles. Neither Tara nor Marika could help glancing down toward the courtyard at the front of St. Vincent's Hospital, where a colorful pond of protesters had gathered along with some of their fellow clinicians, milling about with signs. The group seemed to remain thankfully quiet, except when certain staff entered or exited the hospital, or when someone from the media arrived, which was actually rare. Doubtless they were upset their story wasn't getting much press.

Tara, of course, hardly sympathized.

Down the hall, two other doctors watched the scene below: Dr. Raymond Stiles—a silver-haired neurosurgeon—and Dr. Steven Aronson, an ear-nose-and-throat specialist and more Tara's contemporary in age. They were paired tight, mumbling amongst themselves.

Stiles looked askance at Tara and Marika.

"…getting in the way… all these witch doctors…"

"Okay, sorry," said Tara, stopping. "Did I really just hear that?"

With an imperious sigh, Stiles turned to Tara. Marika stood behind her, biting her lip, fingers curled and dancing repeatedly across her palms.

"Hear what?" Stiles said, with an expectant smirk.

"In a twenty-first century hospital, in America," Tara said, "in Los Angeles, did I just hear 'witch doctor?'"

The two men looked at one another, with forced smiles.

"That's not our choice of words," Aronson said, gesturing outside. "It's theirs."

He looked furtively at Marika.

"Dr. Javid is American," said Tara.

Marika bit her lip, took Tara lightly by the arm. "Tara, let's go."

What are you going to do? Tara asked herself. *Throw down a fight?* Part of her wanted to, a larger part than she ever would've admitted. Dismantling in one violent sweep the emboldened resentment, that smugness, on Stiles' and Aronson's faces—more so Stiles—was in that moment worth her career.

Without another word, Tara turned and left. Marika walked

briskly a few steps ahead of her, arms crossed.

Despite average food, Tara admired the playful humor that had named their frequent lunch-stop *Hava Java*. Something about its rhyme was charming. Located directly across the street from St. Vincent's, it was also convenient.

They took a corner table, next to a window looking out on the palm-lined streets and the massive punchcard slab of the hospital looming nearby, its whiteness stark in the low autumnal sun.

"We're lucky they're only at the front entrance," Marika said, with a wan smile. "What'll we do when they think to cover all the doors? I couldn't leave." She blew on her tea. "Of course, it's not like I have much waiting for me outside this place."

Tara felt exposed. It might've been sympathetic anxiety, she wondered. Though, with more eyes lately on Marika, by default Tara also felt conspicuous.

But it was really *that* place, that place across the street with all its raw, untended humanity that got to her. Hospitals were a throbbing nexus of life and death, a paradigm that could easily open people, exposing a questionable, even wretched, core.

At least, that was the more philosophical excuse. In truth, these people were high-schoolers in white coats. Many of them had spent their cognitive budget on the intellect, leaving little room for any real social consciousness. To them, people were three-dimensional extensions of the textbook page.

Their dishes came. Chicken and rice for Marika and a salmon salad for Tara.

"I think I need someone," Marika said, picking at her rice.

"What do you mean?"

"Someone's who's there for me. All the time." Marika lowered her head, shook her head in what seemed self-condemnation. "I'm sorry. Don't mean to rant—"

"You're not ranting."

"I know you understand. It's just sometimes hard being alone. And the job can be so overwhelming."

"It's about to become more overwhelming," Tara said. Instantly she regretted the comment, however true or obvious, as Marika's blank expression was not unlike that of a stunned child's. "Sorry. You know that."

"Of course I know that," Marika said. "I can't wait to get started, really. In some ways it's cleansing, a new slate, right? But I'd be lying if I said I wasn't worried. This new position could abolish what's at all left of my personal life. I mean, is this a turning point? Will I have time for anything or anyone again? I barely have time now, you know." Marika waved her hand in the air. "I'm sorry, Tara, I don't want to dump all this on you."

"Don't worry about it."

"I don't want to sound melodramatic, but I feel like there's a weird, unquenchable black hole in me. I don't know if more work will fill it. I actually don't know what *can* fill it. It just seems to be getting larger."

Tara chewed and absorbed, best she could, unsure how to respond. Suddenly she felt trapped, ambushed by the spiritual pain she was not qualified to counsel. She had never heard Marika reveal anything so deep and personal.

She feels unwanted here.

On impulse, Tara tried for lightheartedness. "Well, you could always ring up the Kid." She tried to temper her smile with an expression of sadness, of understanding.

"No," Marika said. She studied Tara. "Just, no."

After a short pause, Marika chuckled a little, a pinhole release that relieved some of the pressure, and vindicated Tara.

"Sorry," Tara said anyway.

"Do you think I'm getting too greedy?" Marika said. "That I want it all?"

"Of course not."

Marika straightened her back, eyes fluttering about the rest of the cafe.

"But as you say, I have to keep walking the tightrope, right? Not let myself fall too far one way or the other?"

"I was wrong when I said that. We've already fallen, on the work side. We've gotta get back up on the rope."

Marika blinked. "I'm surprised to hear you say that."

"Why?" Tara smirked. "I think having a life is important, too, you know."

"Sure." Marika's eyes went to the window again. She sighed. "It doesn't help that I don't feel welcome here all of a sudden. I always thought medicine was the one area of life where I could never be rejected or unwanted, not to the degree I can be in other areas of life."

Tara shook her head. "It's bullshit."

"And it's hard to believe this crap is happening in L.A.," said Marika. "I thought I'd just blend into the rainbow, so to speak."

"Stop taking it all on yourself," Tara said. "You know it's not just you they're talking about."

"I know."

"And a man never solves anything," Tara said. "Usually it's just more trouble."

"Like taking a new job?"

"Maybe. Kind of. But as you said, a job is more under your control." Tara stabbed at her salad, more meditatively than hungrily. "Of course, it depends on the guy."

Marika widened her eyes in a *we'll see* look.

The rest of the meal played out mostly in silence. Mentally, the day was over for Tara. This had been happening more and more, and earlier, too. She had no more patients that day, just reviewing lab results and returning calls. She anticipated her rock-climb, which she normally did in the early hours before work, but today had postponed until evening.

More than anything, she thought of disrobing these chemical-smelling clothes, of the energetic catharsis of rock climbing, then slipping seamlessly into the warm embrace of a bath.

Rock climbing for her was a test of humanity's innate and curious restlessness. It was petting nature's fur backwards, this climbing straight up. Flying was more universal. And yet with a few knots and buckles in place, it was a challenge easily surmountable.

At the top of the wall, Tara peered down at the evening gym crowd, the milling bodies and the splayed, sweat-soaked limbs at the weights and ab machines. They looked farther away than they were. Somehow, the enclosed immediacy of the gym made for a scarier prospective fall than the wide landscapes viewed from the Malibu cliffs, where she rode her horse Toby and did her outdoor climbing. There she would keep her eyes on the distance, the sloping hills, the light-tinseled sea, a nice distraction from the sheer drop beneath her soles.

Morbid thoughts came to her. How many of those people had she seen, or might she see, before her in the hospital, sunken and pale and pleading? How many on her table, under her knife? Who of these people, despite their toning and cardio, despite any grand future plans, would not last the next decade? The next year?

Such imaginings, Tara thought, might just be the evolution of her childhood tendency to look down on people from distant high places and squint, pretending that, like some unmerciful deity, she could flick them off the Earth. Playing with bugs.

Marika Javid had one more patient. He was running late, too. Dammit.

I want to get out of here.

She bustled about the office, organizing personal items into packing boxes, trying to burn off her agitation. She had been so excited for the job. Had, in seeing the breast X-ray Tara had shown her, suffered terrible concern that fate would so ironically snatch it from her, when she seemed a shoe-in.

But she had made it. She knew she had fibrous breasts. But Tara had been smart. Insisting. If it turned out to be cancer, no one else need know. She would help Marika find out, clandestinely. No paper trail. No big deal. And like that, the lump was gone. No deadly cells left. Tara was thorough and Dr. Javid's secret was safe. Especially from all the gossip mongers in the department.

Now, Marika would be lying if she said she weren't feeling ambivalence creeping up on her. It was a generous promotion, of course, but, quite honestly, she was a doctor, and the Chief of Surgical Oncology required more managerial leadership than she felt she had reason to expect from herself.

Stop doubting yourself so much.

She also wondered if it was worth the outcry, ridiculous as it was. Perhaps the committee had given her the job as a defiant response to the bigotry of some of the staff. If that was indeed the case, then Marika was merely a pawn on a florescent chess board, and all parties were to be resented.

In the dark front lobby of her office, there was a noise. She stopped and listened.

Nothing.

She went out into the lobby, in time to see the wooden front door click delicately closed, shutting out the white hallway beyond. A tickle in her chest.

"Hello?"

This is not worth it, she thought, sitting at her desk.

Again, the front lobby door clicked open. There was a voice. A familiar one.

"Marika?"

"Yes?"

From the darkened room, Dr. Willem Thomas cautiously approached the lighted reach of her office. The Kid, as she referred to him in closed circles. In his doctor's coat, his youth made him look like an imposter, a teenager in costume. Consistently uneasy, the world to him seemed a slim passage of fragile antiques. It had once been an attractive quality, briefly, the way sensitive coffee-house brooders were attractive—briefly. But Marika had found it contagious, and hardly ideal for any kind of real professional. She did not envy his patients or colleagues in radiology.

Thomas smiled an awkward smile. "You get the report I emailed you?"

Email? Report?

"I did. Thank you." She kept her sentences short and clipped, the polite sign of preoccupation. It seldom had an effect on Thomas, though, who would stand there as he did now with that grin, awaiting, craving, more interaction.

"Congratulations on the new job," said Thomas. "I guess I'll be seeing even less of you."

"I imagine I'll be seeing less of everyone," Marika said. "And thank you." She looked at him. His youthful cuteness, that smoothness that made him like a plaything, had contributed to the one night he *had* been a plaything. Shameful. There was only a six-year difference between them, but in the era of the late-twenties to mid-thirties, such difference was almost generational.

"How is Dr. Stiles, by the way?" Thomas asked.

She was able to disguise her reaction, or so she hoped.

He knows.

Marika kept her head buried in forms and folders. "He's… Stiles. Why do you ask?"

"I'd better get going," said Thomas abruptly. "Keep safe, okay, Marika?"

Keep safe? She assumed he was referring to the political turmoil, which to her wasn't really turmoil so much as a stain.

Quietly, Thomas left. She heard the door click.

Minutes passed. She heard the door open once again. She waited but no one entered. She got up to make sure, but the room was empty, the door slightly ajar.

From her office, the electronic gurgle of the phone. She went to get it.

"Yes?"

The caller didn't answer right away. She hung up.

Come time for her last appointment, she gathered the chart and her laptop and made her way down the hall to the examination room, entering with a lowered head.

Then she looked up and he was there.

"Oh, hello," she said. "Wasn't sure you were coming."

"I know I'm late," the man said. "Sincerest apologies."

The man sat perched on the edge of the exam table, hands pressed hard into the cushion, body rigid. She greeted him with professional calm, "I'm Dr. Javid."

The man stared at her, fiercely contemplative, before grunting a tepid, "Hello, doctor."

A fine gloss of sweat shone on his face. His breathing pulsed rapid and anxious from his mouth.

"How are you feeling?" Marika asked.

He nodded. "I'm all right. Nervous."

"I understand."

"I'm just not used to seeing," he stared at her intently, "...a woman doctor."

"I'll be gentle," she smiled, then felt a twinge of guilt, realizing he did not seem the sort for levity.

His eyes bulged with a kind of manic energy, a lost, disconnected look that spoke of many varieties of thoughts or excitements or fears, any one of which was indecipherable in that formless intensity.

"It says here," she said, perusing the paperwork, "you've been feeling abdominal pain?"

He nodded fast, then rubbed the affected area. "I feel something."

"Could you remove your shirt and jacket for me, please?"

The patient blinked, as if not comprehending. While not the greatest display of bedside (or examside) manners, Marika strayed from much eye contact. In the whirlpool of his gaze, some part of her thought she could drown.

The patient remained still, hardened. Ambivalent. Something was odd, like a bottle top that doesn't quite fit.

"I'd like to examine you," Marika said. Suddenly she had been thrust into some titanic boulder-pushing conflict, or so it felt: her simple, universal request having somehow violated all things believed or cherished by this man.

Slowly, he acquiesced. The shirt and jacket slid off, his copper-dark flesh thin and lean.

"You said you felt something there," Marika said, "in addition to your pain." This was a little curious—with the exception of skin cancer, it was unlikely any lay person without some medical knowledge could detect a growth in the abdomen.

"Yes," he said, eyes fixed.

He looks sick.

"Where, exactly?"

With two long fingers he indicated the region. She moved in, halted. His breathing increased, a stertorous rasping, nostrils flaring to the beat. Either a panic attack or something much worse, and very imminent.

"Are you sure you're all right?" she said. "You look faint."

"Okay," he said. "I am okay."

"Here." Hurriedly she went and fixed a small paper cup of water and handed it to him. Another flash of disbelief—or resentment?—crossed his face.

What are you even doing here? Marika thought. *Why did you come to me?*

The patient took the cup from her, downed it. She leaned in and felt the indicated area, pressed. He winced.

"Sorry," she said. "I don't notice anything, though."

"It hurts."

"It could be for any number of reasons." Half turning, she retrieved the stethoscope, his watchfulness now a source of prickly self-awareness. God, how she wanted to be done, to leave, to be out of sight of this man. *Tell him there's nothing at all to worry about and to just go home. Tell him to stop fretting. Tell him to never come back.*

During her early residency on psychiatric shifts, Marika had encountered disturbed people, and had learned quickly in their presence to be vigilant. She wasn't sure if this man was disturbed, but she kept instinctually on guard.

Dammit, why did they let him come late? She could be on her way home now. *It'll be over soon —then I can go.* Maybe the promotion was the best thing to happen. No more having patients unhappy that they only rated a female doctor. An olive-skinned doctor. An "A-rab."

She'd be interacting mostly with other surgeons, not the patients — unless she was stepping in for a surgery…and by then, they'd be out cold.

"Just lay back so I can examine you better," she said. "I'm going to press hard, so you will feel a poking sensation. That's quite normal."

Then suddenly, everything changed. It wasn't her examining him anymore. As she leaned down to press on his stomach, he pushed her on the shoulders. Hard. Fierce. She stumbled backward, shocked at the assault.

Then Marika looked at him and saw it: a storm had settled in his eyes, leaving erect a singular, cold intent. He pulled a knife from somewhere—a pocket, his pants. Really she couldn't tell. But it was suddenly in his hand and looming above her.

He was not here for him. He was here for her.

A static charge went off in her stomach. "Oh my God."

She lunged for the door. He moved after her. He was tall, so tall, though surely the shadows exaggerated his height, as did the explosiveness of his attack. And it *was* an attack—in smears of motion she saw the wild grimace, the primitive eyes. She made it to the door and nearly opened it when he caught her with fierce determination, slamming her head against the door. Blackness spotted her vision. The room swayed. He clamped a spidery hand over her mouth, and as she re-inhaled the screams rising in her throat she thought, *What is he doing?*

But she knew.

He's here to kill me.

The violent dance staggered across the linoleum. With what felt like one of many clawing hands, the man tore at her lab coat, then viciously ripped her blouse under it, raggedly exposing her bra which he yanked down to bare her breasts. *Allah save me! He is going to rape me.* The sight of her naked chest seemed to galvanize the attacker and his grip on her mouth tightened and all she could smell was the expelled rankness of her own terror. Briefly he released her torso and

Marika managed to spasm away from him enough to reach for something, anything, that could help.

A weapon. She grabbed for a top drawer, her hands flailing. Her mind sped from the percussion hammer to the shears to the stethoscope—*strangle, yes strangle him*—

But wait: on the desk—a stapler. She grabbed it and wrenched from his grasp. In turning, her elbow caught him in the temple and he stopped, though his hand still held her clothes while the other brandished the blade. It was at her face now. And he was looking right into her eyes.

She swung the stapler at his head. But he was faster. A swift arc of his arm and a pain unlike any other entered her abdomen, flared like lightning across her system. Hot and searing. Her legs turned rubbery. Once more he plastered a palm over her mouth, stifling her choked cry. A gown of blood draped down her hips, legs, streaking and dotting the floor to which he forced her down as he sent into her flesh yet more of this bladed storm, erupting founts of blood, and then he lorded closer to her face again, pulled her head back and drew a fiery streak across the softness of her throat, a crescendo fitting for the symphony of agony which seemed ongoing, terribly and unmercifully eternal.

Her vision blurred. Suddenly she was light. The feeling of life itself draining, jumping away. After sliding faster and faster on a terrifying descent, this moment now, this static moment of the man over her, the blade dripping with her gore, was a temporary plateau. The seconds slowed long enough to ensure cognizance of them, to instill final clarity in what they now wrought, before she was sent further down, down into crimson darkness.

CHAPTER THREE

TOWARD THE CENTER OF his soft eyes, there was a steeliness, a spirit hardening with years. For Detective Mike Tucci, who had long thought himself too short and too gentle-faced, this was a welcomed trait, because it made people assume he'd "seen it all." And people who assumed such tended to fuck with him less.

Truthfully, however, he had very rarely seen a thing like this. Something about the young doctor's position made him think she was still alive, that perhaps, in attempting some athletic feat, she'd taken a bad fall and was merely resting it off. A vibrancy shone in her face, a sad afterglow of life.

Tucci sifted through his pocket and crinkled open a Jolly Rancher and popped it in his mouth. He knelt by the corpse, careful not to step in the congealing blood, spilt so profusely by the multiple stab wounds about her chest and the hasty slash to her throat.

How do you rip up something so beautiful? he thought.

Around him, blue suits took statements and forensics scrutinized the scene, flashing photos of the body and the disarrayed office, dusting, bagging, sampling.

"We gettin' everyone out?" he asked a nearby officer.

The blue suit nodded, indicating the slow procession of cots and patients wheeling away down the hall. The entire area floor was to be taped off. "Everyone. They're transferring them to different wings, wherever's there's space."

Associate detective David Bashir stood, hands pocketed, by the exam table, unable to withhold from his lean bronzed face the shock or morbid fascination living there.

"Put up a fight, looks like," Tucci said. He knelt by the body. Gloves on, he examined the stapler clutched tight in her right hand. "Went for the stapler as a blunt weapon. Didn't seem like she could do much though."

"I don't see a patient chart anywhere," said Bashir. "Perp may have taken it with him."

A Dr. Willem Thomas had discovered the body. He was a younger man, late-twenties, but carrying on him much of the antsy uncertainty of his early twenties. Pale skin with shaggy brown hair and equine face, he had a vaguely rural, Midwestern air. Tucci had a gut dislike of the young doctor. If he was honest, though, he had been feeling a recent dislike for everyone. Either it was self-loathing projected outward, as Miranda, only a semester into her therapy studies, had once said, or people were just getting worse. But that was forever the cop's problem, wasn't it? Increasing bitterness at the constant dumbness and degradation. Once, Tucci had vowed not to adopt such a mindset. But maybe that was like an unapologetic smoker vowing not to have black lungs.

Dr. Thomas stood there in emotional paralysis, eyes fixed on the floor, avoiding Tucci's as they spoke. Continually, his right hand scratched the back of his left, covering the same area over and over.

"This just isn't real," Thomas said. "I don't... It's just... how could it be real? How the fuck could this be *real?*"

"Did you know Dr. Javid well?" Tucci asked. He saw Thomas perk up at this question, what might have been a defensive gesture. The reaction was visceral, but clearly restrained. There was also the "Twitch," Tucci noticed—that flutter of the eyelid. So often it indicated withheld paranoia. Accompanied by a long breath, as the young doctor's was, it could mean strong paranoia. Of course, this in itself was not a sign of complicity. Many people were walking nerves. But in the doctor's case it could indicate regretful closeness to the situation. To the victim.

"Sure I knew her. I—"

"Know her well, I said."

"What do you mean?" Thomas said. "Like was I friends with her? I don't know. She wasn't really friendly back. I like to think we were friends…"

Plain puppy love in this kid, Tucci thought. Intentions thwarted. Assurances gone awry.

"Who might've been this… motivated?" Tucci asked.

Thomas's eyes bulged. "How the hell should I know? I don't run around with sickos. Neither did Marika. Maybe it was a robbery —"

"Doesn't look like it," Tucci said. Dr. Javid's bag and wallet were intact in her office drawer, untouched. No drugs were missing from any of the cabinets.

Within the space of a few feet, Thomas paced back and forth, moved his hands like an anxious thinker on the edge of a grand thought.

"Someone," Tucci said, "had some serious business with her."

Thomas nodded, still evading eye contact as Tucci studied him.

"You say you talked to her last night?"

"Yes."

"About what?"

"Does it matter? I didn't do this. I cared about her. We were… I don't know what we were. I liked her."

Tucci snorted. "Unrequited love? Jilted lover?"

Thomas rubbed his face. "No. Jesus, you know who you really should talk to is Dr. Stiles. Raymond Stiles. He led the crusade against her. He was the one making things difficult for her. He was sympathetic to the protestors—"

"We're talking about you right now," Tucci said. "Tell me how and what happened when you found her."

Thomas sniffed, struggling hard to suppress more tears. "I was tired of her brushing me off, that's why I came in early this morning." He laughed, absurdly. "I… hooked up with her like half a year ago. Like always, though, it meant more to one of us. Guess who?"

"Uh huh… the cougar cub," Tucci answered. "But you weren't in it just for the fun."

"She seemed embarrassed by it. I resented it. I thought we could be good together, but it got to a breaking point. She wanted to end it. So, whatever, it was a fling."

"And last night?" Tucci probed.

"Last night, I stopped by to congratulate her on her new job, but she was so cold and distant. I went on my way but couldn't let it slide any longer so I decided to come in early today— before anyone else— so I could tell her my feelings, no matter what. I went to her office to wait for her. I was sort of nervous and futzing around, so I just meandered into the exam room. That's… that's when I found her."

This late Doogie Howser, bundle of nerves he may have been, hardly seemed a suspect. Just someone slow in getting used to the fast lane.

"Anybody know about you two?" Tucci asked. "Someone who… might've disapproved?"

"I dunno. There's her office mate, Tara. I mean, Dr. White. They have lunch together and stuff. I'm sure they talk about things. You know women. But… I don't know, Marika wasn't like that. Except I know she felt weird about us. I heard they referred to me as the Kid."

"Was there anyone else she may have been with, you know, had a thing with? That you might know of?"

The Kid shook his head, expression blank.

"Who's this Stiles you mentioned?"

"Dr. Stiles... Raymond Stiles... he's strange. He's a bigwig around here. I know she looked up to him. They shared patient material—he does neurosurgery. But he was one of the first big names to come out against hiring non-American doctors. That is, after the protests began. They started sort of small, but really grew. Once Stiles opened his mouth, others felt okay doing it, too. I felt... I felt bad for her... She seemed so lonely... And she was so beautiful... And..."

Dr. Thomas appeared to be going off on a tangent, forgetting he wasn't alone. If Tucci up and left him where he was, the guy probably would have continued talking, back-and-forthing.

Despite the Kid's clear hurt, Tucci still wanted to punch him, to snap him back to, or up to, manhood. At least the "Twitch" had left his face.

"We're going to need you at the station," said Tucci. "Fill out some paperwork, get your prints."

"Yeah... yeah, right."

Officer Eric Connors approached and relayed Dr. Thomas to another officer, then approached Tucci, a cold defensiveness about him. In his hand was a ledger, scribbled with information.

"Ran down the immediate witnesses," said Connors. "The night clerk, two nurses and a janitor. We're canvasing more. But three of the four said they thought they saw a Latino man, or Hispanic, or whatever. This Latin guy was walking fast down the hall not long after the time of the murder. Night clerk said he stopped to ask her a question in Spanish. She went to get a translator, but the guy left while she was away."

"The fourth?"

"Sorry?"

"What did the fourth witness say?"

"Oh. Said he saw a 'dark man' go down the stairwell. Said he had gloves on." Connors stared at the page, eyes narrowed. "This was the custodian whose name is Emmanuel Garcia. Speaks limited English but even when I spoke to him in Spanish he referred to the guy as *'hombre oscuro'*—dark man."

Other surface testimonies trickled in, some of maddening discrepancy. An orderly thought he'd seen a dark, bushy-haired woman enter Dr. Javid's office twenty or so minutes before the slaying. Physical details varied from mouth to mouth, much to Tucci's mounting irritation. Some were directly contradictory, such as the height: "There was a stocky man in black clothing and a real serious face I saw on the floor," versus "I think he was thin… tall, but crouching-or-something— like he didn't *wanna* be tall, you know?"

Dr. Willem Thomas claimed no sighting of anyone suspicious, probably because he was holed up in his own little corner, stewing in his little crush. He'd had blinders on, as Tucci imagined a lot of people did in places such as these, and especially at this hour, as they followed the singular track of their duties. Much of the faculty here was understandably tired and strained. They'd worked the night shift, some of them taking on double consecutive shifts, and enough occupied them so that anything in between was mere shadow.

As medics prepared the body for transfer, Tucci met Bashir in Dr. Javid's office.

"Chief of Security has been notified," Bashir said. "Be here in twenty."

Tucci perused Dr. Javid's desk. Files were stacked and color-coded and pristinely symmetrical. Amid the outer disarray of paper and boxes strewn about, her desk was an oasis of feng-shui.

Tucci drifted toward the office lobby. "We'll have to see what Big Brother tells us," he said.

"What?"

He pointed to the security camera mounted in the upper west corner of the lobby.

"Got it," Bashir said. "I'm gonna grab a coffee. You want one?"

A veritable media potpourri, St. Vincent's surveillance room contained three rows of monitors stacked atop one another, aglow in their electric indifference, blinking back the cold hollow corners and hallways and offices and waiting rooms. Shadowed people moved like insects across some massive buglight.

Chief of Security Aaron Stanton, a stout African-American man with bold-rimmed glasses and wise gray curls, introduced Tucci to the two guards on duty. Tucci noticed a drained pallor in all of them, and a considerable effort to not betray the shock and the terror they must have been feeling.

"Not long ago we invested in a digital overhaul of our system," Stanton said. He showed Tucci his smartphone, its small screen cycling through feeds from around the hospital. "We have things logged on phones and on the internet. Sadly, in the transition there's been a few hiccups, so we lose a feed from time to time."

According to Stanton, cameras weren't allowed in the examination room, where the incident had occurred, and sadly, the one in the waiting room hadn't yet been installed. Plus, the feed from that floor's lobby, which might have caught the face of any passing suspect, had broken down. Figures—Murphy was, after all, God's favorite philosopher.

The best they could dredge up was the time-coded video from Dr. Javid's office lobby. Tucci watched Dr. Thomas enter and exit moments later. Another camera, positioned farther down the hall, captured what indeed must've been the killer leaving the exam room. Tucci could see only his back, but in the distant jerky pixels, ascertained dark hair, a dark jacket, and jeans.

Notions of any grander scheme dwindled. He sensed this fucker, in the vicious eagerness so evident in his method (a "crime of passion," as went the well-worn cliche), had little foreknowledge of the hospital's security system, and perhaps didn't even care if he'd been caught on video. He might've even uploaded it to YouTube, the way this world was now.

There was also the potential complication of her patient, who could've walked in at any time, unless the perp had contrived some delay. Maybe he did have foreknowledge, a tip from someone within the hospital—an accomplice or relative—privy to the convenient holes. Or did he make an appointment as the supposed patient?

"Let's get all the exits," Tucci said. "They up?"

Stanton nodded and one of the guards at the station, a skinny young black man, began work on pulling up the feeds.

They watched two before Tucci spotted a figure exiting from the east side of the hospital that resembled the one that had left the office. The elapsed time matched, too. Briefly the man came into profile before moving into the sanctuary of shadow. Tucci discerned a tight-fitted ballcap; doubt stung him and he wondered why none of the witnesses had thus far mentioned a hat, though the man easily could have not been wearing it at the time they saw him. The skin was a darker shade, in line with reports of a Latino ethnicity.

Tucci asked for a zoom and multiple stills. Four times he watched the figure walk from the hospital into the grainy darkness, dissolving so swiftly from sight.

Fucking ghost perp, he thought, considering the musings of an old colleague Dick Pervis, or Dickey, as they'd called him. "Sometimes you get 'em," Dickey had said, running his sausage-finger through a jar of peanut butter and licking it clean. "The ghost perps come from nowhere and they go nowhere. They got a shell in this world but nothin' else, and they slide through your fingers and you ain't none the wiser."

Tucci collected everything he could from the surveillance station, his skin prickly, his head full of late-night helium. Coffee-crash was coming on fast, the caffeine weak against an onslaught of post-midnight, early-morning exhaustion. Either he needed several more cups or a nap, if he could sneak one in.

Bashir saw him in the waiting lobby. "You okay?"

Tucci nodded. "Not thinking very straight. I'm gonna grab a quick Z in the car then head to county."

Bashir nodded.

Tucci hurried down the hallway, head lowered. The gazes of passersby rolled over him cold and total, like streamwater over a rock. He took a solo elevator trip to the ground floor and went out into the darkness kept at bay by the hospital's flourescent lights. Probably there was a lounge or something where he might be able to rest, but sleep for him was fickle, and it came best in a place familiar and isolated.

In the dead autumnal chill, his breath was a series of phantoms, lost to the night. Thoughts of Dickey persisted.

"That gets me thinking," Dickey had said. "You know, there can't be heaven and hell, cause that means they got good ghosts and bad ghosts. So why don't the bad ghosts always try to fuck shit up around here and why don't the good ghosts stop 'em?"

"Maybe they do," Tucci had said.

"Maybe. But why don't the good ghosts stop these cocksuckers we get around here all the time?"

"Maybe they're overwhelmed. Or no ghost can touch the living."

Dickey had stared at him over a finger gooped with peanut butter. "Maybe maybe maybe. It's all one giant ass-swelling 'Maybe.' Maybe we're entertainment. Maybe when you bonk off, you go from the show to the stands, and maybe you get to laugh for all eternity. Maybe these schmoes in bags and morgues and graves are just off havin' fun and we shouldn't fucking worry about it anymore."

He was beginning to think she couldn't *not* smile. Having first taken her chronic grin as a flattering flirt, as any guy does when a woman flashes teeth like that, Tucci had begun to think it a tattoo or a clown-grin painted on.

After all, Dr. Lindsey Garb was the goddamn coroner. And she seemed to love her job, maybe perversely. Morbidly. It was good for him. She was here early, here late.

The smell of an autopsy, a potent cocktail of chemicals and rot, was always difficult to acclimate to, but he was getting there. Gray and amphibious, Marika Javid's nude body lay stretched upon the slab, her cleansed wounds reduced to terse, thin lips in her skin. The sight of those stab wounds—eight in total—scattered across her torso like volcanic ruptures, cleaned to their humble-yet-horrific essence, was for Tucci worse than seeing her with blood-soaked clothes. Moving about the body, absorbing each individual wound, he experienced sympathy pains, psycho-stigmata of sorts, knowing firsthand the searing heat of a blade below skin. To know that repeatedly, to know it dragged across the softness of one's throat, could only be unfathomable, hellish pain.

Tucci readied his camera. Garb measured the wounds, a necessary formality even if, with stab wounds, it was unreliable information given skin elasticity and various angles of the blade. It may not have even been a blade, as the marks on the body were often misleading as to the type of device used. Conical objects, such as a tooth-shaped souvenir pen that had once been used as the bloody resolution to a domestic dispute, could leave slits and cuts analogous to a blade five millimeters thick.

The width of Marika Javid's wounds ranged from six to nine millimeters.

"I'm going to measure them again," Garb said. "Once I appose the edges. You'll get all the pics."

"You know me," Tucci smiled. "I like to have my own."

Garb stepped back. "Be my guest, snap away."

Garb placed upon each wound a steristrip, a clear tape always reminiscent to Tucci of the nasal strips Miranda made him wear to reduce his snoring. He began photographing the body, close in and far, a singular and morbid paparazzi. Garb, still bright-eyed, still smiling, unloaded rudimentary details into a tape recorder.

"…entries near the clavicle, top of the sternum, beneath the solar plexus. Unsure from surface analysis if the wounds indicate the full dimensions of the stabbing instruments. Will see once we get in there…"

In quirky coincidence, both Tucci and Garb noticed the area of the body's right breast. Tucci stepped closer and photographed it.

"This looks like a previous wound," said Garb, running a latex-gloved finger over the faint scar. She did this so gingerly Tucci thought maybe she was afraid of rousing the body from sleep. "But it's clearly healed."

From another angle, Tucci took a second photo of the old scar, which he knew could have been anything, from a childhood bike accident to a schoolyard fight.

There was no telling. Never any telling. With one's death being his cause, his industry, his central relation to any victim, everything of a victim's life became about the death, even childhood bike accidents. But that's the way it was, wasn't it? All led to crawling, walking, running, creaking to That Moment, the masterstroke of finality the world intended for us all.

"What about that one?" Tucci asked, pointing.

Garb shrugged as she strapped on a clear shower cap. "Might be surgical. Certainly has the cleanness of a surgical scar. But it's strangely irregular. Could be a biopsy."

Tucci took another closer-in photo of the mark.

If there'd been any intention of gentleness prior, none remained in Dr. Garb's alacritous hand as she made the first incision toward deeper, darker tissue.

In the sun-bleached morning, Tucci returned to St. Vincent's, where he noticed a blue news van parked out front, amid a small crowd and a smattering of police.

Fucking hell. The case was only hours old and already someone had leaked to the media. Or did anyone really have to leak it? The media's eye had already been on the protestors. With these latest developments, it would gorge itself.

He parked and approached the scene. A headache played at his temples. Having eaten nothing since yesterday afternoon, he felt a raw hollowness in his gut that had begun to spread to the rest of his body.

"We have every right to be here!" shouted one of the civilians.

Some held signs. The protestors, he realized. Several blue suits engaged them, arms gesturing diplomatically. Off to the side stood a crisply-attired female reporter, her cameraman and one or two crew members.

"We're just asking that you move to a less high-traffic area," said one of the officers, with calmness only a blue-suited rookie could muster.

Tucci couldn't help admiring the twisted tenacity that had the protestors arriving so early, that gave them the gumption to tussle with officers at such an hour. He had a notion this investigation might not have to extend beyond hospital parameters, that the victim, the suspects, the motive, could all exist within a block of one another.

One of the newspeople approached and he waved them away, telling them to wait for the official press conference later that morning.

The hospital was much livelier, a frenzy of new faces, all so haggard. Undone. Like the wounds sustained by Dr. Javid, impact of the incident had bled fast and wide, seeped across floors and rooms and offices. Tucci could feel it. Hospitals were places to escape or alleviate pain. That such gruesomeness actually spawned here appeared to be a source of terribly unsettling confusion. As though some elementary law of nature had been overturned.

Bashir was stretched out in one of the waiting room lounge chairs, eyes red, coffee cup in hand, nodding off. Tucci bopped him on the shoulder and he righted.

"Colleague's here," Bashir said.

"Who?"

He gestured.

"Dr. White?"

Bashir nodded.

Tucci took a few steps down the hall. When he saw her, he stiffened.

Dr. Tara White sat on a bench in the hallway outside Javid's office, issuing a statement to one of the officers. The pure physicality of the woman was stunning: her solar-gold hair, tied back, the crystalline blue eyes so sharp against the olive smoothness of her skin.

He approached her. Though tempted to sit next to her, he stood. More formidable that way, even when volleying hard candy around one's mouth.

"Dr. White?" he said. "I'm Detective Tucci."

Lightly, she took his hand. "Hello."

She looks remarkably composed.

"May I ask you a few questions? We can go somewhere a little more private if you'd like."

"I gave that officer information."

"I realize. That's a formality —"

Abruptly she stood, only a foot from him. "We can go to my office."

They moved down the hall, Tucci a couple steps behind. He couldn't help but admire her figure, nicely disclosed by the tautness of her coat and her baby-blue skirt.

"I'm very sorry about Dr. Javid," he said, as they entered her office, taking seats across the desk from one another. "I'm guessing she was more than a co-worker to you."

Tara nodded, slowly. "We were partners, and friends. Sort of. We were pretty similar, so ironically that kept us from being too close. Funny, huh? Similarities keeping people apart."

"Would you mind expanding?" *This office is so immaculate,* Tucci thought, furtively scanning the gleaming organization of the place, the perfect stack of forms, the fussed-over utensils and laptop, the tight baleen-alignment of hundreds of folders and books flanking the desk. All business and expedience, nothing overtly personal save for a butterfly motif in the scattered bits of decoration.

"We found solace in each other," Tara said. "Of the faculty here, we're on the younger side. We're also women. I know that sounds like a tired complaint, but it's not. Women of any profession have to work harder to be taken seriously."

Tucci studied her.

"Don't worry," she said. "I'm not about to go off on a rant."

"I enjoy monologues," he said, with a tiny smirk.

"Okay." She looped two blonde parentheses behind her ears. "But Marika and I would joke that we kept one another on the tightrope. We had a kind of pact to walk diligently, balanced, in our careers, and not succumb to personal distractions. Not in these tender years of our 'hazing,' so to speak. So we saw each other only briefly outside work. Neither of us have, or had, a significant other. She was often tempted. I steered her accordingly."

"Sounds like the system worked," Tucci said. "What about family? Any mentions of boyfriends, ex-husbands, confrontations?"

Tara shrugged. "She was never married, and she hardly, hardly dated. From what I gathered, pretty much all her family is back in Iran. I think she might have had a bad relationship with them. Not sure. I know she had some acquaintances through her mosque. But how close she was with them, I don't know."

"She was recently promoted, wasn't she?"

Tara nodded. "Chief of Surgical Oncology. Though I feel it was not just a promotion, more of an honor. Certainly it meant a lot more on her plate, or was going to…"

"As I understand it, some weren't too happy with this honor. And it wasn't because she was young, or her sex."

"I'd say so, yes. God, I hope this whole thing will shut them down once and for all." Tara paused, lost in a strange meditation that had in it a hint of malice. "They were upset about a lot of what they perceived as threats, little things adding up to big things, in their paranoid minds. Marika getting the position was just a big concrete example for them to blow up their stupid cause. Of course, that was sort of the goal of the committee in promoting her, I think. The committee wanted to make a statement."

"And some of the staff in the hospital had problems with that?"

"Believe it or not, yes. Other doctors. Nurses. Patients who thought they saw sketchy things happening here." Tara picked at her fingernails. "It got them only more upset when most people denied them, or ignored them. And before you ask, as much as I dislike them, I'd rather not name names."

"Dr. Thomas did," Tucci said. "He mentioned a Dr. Stiles."

Tara's eyes widened. "Stiles didn't make her life easy. He turned on her, I think. He kept saying he sympathized with the protestors in basic theory, not in specifics. Whatever that meant. He knew she was a good doctor, but he didn't know much about her. None of us did, really. And like any xenophobe, he was suspicious of that. How's Willem doing, by the way?"

The jump in subject disoriented Tucci, but he caught on. "Willem? You mean Dr. Thomas?"

"Yes. He… found her, right?"

"He did. He was a little out of it. Something tells me that's not unlike him, though."

"You don't think he did anything, right?"

"You tell me."

"He was head-over-heels with Marika. That was pretty obvious. Conversations about him that he's never heard could probably come in volumes. People talk around here. Gossip. I think he's got a good heart, though."

Tucci said, "The protestors."

She nodded. "Occasionally."

"You think any of their camp might stoop to this? Maybe to fire up PR for their cause?"

Her entire body heaved with a portentous breath. "I don't know," she said. "I suppose it's possible."

"Dr. White," Tucci said. He leaned back in his chair. He felt oddly comfortable with this woman. "Can I call you Tara?"

She paused a moment, then waved him on. "Sure."

"Tara—were you at all upset yourself with Dr. Javid getting this job?"

Tara crossed her arms. Secrets to protect, Tucci thought.

"No," she said. "Not like the others. We were friends, for God's sake."

"No resentment?"

"Why would I feel resentment?"

"Why wouldn't you? Dr. Javid's appointment was somewhat of a political move itself, wasn't it? As you said."

"I'm not the type to subscribe to that reverse-racism crap."

"Doesn't really matter." The candy in his mouth was down to a slippery nub, and he swallowed it and unfurled a fresh one—watermelon—and popped it in his mouth.

"How many of those do you eat?" Tara said.

He ignored her. "Where were you during the murder?"

Tara looked at him. "You're going after the chicken in the fox den."

"Pardon?"

"I grew up on a farm. It was something my dad used to say when he felt the wrong person was clearly being fingered. There are two chickens in a fox den. One is killed. You're accusing the other chicken."

"I'm not accusing you at all."

"I went rock climbing at the gym. You can check the sign-in records. Then I went home, binged on ice cream, and took a bubble bath."

"I have no trouble believing that."

"What? The bingeing on ice cream?"

"No, the bath. Your skin looks it."

"Thanks. You're secretly pushing for a rant, aren't you?"

"Why would you rant about a compliment?"

Tara narrowed her eyes at him. He found it difficult not to stare at her.

"If you'll excuse me," she said, getting up. "I have no more time now. I have patients."

"Right." Tucci cleared his throat. He reached into his breast pocket and handed her his card. "If you think of anything else, give me a call."

Tara gave him her cell number.

"Thanks," he said. "I'm sorry for taking up your time. But I'm probably going to need more of it soon."

Tara cast her first genuine smile, though it was still hesitant. "I understand, Detective Tucci."

"Mike." He smiled.

"After all, Mike," said Tara. "I imagine our jobs aren't too different."

He looked at her, puzzled.

"Protecting life," she said. "Confronting death."

There weren't many of them, but with their protest signs, they were conspicuous enough. Some held their signs up, though somewhat half-heartedly. *Preserve Lives, Not Politics!* and *This Cancer Has a Cure!* were ones he noticed—they in particular were held at eye level, covering the faces of those who held them.

Tucci strode toward the small group. A few were seated on folding chairs. He glanced at the other signs lying on the ground or propped against a wall, no doubt left there by people who chose to stay home after hearing the news. Those remaining were clearly conflicted in the wake of the murder. Tucci was surprised any of these folks had opted to stick around, though not too.

There were five of them. The most authoritative stood in front, looking lost but determined. Determined exactly about what, Tucci couldn't say. Maybe determined not to look lost. Hopeless cause, though; the man, a younger, pale-faced individual with a volatile demeanor, was patently transparent.

Tucci approached him and flashed tin.

"Ask you a few questions?" Tucci said, slipping his badge back onto his belt.

"We didn't do anything," piped up one woman, a frizzy blonde who looked the eldest of the current group.

"You're doing 'somethin',' I hear," Tucci said. He readied his notepad, popped a raspberry candy into his mouth. "I'm honestly a little surprised to find any of you around right now. You sure it's the best time to be out here?"

"We—well, some of us—figured this was the best approach," said the man. "We couldn't protest as planned, on account of it being disrespectful, right...?"

"Okay." Tucci could tell the man resented his unflinching expression. As if this prick expected brownie points for his lame show of 'respect.'

"But we couldn't exactly all beat feet home, either," the man continued. "Because that would be suspicious. Right? You tell me."

"I would've stayed home," Tucci said. "But then again, you being here is convenient for me. What is it that's gotten you so twisted up?"

"I can already tell which side you're on."

"I don't have a side," said Tucci. "I have a bunch of you with signs down here, and a murdered female doctor upstairs. I've heard you all have been making a bit of a ruckus around the hospital. Don't yell if you don't want to be heard."

"We're expressing rightful concern," he said. "That's all. When you have an open-ended system of political correctness and lax policies, you're bound to get people who exploit that system, people who shouldn't be there. *Here.* It may not amount to much in other areas but this is medicine, goddammit. This is your life and mine. Our lives. Our lives in this country. When you have people from

Harvard getting passed over for doctors from some Saggypants Reggae University in Jamaica, when is someone going to draw a line?"

Tucci smiled, which he could tell irritated the man. "Do you work at this hospital? Or just hangin' around for the fun of it?"

"I did, yeah, I used to work here. I was a nurse. Three years. Most of us worked here, or knew someone who was treated here… or died here."

"Wanna tell me your name?"

The man hesitated. "Carter Graham."

Just then, the man's eyes strayed, fixed on something nearby. Tucci followed his gaze to the small group of passersby, one of whom, a fit-looking male nurse, had stopped to stare blankly at the protestors. The nurse looked exotic, Tucci thought, like he had southeast Asian, maybe Korean, maybe Thai, in him. Far less clear was the man's unthinking, deadpan expression.

"You happy?" the nurse said. "You fucking *happy*?"

The nurse advanced. The group stirred. Tucci could smell the intentions, intentions indifferent to the police presence. He held up his arm toward the nurse.

"I got these guys, okay?" said Tucci. "Back off."

"What do you mean 'got us?'" said one of the women behind him, the one with the frizzy blonde hair. "We aren't under arrest, are we?"

"Means you're fucking history," rasped the nurse.

In a spurt of confidence that probably came from the cop presence between them, this Carter Graham said, "You're the one that's history. You shouldn't *be* here."

The nurse didn't think—nobody thought. No one had time between the second of reflex and the moment of attack, during which Tucci was sideswiped. He quickly regained his footing.

The other protestors shot up out of their seats. The police nearby moved in fast on the fury. As a lame shield, Graham held up his sign, cowering beneath the blows of the nurse's fist which, while of vicious momentum, struck only the shoulders and the back of his neck. People screamed, shouted, the air fluttering with rage.

Tucci moved in and gripped the attacking nurse by the neck, suppressing the man's left arm. He pulled him back, vicariously empowered by the strength trembling through the nurse's body.

Tucci sensed a slow return of faculties to the nurse, the power waning as if he'd begun to fully realize his actions. Yet, perhaps to save face, the man did not stop thrashing altogether, and his elbow struck Tucci square in the face.

The blow was hardly severe, but the ache of his nose sent Tucci stumbling from the scene. The pain vibrated, like fiery guitar cords strung just below the middle of his face. The point of the elbow had struck the bottom-left side of his nose, just above his lip. Cautiously he tongued his teeth, checked also with his finger. None seemed broken or loose. Thankfully he'd finished his last candy before the incident. There also seemed to be no—

Shit.

He dabbed his nose, his finger coming away with a splotch of blood. Blood. Fuck. Streaming from his left nostril. His sinuses swelled, an aching drumbeat on his eyes. He retrieved his handkerchief and sat by the floral decor several feet from the protestors, his head tilted back. The nearby cameramen had mobilized, trained their big dilating irises on the scene. Officers kept them back.

One officer approached him.

"You all right, detective?"

"I'm okay."

This being only the second nosebleed in his life, he was a little more shaken than was probably warranted. It was so funny, the brain, the stuff it chose to be afraid of. He'd felt a bullet whiz past him, felt the heated displacement of air. He'd nearly flipped cars, when he was a teenager. He'd been fucking stabbed, felt perhaps a tenth of the agony that had seen Dr. Marika Javid off the planet. But nosebleeds did it. Ever since he was a boy, the sight of friends' nosebleeds had terrified him, and, with every harsh facial contact, he'd tested for one of his own, dabbing with caution. Then, finally, there'd been that afternoon in seventh grade when he'd torn around that corner and smashed into Eddie Brenner and all his thick red worries had come flooding out, ruining his shirt. He'd thought his brains were leaking out.

Blue suits cuffed the nurse and led him to a squad car. The mania in the man's eyes had subsided, given over to a sad, quiet acquiescence. Two officers addressed the protestors, recommending they leave or move to another location. The newsmen captured it all. The gaunt-faced Carter Graham appeared woozy but whole. He complained of no acute pain but was nonetheless steered toward the emergency room.

One of the protestors, a young woman of about thirty, eyed Tucci. She seemed willing but very hesitant to engage him. He would address her in a moment, once the bleeding had stopped. He was mildly embarrassed at his perceived vulnerability.

Finally, the woman approached him.

"I know a lot of people think we're a bunch of crazy bigots," she said. "But some of us have a good reason for being out here."

Tucci nodded. "I'm sure." He didn't know himself whether his reply was sarcastic or genuine.

"My mother died of cancer two years ago," said the woman. "An Asian doctor here recommended this holistic healer to her, who made her get off chemo. My sister and I were nervous about this, and we asked her doctor and the doctor seemed non-committal, almost. He thought she should keep doing chemo, but seemed to have faith that my mother ought to try this healer first, based on her body and the stage of her cancer, or something. I didn't understand it. Wouldn't you want to throw everything at it? I feel like if my father'd been around he wouldn't have let her do it. But Mom was kinda disillusioned with western medicine, and honestly gullible. She ended up dying a month later."

"I'm sorry," Tucci said. "But that's one doctor giving his opinion, makin' a referral or whatever."

"Maybe," she said flatly. "But it sets a dangerous precedent. Some of these doctors are steeped in cultural traditions. They may not directly administer bogus treatments, but they may recommend them and point patients in certain directions; y'know, do it indirectly. And we're not overreacting. It's a problem that involves our health and our lives, and the health of our families."

Hesitating, he said, "What do you —"

Tucci glanced up, saw the woman had moved away. He lowered his head again and sat for several more moments when another female voice, this one more familiar, brought him back up.

"Detective?"

Tucci looked. It was Tara—Dr. White.

"Doctor?" he said.

"What happened?" She stepped closer. He hoped she wouldn't. "Are you okay?"

"Sure. Just an elbow to the face." He watched for a recoil, a gasp, but there was none of that from Dr. White. A distant piece of him was disappointed. "Got caught in a minor scuffle out here a moment ago."

"Someone wasn't cooperating?"

While her expression remained unchanged, Tucci noted a slight tongue-in-cheek quality to the question. Taken with her obvious empathy, it was a strange mixture.

"No. Not exactly."

"I understand."

Understand what, Dr. White?

"I thought you had patients," Tucci said.

"I did. I had a consultation. I need to get out of here for a while, though."

He looked at her. There were fathoms to this woman, but then, what else could one expect from someone who dealt in cancer? Tucci could also readily admit the affect of noir lore in his stirring curiosity: the breathtaking dame, the rugged cop—or, in this case, the candy-addicted, bloody-nosed cop.

"Let me know if you ever need anything, detective," she said. Her tone was more amenable than it'd been in the interview not an hour ago. "Like a fresh handkerchief."

"Thanks."

Tara walked away. Tucci's gaze followed her through the bustle. Near the curb she turned and gave him a wan smile, then continued on. His expression, largely veiled by the handkerchief, went unchanged.

❧

Chair Department of Surgery, Dr. Janice P. Parsons was dwarfed by her own energy; the anxiety that glutted her office clouded every word. Stylistically, she looked like someone out of the sixties or seventies. Tucci was reminded of his ex-girlfriend Miranda's neighbor, who not only shared Parsons' bob haircut and full palette of makeup, but a prideful, irrevocable bitterness; what Tucci privately referred to as the Cat Lady Syndrome, or at least the beginning of it. She was the type to choose teams quickly, and to designate in moments whether one was with her, or against her.

"Thank you for seeing me, Dr. Parsons," said Tucci, taking a seat.

He sniffed hard. His nose was clogged. Sinus pressure thickened behind his right eye.

"We're all in absolute shock here," Parsons said. "Something like this… you know, I feel responsible. In some ways." The latter portion she added hastily.

"How so?" Tucci said, though already he had a good sense of why.

Parsons sighed. "It was my responsibility to present her with the appointment. I'm almost certain that's why she was… God, I can't even bring myself to say it."

"I'm sorry."

"I never thought they'd come to this level —"

"Let's not jump to conclusions, Dr. Parsons." He popped another Jolly Rancher—cherry—into his mouth. There were only two left in his pocket. He'd have to stock up later.

"It's difficult not to," she said. "Mr. Tucci, I'm very much a believer of attitude into action. There are forces in this hospital that, to put it bluntly, affect the health of everyone, mentally and physically, and in turn affect those we're trying to help. It's honestly like a social disease."

"How long has this been a problem? I'm guessing it wasn't just centered on Dr. Javid…"

"Of course not. It did flare up when she was appointed Chief of Surgical Oncology. But truth be told it's been building. There's kind of an old boys' network in this hospital. Combine that with reflexive scientific arrogance in the face of alternative therapies, some of which were starting to be introduced… um, it was a flammable mix, I suppose. But as far as I know, Dr. Javid was very westernized, very by the book. It was one of the reasons we gave her the job."

"It wasn't a response to the complaints?"

"To a degree. But look, that's not my M.O. I hate to start fights, but if there's a fight going on around me, I can throw a punch if I have to. But Dr. Javid was very officious, too. She took courses in human dynamics and management. I was impressed with her."

"Was there anyone you can think of that seemed more on the fringe? Anyone who made out of line comments or threats?"

"No one specifically, though it was easy for me to tell who stood where. In fact, I remember... a former colleague of hers, a Dr. Osman, also a cancer surgeon—Dr. Patrick Osman. He mentioned to me—I think it must've been about six months ago—that he was concerned about Dr. Javid. He had a smugness when he talked about her, and I knew he was friends with Dr. Stiles, one of the more vocal... um, dissenters, I guess.

"I asked him what he was concerned about. He said he was afraid Dr. Javid was emotionally unstable. He said he'd heard her ranting on her cell in a foreign language. I'm guessing it was Farsi—and that she started to cry afterward. The fact he even mentioned the language thing was weird. I assumed he was trying to be subtle about it. To make me think about her competence or reliability or something like that."

"Any idea why she might've been crying?"

Parsons shook her head. "That was her business. The way Dr. Osman told it, it didn't sound like anyone was supposed to hear or know about it."

"I'd like to talk to him — Dr. Osman."

"I'm afraid you won't be able to. He passed away last month. A stroke."

Tucci thought about Tara—wondered if she knew anything about Marika's crying jag. He suspected she didn't, given the hard-shelled doctrine of "no personal distractions" that White seemed to promote. Despite their friendship, Dr. Javid likely would have been embarrassed about confiding in her, whatever the problem.

St. Vincent's appeared to attract, or breed, tough and

independent (if a touch paranoid) women. While half of Tucci admired this burgeoning portrait of focus and tenacity, the lesser half wondered if these women just needed a good solid fuck.

After several more questions, Tucci wrapped the interview.

"Where can I find Dr. Stiles?" he said.

Parsons jumped slightly, as if at a static shock. "He's in neurology. Sixth floor."

In leaving, he took the last candy and whirled it around his mouth, its clicks against his teeth apocalyptic in his skull. He went to the sixth floor neurology wing but found Stiles wasn't in. He took one of the cards available at the desk.

A familiar sensation, never missing from a new investigation, began to boil up within him. He closed his eyes, took a deep breath.

How the hell do I do this? How the hell did I ever do this?

Of course, he knew the utter egotism in thinking he was solely responsible for such cases. Silly as it might be, though, part of him needed to feel that way, that he was the only one on the path, the only one holding the magnifying lens to the footprints. Yet this mild delusion, while giving the job a kind of divine weight, invariably threatened to overwhelm him in the beginning of a case, when the path branched off into numerous hazy possibilities, and he stood bleary-eyed at the trailhead.

Rape tests were clean. Maybe perversely, this disappointed Tucci. It frightened him more, too. Having rape in the equation, vicious as it was, would have familiarized the case, categorized it as something mostly primitive, free of complex legwork and politics. A former lover, an unknown stalker, coming in and launching himself at her, not intending to kill her until faced with violent resistance: such a scenario was simply easier.

He was now looking at something even more premeditated, someone who had chosen her, despised her enough to succumb to such a gruesome and, Tucci thought, desperate remedy.

Only a year prior to her death, Dr. Javid had put down the last signature for a studio condominium. The finality of it—that she should desire, or assume, nothing more in her life —struck Tucci as a little sad. Javid made good money, certainly, but wanted nothing of a larger place, nor anyone with whom to share it.

Perched on one of the earthen ligatures of the Hollywood Hills, the complex, in its sleek, metallic facade—"so po-mo," as Miranda would have said—seemed to Tucci more like a top-secret facility.

He understood its appeal to Dr. Javid, who, in personal design, indicated a taste for minimalism. What was with these doctors? Maybe there was something about cancer surgery that inspired preference for the superlean, the streamlined. The catharsis of cutting out invasive masses carried over into lifestyle, into carving everything into aerodynamic sharpness, ostensible control.

It didn't take long for him and Bashir to make their way through the place. Tucci had a creeping notion that Marika Javid had in fact set it up in such a way to streamline any inevitable investigation. This idea of dark foresight on her part came mostly from her phone logs and online records, all of which she'd cleared. Probably paranoid. They'd had to elicit her logs from Verizon.

With the brewing climate at the hospital, some paranoia was warranted, but there seemed more here. Shadow-worries beyond the obvious.

In manipulating a folder beneath the living room desk, a tri-folded paper slid out. A letter, written in...

Tucci called Bashir over and handed him the letter. "This Farsi, I take it?"

Bashir nodded.

"You read it?"

As Bashir's eyes crawled across the lines, Tucci watched for a reaction but the young man (or young*er*, dammit), gave none, until the end when he perked up, as if with fascination.

"What's it say?"

"Dear Aadila —"

"Do we have an Aadila here?" Tucci said. He went to the only photo album they had found—barely half-full—and flipped through it. Bashir stood beside him. Mostly they were old photos, some even Polaroids. The front photos in which Marika was featured were washed out, taken years ago in another world, another life. Her dark headscarf starkly highlighted the caramel tenderness of her face.

The album's chronology leapt from the distant past to a much more contemporary, and relevant, period. There were photos of her medical school graduation, a shot of her at some gathering, smiling and clutching a drink, and a group photo outside a mosque.

Do Muslims drink alcohol? He knew Bashir did, but Tucci couldn't be sure.

"Aadila Zuabi," Bashir noted, pointing out a name scribbled in Farsi. "Third from the left."

The woman wore a diminutive grin, like she had a daily allotment of smiles and was conscious not to exhaust them. Next to her was a man of strict countenance, utterly bankrupt of smiles. Marika stood on the other side of the group, beaming.

"What's the letter say?"

"Dear Aadila," Bashir read. "You are my friend, and I cherish your presence and your devotion, regardless if the distractions of life or career put us out of touch for long periods. You are always there for me and you know that I am always here for you. I don't want anything to upset you. But after our last phone conversation, I feel I must speak from my heart. Please know I am only being honest.

"You disapprove of my ways. Liath far more so. This is not new to either of us. Forgive me if I exaggerate, but I believe you think I've sold out my faith, and I want to assure you I have not. Perhaps you might say I'm too Americanized. But Allah is everything, right? Allah is in every person, in every country. What difference then, I ask you, does it make of the culture in which I choose to live? Of course, saying Allah is in everything is like saying the parent is in the child—while the parent created the child, and the parent's blood runs in the child, they are nonetheless two separate beings with separate minds and separate wills, and there is no guarantee of the child obeying.

"You might believe I, as the child of Allah, have disobeyed Him. But I do not believe so. I do not believe our relationship with Allah is parent-child. Forgive whatever blasphemy you might perceive, but I believe we *are* Allah. We are the cells that compose His body. Islam knows this and asks us not to so much 'submit' to a father, but rather to accept our identity as Him. To pray five times a day is to acknowledge our inextricable part in the divine, to never live separate from it, to never forget it. To the same ends, other faiths practice mindfulness, or meditation. There are many roads to mercy and to peace, and to love, and all roads lead to Allah. Not just yours, not just Liath's.

"I pray you understand," he read. "Love, Marika."

Carrying from the apartment only four boxes of materials—mostly files, bills, any correspondence and Dr. Javid's only photo album—they sat it all on the backseat of Tucci's sedan, next to several other records they'd taken from the hospital.

Tucci nestled into the driver's seat, Bashir beside him. He started the ignition and drifted toward Mulholland.

"Choir practice?" Tucci said.

"Sure."

They entered the main road, snaking dark and long through wilds and wealth.

"O'Brien's?" Bashir said.

Tucci gazed out the window. "Kind of feeling a new place, actually."

"Where's that?"

"I'll tell you. Just keep going."

Save for one or two westbound headlights, they were alone upon this narrow, pale-lit road that wound across the top of the city. The contrast was striking: side by side sat hyper-modern affluence, aglow in self-aware security, and the gnarled bush untouched for millennia. Wilds and wealth, yes. Between these two ends had accumulated a history that lived and watched and was palpable, a construct of glory and broken souls and dreams that was the painfully compacted soul of Hollywood. Tucci had not been up here in some time. He appreciated its power.

Tucci had seen Los Angeles through a child's eyes. Teenage eyes. Man's eyes. For so long now, through a cop's eyes. All pores open, all veils lifted. The city was in him, the city was a constant wonder and it was a chronic disease. The United States of America had been dubbed by its founders a grand experiment; it had been an experiment driven by the deepest desires for freedom and for unity, because unity was, after all, the ultimate freedom: the relinquishment of fear of another. In many places in the country, however, such drives seemed to have thinned out, but in cities like Los Angeles the experiment persisted, the concrete petri dish still swarming, the tall glass-and-steel test tubes still bubbling. Ready to explode? Maybe.

Who the fuck knew.

They took window seats, in full view of outside passersby and the high-ceiling lobby, where a chandelier hung like some crystalline uvula over a marble fountain, where people, many tired with travel, milled about toting bags and suitcases. Not twenty feet away stood the hotel bar, from which they'd gotten their drinks, a Jack and Coke for Tucci and scotch for Bashir.

"Kind of classier than I was expectin'," said Bashir. "I like it, though. Quieter than O'Brien's."

"O'Bie's ain't bad," Tucci said. "Depends on my mood. I like to watch the people here. A lot of them are a unique kind of people. I been here so long I don't know what to feel about this city. But the people coming in and going out—I like seeing the city in their faces. What they think it's gonna be like. What it does to them."

"You know, I'm beginning to think that for a cop you actually think too much." Bashir looked at him amusedly, adjusting his tie and sipping from his glass.

"Thinking's all I have."

"Yeah but there's a limit. You can think yourself right over the cliff if you're not careful."

Tucci nodded, his gaze unbroken on the street where darkness drifted into all hollow places, the streetlights burning like giant pebbled cigarettes. "I got a lot of thinking in me that I gotta direct somewhere or else it's all settling in the wrong places." He looked at Bashir. "Like you."

"What's that?"

"You're still thinking about Dr. Javid."

"So are you."

Tucci took a long sip of his drink. Good time to stop that bullshit. And of course he still dwelt on Marika Javid. Heavily. Some homicides were packages, others people. His increasing years had rendered more and more of the bodies mere packages, soul-deadened deliveries from dark corners, so many alike. Those who transcended this belittling label—people—were nowadays especially distinguished. What had Dr. Javid done to deserve this dubious honor?

"You hear, by the way?" Bashir asked.

"Hear what?"

"Olin."

Nearing the end of his drink, Tucci swirled the glass, shifting the ice. "Yeah, 'course I heard. The hell can I do?"

Tucci kept his eyes down, not wanting to meet those dark pupils of Bashir's.

"Maybe buy an extra piece," Bashir said. "If you haven't already."

"He ain't going to come for me."

"How do you know that?"

In seconds, Tucci reran these past five years since Zedd "The Mouse" Olin had gone to prison. Whether from current distractions or drink, or something deeper, he struck a wall in his memory. Most of that half-decade in between he realized he couldn't recall, that it was a stone strip of weeks and months through which occasional memories winked from occasional cracks.

Olin was being released. The fucking mutt was getting out.

"I don't know," Tucci said. He put his glass down, popped a raspberry Jolly Rancher into his mouth. "But you don't spend healthy days waitin' on the flu. Flu's gonna come, it's gonna come."

Thankfully, Tara's last patient canceled, likely spooked by the now-public news of Marika's death. She was able to go home earlier than expected.

While normally she took the elevator to her floor, tonight she climbed the stairs; the slower pace, the mild rigor, somehow jibed with her mood. As if she wanted to burn off her thoughts. But that was impossible, of course—these thoughts would fill every shadowed crevice, tail each waking thought, infect her dreams. Such was the price of closeness, she thought.

Tara had encountered much death, but Marika's would be with her for a long time, probably forever. Of course, adding to the impact was the particularly savage manner of her demise, so at odds with the usual, final exhale of a patient.

Her hope of not running into anyone was, as usual, instantly vetoed by the universe. Her neighbor, a man five years her senior named Randolph Malick, was on his way to the elevator, a cigarette behind his ear.

"Hey Tara," he said. "How are you? Susan was telling me she heard something about St. Vincent's on the news today. Are you okay?"

"I'm okay," she said.

The dazed way Randolph would stare at her during conversations made her uneasy. She could see, distantly in his eyes, the secretly-held turmoil of a mid-life crisis. She sensed numerous creepy fantasies playing out in his head, particularly ignoble given the man had a wife and two young children.

"I'd rather not talk about it, if it's all the same to you," she said.

Randolph gave an exaggerated nod. "I got ya. Just let me know if you ever need anything. Me or Susie."

"Thanks."

She started once more toward her door, but he reeled her back.

"I know I should quit," he said, taking a drag on his cigarette. "Here I have a cancer doctor right across the hall from me. 'Course, maybe that's why I don't quit."

Tara just smiled, vaguely.

"But I'm heading on down to get the mail. Figured it'd be a good time to light up."

Leave me the hell alone.

"Did you have a good time in San Diego, by the way?" he asked. "I don't think I've really talked to you since then."

"I did. Thanks."

"You said you have family there…?"

Randolph's apartment door popped timidly open and his son, about eight years old and clad in Spiderman pajamas, emerged as Tara's savior from this conversation.

"Daddy?" he said.

"I'll see you later, Randolph," Tara said. She swooped into her apartment before he could properly finish his reply.

She was alone.

Marika is dead. You will never see her again. You will never hear her voice. Talk to her. Have lunch with her.

She went about the apartment switching on lights, trying to diminish paranoid stirrings within. In unloading loose items from her pockets, she came to Detective Tucci's card and paused. She placed it on the edge of her nightstand.

She didn't notice the kitchen until she emerged from the newly-lit bedroom.

A recently purchased baguette she'd left out on the counter had been gnawed upon, the wrapper torn open, the telltale crumbs of a little feast scattered across the marble toward the sink. In the nearby fruit bowl, two plums and a banana also bore the irregular nibble-marks of what could only have been an investigative rodent.

Tara stared at the vandalized food, and started to cry. Fucking ridiculous, she thought, Marika dies and there's not a single tear—but a rat helps itself to some bread and…

The tears came fast and hard, so much so she had to steady herself on the way to the couch, where she slumped down and sobbed.

It was the invasiveness, is what it was. Her world, her refuge, had been invaded. The world of the hospital had been invaded, and here, albeit with a comparably tiny example, such malignant agents had reminded her that the world of her home was no different, no safer from the blood and the filth. Vermin could come and go as they pleased, ravaging and taking what they wanted.

Tara drove to the store, bought several traps and put them out near the kitchen. In adjourning to bed, she closed the door and left the light on, but it was her anticipation of any noise, whether a soft rustle of the rodent's return or the snap of its demise, that kept her awake long into the night.

CHAPTER FOUR

IN REGAINING HIS COMPOSURE, it always frightened Tucci a bit just how easy it was to project all aggression into the singular focus of that limp, ten-pound bag hanging before him. Likewise, he could fold everything of himself into his inner-reptile, collapse all but some burning portion of his lower self to unleash with abandon all violence once imagined, wished or willed.

There was physical catharsis, sure, though, ultimately, little was actually assuaged. Once the endorphin high wore off, that pesky Mike Tucci, that Tucci that spoke, reasoned, opined, would cloud him once more.

His last round he went full at it, deliriously pummeling the bag, his arms no longer attached but things shooting in raging release from his person. Sweat shone, streamed, flew. It was addictive. Then, black spots appeared on his vision and Tucci stopped, bending at the waist, the gym around him on a sickening sway.

Enough.

He threw a towel around his neck and sat down, head lowered, eyes closed. From an Arrowhead bottle he squirted water into his mouth. He felt drunk, though enlivened. Was this what they meant by "drunk with power?"

He chuckled.

Tucci stood and made his way to the locker room. Over the

squeal-and-clang of the lockers, voices carried loud and raucous. Booming laughter. Shop talk. Titties and pussy talk. The air stained chemical-sweet with chlorine and the raw earthen odor of bodies and simmering sex. In locker rooms, he'd always thought, words and ideas had smells.

He thought of Dr. Tara White, even as he told himself not to. Not now.

Not like that.

Tucci showered. As he lathered himself, his fingers ran gently over the loose S-shaped scar in his lower right abdomen, which he would nowadays say came from an appendectomy. Having once taken a kind of macho thrill in telling the story, relating to gratifying squirms and winces the feel of a blade in his tissue, the agony of its twisting, Tucci had fallen to a tired humility about the whole thing. Even that, he thought, might be giving himself too much credit. Likely he was just getting old and fucking lazy about telling stories to beef himself up.

Beneath the bumpy tracing of his fingertips, he felt a small protrusion by his shoulder blades. It seemed new. He shut off the water and stood there, fingering it. It was attached. It had come from him.

Tucci dried off, returned to his locker, dressed his lower half, then went and stood before the long array of sinks and mirrors. He glanced about: one guy shaving, the other leaving, scrubbing his head down with a towel. From a nearby toilet stall bellowed a truly triumphant shit. He leaned in close toward the mirror and turned awkwardly to glimpse whatever was on his back.

A dark mole, that was his first impression. Probably what it was. But wasn't dark bad? In a certain light this thing almost looked black. The more he studied it, the more irregular it looked, too.

Shit. A freak windstorm battered his brain. What was up? What was fucking *up*? Couldn't things just *stop*? Didn't Whatever It Was have a sense of enough?

Tucci pulled himself away from the mirror, splashed his face with cold water, then went to dry off.

"Hey, Dad, I'm here."

The first surprise: the minor pile-up of dishes in the sink, some of which, judging by the congealed sauces and encrusted food, looked to be several days old. Tucci put the two bulging grocery bags on the counter.

From the other end of the house came the reply, "Yeah!"

Tucci removed his coat, hung it on the back of his chair in the dinette then headed down the long dim hallway. His own faces of five, ten, twenty or more years ago smiled or laughed at him from the pictures hung on both walls.

His father, Dan Tucci, sat at his desk in the den, clad in his bathrobe, glasses perched at the end of his nose. As the blinds were shut, the thin slivers of sunlight proved weak complements to the throbbing computer monitor, the room's main source of illumination.

"Hiya Mikey," Dan said, turning only half-heartedly as Tucci entered. "Sorry, I'm almost done here."

Tucci went over to one of the blinds. "You're not going to recoil like a vampire if I pull this up, are you?"

"No, but I'm almost done here, like I said."

He drew up the blinds halfway. A rush of late-afternoon sun flooded away the shadow. "Dad, what's with this old-man cliché?"

Eyes mostly focused on a website, Dan said, "What do you mean? I *am* an old man."

"Sitting in the dark in your bathrobe with the dishes piled up. I shouldn't be at all worried, should I?"

"Hey, if I spiral into dementia, it'll be by my watch."

"After you're rich."

"After I'm rich."

"Your place is opening soon, right?"

Dan turned to his son, tilted his head to look through his glasses. "Just two weeks. I'm lookin' over the website now."

Tucci glanced at the screen. For a year now, his father, alongside a group of his white-haired golfing buddies who called themselves The Eagles, had invested in a franchise called *Chago*, which, after ten years of filling blocks in San Francisco, had made its way to Los Angeles.

"This stuff is Mexican and what else?" Tucci asked.

"Korean," said Dan. "And bits of Italian."

"Have you ever had Korean food, Dad?"

"I went to a McDonald's in Koreatown, once."

Tucci smiled, shook his head.

"This is going to be big, Mikey," Dan said. "I know, I know I've said that many a time before. But this…" He made a clutching, arthritic gesture with his fingers, as if holding a crystal ball. To Tucci he looked like a cartoonish supervillain, still trying for conquest well into old age.

"This is gonna pay for my funeral and yours."

Tucci blinked. "Thanks, Dad."

"You know what I mean. Way down the line."

"Let's hope."

In his father was a childish glow very familiar to Tucci. He enjoyed seeing the old man excited—especially at this age, when most fathers might be cursing (or forgetting) the world. In Dan Tucci thrived still the fiery, youthful notions of seeing every corner of the world. In Dan Tucci thrived still the genetic guarantee, innate to most Americans, of supreme wealth in this lifetime.

"I brought salmon and pasta for dinner," Tucci said. "Want to help me clean the dishes?"

His job being what it was, for a long time Tucci hadn't really had pursuits or hobbies of his own. The more this persisted, the more he became aware of a lack, of having lost some dimension of his humanity.

Tucci considered practical hobbies that also satisfied base needs, thinking back to a patrol officer he once knew who claimed sex amongst his hobbies. While Tucci wished sex came regularly enough to call it a hobby, he did enjoy food—good food—and, when the opportunity presented itself, he did enjoy cooking. It proved a form of meditation.

Cooking alone, however, eliminated a necessary element. He needed an audience, even of just another, and had every Wednesday evening found one in his father.

They ate in the dinette. The nineteen-inch television before them flashed a rerun of some old 70s sitcom. Conversation was minimal. Tucci was glad for the wine he'd brought.

"How's Charlie?" Dan said.

"He's doing fine. I haven't seen him in over a week, though. We're supposed to get together Friday."

"I see."

More silence. His father seldom asked about his job.

"Dad," he said, "I'm sorry if I've been short or anythin' like that —"

Dan waved him off.

"You know, I think it's good you got something going again," said Tucci. "With this restaurant thing."

"We'll see," Dan said. "Just hope this one works out. I think it will. I've been needing to get my hands dirty again. Got that itch you know. A man always needs something. And plus…"

"What?"

"I been feeling her lately. Like your mother's been tapping me on the shoulder and I turn around and she's not there. Not really. Not saying I'm seeing ghosts. I just—"

"I know what you mean. I've felt her, too."

Tucci studied his father.

"You know it?" Dan said. "Craziest thing, that's for sure. Even crazier… I still want to impress her. I know, right? I think that's why I need to move. I gotta do something. My reflex is to still give her things. To know I'm there for her."

He admired his father's spirituality, if it could be called that. Never one for fervent belief of any stripe, Dan Tucci had always approached life practically, with a calm and unbroken assumption, sans drama, that "something else" was just out there.

"She used to say we're all here to peel away the lie, to get at the 'big truth,' as she called it," Dan said idly. "Not even sure what exactly she meant by that. Not sure she did, either."

Tucci nodded and drank his wine. He thought he might have something to say to that, but just remained silent and continued eating.

Slowly the marine layer eddied in, tinting in gloomy shade the hills and the oak trees and the solemn faces gathered about the body wrapped in white cloth.

Tucci stood at the perimeter of the crowd. Here in the Islamic section of the Roseland Cemetery, Dr. Marika Javid's funeral was taking place, and, despite the media attention, despite the sizable melting pot of people attending (all of whom, Tucci estimated, could be generally categorized as either a colleague or fellow faithful) the event felt small, fragmented. Standing next to him, observing it all through a stoicism that was a fine meeting point between the cop and the solemn Muslim, was David Bashir.

Next to the body, the imam, standing away from the crowd, led the gathering in the *salat-l-janazah*, the prayers. The congregation kept their heads lowered, as did Tucci, though his eyes remained open, surveying all those before him. Through the lumpy forest of scalps and veils he caught the golden gleam of who he thought might be Dr. Tara White.

Following the prayers, younger males of the mosque picked up the body and, along with the imam, took it away to be buried. The rest of the congregation began to scatter. A somber hum of conversation took over.

Staying toward the back of the crowd, Tucci watched Tara. She kept her head lowered, making furtive, almost embarrassed eye contact with those around her. She seemed to actively avoid one person in particular, a tall Middle-Eastern man of about forty.

He was about to approach Tara when a young dark-skinned woman, head wrapped in a black veil, beat him to the punch and pulled her into a conversation. With quick scrutiny Tucci recognized the woman as Aadila, the friend from the album—and letter.

He surveyed the drowsy, mingling crowd. The faces were so detached. Only a handful of people, including Janice Parsons, were visibly upset. Tucci paid particular notice to Dr. Javid's colleagues from St. Vincent's, grouped into one area: a little clique. They appeared lost in a daydream.

He noticed Dr. Stiles and a woman, most likely his wife, speaking with Dr. Parsons. Stiles, however, stood marginally aloof from the conversation, hands in his pockets, his gaze somewhere out among the trees as the two women nodded and gestured. His head moved fitfully, as if pestered by an insect, and there was a slight yellow-hued pallor to his face.

Tucci approached the threesome, followed by Bashir. Janice Parsons saw him first and reacted with ambivalence, but stayed where she was. Tucci kept his eyes trained on Stiles, the last one to register his presence.

"Dr. Stiles?" Tucci said. There was irritation in the doctor's face until Tucci and Bashir showed their badges. Flashing tin seldom failed to whip them in line. "I'm Detective Michael Tucci and this is associate detective David Bashir. May we ask you a few questions?"

Scarcely moving, Stiles kept his hands in his pockets, staring at Tucci, lips terse, eyes pulsing in what Tucci took to be supplication. But he couldn't get ahead of things. Undeniably, though, his entrance into the conversation seemed to be the cherry atop already-palpable awkwardness.

"A little inappropriate, don't you think, detective?" said Stiles. "To be asking questions here?"

Tucci narrowed his eyes at him. "It's protocol. And I think it's more than appropriate. Finding who did this to her would be the best tribute she could have, don't ya think?"

Janice Parsons nodded her head diminutively, then slipped off, acting as if her retreat weren't plainly obvious.

With mechanical tenderness, Stiles' wife, a woman of looser, almost hippier countenance than Tucci would ever have guessed, rubbed his arm.

"We should get going," she said.

Tucci extended his hand to her, introduced himself and Bashir. Stiles observed all this as if behind glass. The wife's handshake was non-existent as she spoke her name.

"Charlotte," she said. "I'm sorry, you caught us at a bad time, detective."

Tucci nodded. "I realize, but it's necessary." He dug into his coat, uprooted his card, and handed it to Stiles who took it between thumb and forefinger like it was a scrap of trash. Tucci's smile didn't waver—he liked smiling at Stiles. Clearly it made him uncomfortable.

"Sooner or later," Tucci said, "we'll need to talk."

"I could never imagine something like this happening," said Stiles. "I still don't believe it."

Tucci sensed a hint of desperation in Stiles' voice, an attempt at acting shocked. Maybe he was. But if not, he wasn't a very good actor. And if he was indeed shocked, he hid it well in his steely countenance.

"Have a good day, doctor," Tucci said. He looked at Charlotte, who smirked at him. While probably delusional thinking, he saw sensual tease in that smirk, and imagined Charlotte might have spoken more to him if not for her husband.

They moved away. Tucci watched them, then was alerted to a voice behind him.

"Detective."

He turned.

Tara.

"I told you," he said, with a minor grin. "You can call me Mike."

"Nice of you to come for the service," Tara said. There was investigation, curiosity, in the way she studied him.

Tucci nodded with gravity, then gestured to Bashir. "This is David, a colleague of mine." They shook. He felt Bashir's eyes on him. Tucci tried not to look at him for fear of having offended him with that condescending introduction. "How're you doing?"

"About as good as one can be doing," Tara said. She bit her lower lip. "You're looking at the new interim Chief of Surgical Oncology."

Her tone was conscientiously neutral, rendering the news more an inevitability than something to be celebrated.

"Congratulations," said Tucci.

Tara crossed her arms. "On a temporary basis, at least."

Tucci used the crowd to keep his eyes busy, so as not to linger long on Tara, whose captivating, penetrative stare he, as a law enforcer, mildly envied. It could ply many men.

"Who was that you were just talking to?" he said, even though he knew.

The Middle-Eastern woman who'd approached Tara moments ago was now speaking with another Muslim woman.

"That's Aadila, I think she was a close friend of Marika's," Tara said. "She stopped by the office a few times." She lowered her head. "I don't know why she's talking to Stiles and his wife. Do you know Dr. Stiles?"

"I know he wasn't a big fan of hers, for whatever reason."

"Call a spade a spade—he's a damn racist," said Tara. "A classist too. Went to Harvard and thinks that anyone not out of there or Princeton is suspect. Even though Marika was educated here, I think he saw her as emblematic of a problem. He was threatened. Plain and simple."

Tucci nodded. Across the way, Aadila had broken from her conversation.

"I think I'm going to go," Tara said. "Many things to do." She turned once more to Bashir. "It was nice meeting you."

"Good to meet you, too."

"Okay," Tucci said. With a sardonic grin, he added, "Make time for me. We may need to talk some more."

"Will do," she said, moving away. "See you later, detective."

"Mike."

"Right, Mike."

Bashir looked at him. "Javid's partner. What's her story?"

"Sticksville, bascially." He stopped there, even though Bashir expected more. Truth was, there wasn't much to tell. Dr. Tara White's background check had come up decidedly natural, spotty and practically non-existent. Not surprising, given her rural midwestern upbringing. Especially since she was a generation ahead of the social networking circle-jerk of today's crowd.

"I think I just met your high school self," Bashir said. "You see yourself talking with her? Not that I blame you."

"Fuck off, man."

The words of his former partner in patrol came to him. *Brain's got three hemispheres. Three. The right, left, the south. You got science in the left, religion in the right, and the great and wise uniter in the south. The oldest. It speaks and everyone listens.*

"I'm fine," Tucci said, watching Tara walk alone across the cemetery.

As if feeling his gaze, Tara turned and dealt him brief acknowledgment, without breaking her stride. Over the treeline, the sun lanced the clouds and shone across the green hills, elongating her bobbing shadow.

Tucci broke his minor spell and approached Aadila, showing his badge.

"Do you—can I—talk not English?" Aadila asked. Every word appeared laborious. It seemed hard for her to take her eyes off the group of men carrying Marika's body across the cemetery.

"Sure." Tucci placed a hand on Bashir's shoulder. "My associate can translate."

He popped a candy into his mouth, then reached into his breast pocket and extracted a tri-folded slip of paper. "First, I think you should know: Marika wrote you a letter."

Bashir zipped off the translation. Aadila's brow furrowed. Then it dawned on her. She pointed a long golden finger at the folded paper in Tucci's hand. He nodded.

Glances were shared, then Tucci handed her the letter. She unfolded it and read it. Her eyes watered, her nostrils flared. She countered the rush of emotion with a sharp inhale.

"Liath is your husband, I take it?" Tucci said.

"Yes."

"He's not here today?"

She shook her head. "No."

"He dislike Marika that much?"

"He is working. He would have come otherwise."

"He couldn't take time off for her funeral?"

Aadila spoke, Bashir listening intently before offering the translation: "He did not approve of the way Marika conducted herself. He thought she had been gifted by Allah with beauty and intelligence and that she was not, in turn, worshipping Him properly. We were good friends. We tried to introduce her to potential husbands. But nothing ever worked out."

"He must've been bothered by that. And by your friendship, no?"

"My husband," she said, Bashir translating for her, "is very strong in his opinions. But he is not a violent man. He knows what is right and what is wrong. He knows from Allah. What happened to Marika was wrong." Aadila's voice cracked. She closed her eyes, as if willing away tears.

"Just how well did you know Marika?" he said.

"We attended the same mosque for ten years now. We bonded—" Bashir leaned in, asked her to clarify or repeat something, then continued, "Like cousins. Or even like sisters, in the beginning. And I knew her enough to know that our drifting apart was not personal."

"What do you mean?"

"We were close because we had no one else. I had my husband, but... I needed a friend. Marika and I sometimes did not speak for almost a year, because of her dedication to her work, but when we would talk it was like we had seen each other every night. We could pick up easily from where we left off."

"Was that something that bothered Liath? That she did not go to mosque regularly?"

"No. Not that. Especially if she was working. Healing others for Allah, as he said. And as long as she prayed five times a day. I do not know if she did."

"So, what exactly did he disapprove of?"

Aadila held up the letter as though its very existence were the answer. "She was very open about things, very questioning of things. Activities that gave her pleasure—she didn't understand why Allah would not permit them. I wondered about her faith, why she came to the mosque. Was it community? Was she truly faithful to Allah?"

Aadila slowed, then paused, allowing Bashir's translating tongue to keep up.

"My husband never liked her," he said, quoting her, "but that may have been because she was forthright. And pretty. At first I didn't like her because she was so pretty. But she had fire in her soul. I responded to it. And of course I admired her work. But… she did lose that fire in the last few months. She came more regularly. She questioned less. I assumed she had given herself over to Allah. Liath did not want me talking to her anymore. He said he had heard things about her that Allah might not forgive her for."

"How did he hear about these things?"

Aadila bowed her head, spoke. "I don't know. That is not my place."

"What did you know of her work situation?" Tucci said. "You know she was caught in the middle of a political fight?"

Breathing hard, Aadila continued, Bashir offering the English between every few sentences.

"I did," she said. "I know she was upset about the whole situation at the hospital. I told her to leave, even though I knew she would not. It's interesting, looking back—I remember when we first met, when we were younger, she was quite sensitive. She always wanted things to be good, to stay good, and she nearly broke down when something went awry. But then, as a doctor, she became so resilient. Determined to get through problems, the kind of doctor you would want if you had terrible diseases."

Tucci was about to speak, when she continued.

"I do think," Aadila said, "that she was seeing someone at her work. Someone she probably should not have been seeing. Liath suspected this, too. One of the reasons why he disapproved of her."

"What makes you think that?"

"It is not based on anything concrete," Aadila said. "It was just her mood. She seemed both excited and gratified, and then turned rather dreadful. I'm sure I'm exaggerating. Of course, we didn't talk all the time, so it's difficult for me to say. But we did talk more in the months leading up to her... terrible passing. My husband didn't know. I didn't tell him." Aadila lowered her head, sniffled.

"I'm sorry."

"Thank you," she said. "If you don't mind, I would like to go."

"Sure."

Aadila moved away.

The burial group was gone, the crowds diminished. Above, the clouds slowly parted at the thickening sunlight which saturated the hills, perhaps to counter the death underground, to heighten the life already evident in the spring-green grass, outshine the colors in the fading trees.

Tara despised working well into the night, regardless of necessity. Yet she resented this contempt of hers, which seemed a holdover from her later high school and college years, tenacious despite the demands of the medical profession to accustom her to the inevitability of long hours. It was that butterfly in her, the wayward girl that, while long tamed, desired total freedom.

One good thing about the night: the drop-off in phone obligations. However in this turnover phase as the Chief of Surgical Oncology the phone had been ringing all day and night, dribbling voices into her ear.

And then, there were the emails. Dear God, getting back to everyone seemed endless.

Twenty minutes from midnight, she put the computer to sleep, darkened the office, and stepped out into the shimmering fluorescent corridors, the pulsing echoes of her high heels on the linoleum like a lonely heartbeat in the hallway. A male nurse passed her and they exchanged curt smiles. She had yet to get used to this section of the hospital. At her request, Dr. Parsons had allowed her transference to a sixth floor office, two above where she and Marika had once been.

Alone for two floors' descent, at her old stop the elevator lurched open. An orderly came aboard, a short round man with many stored-up opinions about the world that exuded from his pores.

"Hi, Dr. White," he said, eyes like glass.

"Hello."

He's one of them, Tara thought.

Them.

While tenuously spiritual (she would often describe herself as an open-minded agnostic, always adding that maybe this was Cosmos Version 1.1, prone to glitches—such as cancer—which God had left us to rectify) and adverse to weighty religious terms, nowhere in her vocabulary was there a better word than "biblical" to describe this situation here. Upon Marika's death, St. Vincent's seemed a battlefield of Good and Evil, demons and angels with nametags.

Diplomatic mostly, but out to destroy. Conquer.

For the few floors they rode together, the vibe in the elevator worsened. Tara knew it could very well be just her, but the glances the orderly would throw her every few seconds, as if waiting to seize an opportunity, validated this feeling.

The first floor opened before them and, without a word, the orderly slipped out and the doors closed. Once more, Tara was alone as the elevator took her and deposited her in the bowels of the parking structure.

She strode toward her car, hand positioned over the mace in her purse. She felt absurdly like a western gunslinger ready to duel.

Parking structures epitomized urbania—all stone and metal and intricate geometry, stained with oil and the remnant fumes of gas and other cultural excretions. A nostalgia for the countryside filled her, and, in a revelatory flash, Tara realized how finite would be her relationship with St. Vincent's.

I can't be here much longer, she thought. *I can't be here. Not like this.*

◈

Outside the complex stood her neighbor Randolph, sucking pensively on a midnight cigarette. The approach of Tara's car brought him back from stargazing. He recognized her vehicle and smiled and started toward the lot to meet her. Tara sighed.

Climbing out, she offered only cursory acknowledgment of Randolph's presence as she bustled about getting her purse and attaché case from the backseat.

"Hi, Tara," Randolph said. "Late night, huh?"

"That it was."

"You need my help with anything?"

"No I'm fine. Thanks."

"My daughter Annie has the flu," he said. "We're taking her to the doctor tomorrow. I say we just take her across the hall! To you!"

Is that supposed to be a joke?

"You didn't get her vaccinated?" Tara said, heading toward the elevator.

"Oh no, we're not the vaccinating types," he said.

This stubborn persistence of ignorance—a ceaseless mystery to her. Why did belief have to wedge itself into things that just were or were not? Were people going to stop believing in electricity? In gravity? Was the necessity of water to survive bound to become a partisan issue?

Randolph joined her at the elevator, put out his cigarette in a nearby ashcan. "I think there was someone at your door earlier tonight," he said.

The temperature dropped in her veins. "Excuse me?"

"There was someone at your door. I was coming back from taking out the trash and I passed him as he went out."

"How'd you know he was at my door?"

The elevator rumbled to a stop before them, opened and they stepped on.

"Seemed like he was. When I arrived, it looked like he'd just been kneeling, I guess maybe from leaving you a note under your door. Then he walked past me. I said hi, but he didn't say anything. He was wearing sunglasses and had a baseball cap on."

"Maybe he was passing out letters to all the tenants."

"No. I didn't get one. And he ignored Ms. Filmore here."

The elevator chimed at their floor, opened. Tara didn't want to move. Didn't want to see.

Run. Run now.

"What else did he look like?" she said.

Randolph shrugged. "Had a goatee I think. Dark pants and a t-shirt maybe. Are you okay? I figured maybe he was a friend, or boyfriend…"

Maybe Mike Tucci?

"I don't know," said Tara.

They moved in slow tandem down the hallway.

"Would you like me to come in with you?" Randolph asked.

Fumbling for her keys, she said, "No. No. Thanks, Randy. I'll be fine."

"You're sure?"

"Yes."

Randolph stood and watched as she opened the door and quickly went for the lights. At her feet lay a clean white envelope, unsealed, unmarked, but containing something.

"Guess that's it," Randolph said. "Good night, Tara. Let me know if you need anything."

"Thanks. I will."

Across the hall, the door shut. She was alone. Alone with this envelope.

Make sure.

As if determined to meet her stalker head-on, face to blade, she unleashed herself among the furniture, scouring every crevice, plunging into every room, overthrowing blankets, drawing back curtains, checking under the bed much as she imagined any monster-fearing child might be doing that moment.

She went to the letter, nudging it first with her foot the way she would a dead animal. Then she warily picked it up and dumped it on the kitchen counter and stared at it for a long time.

After furtively surveying her apartment once more, Tara closed her eyes and pulled out the single sheet of paper tri-folded in the envelope.

In a bold reflex she forced them open and saw, typed:

"you protect your fuckin sand nigger and voodoo friends and you're just like them so eyes open you might be next you cunt"

⌒∾○

"Thanks so much for coming, over," Tara said, holding the door open. "I didn't know who else to call. Not about this."

"Don't worry about it," Tucci said. "Let me see it."

She gestured to the counter, where sat the envelope and letter. She stayed put as Tucci went and picked it up. Read it.

He was not too alarmed. First impression was that it had not been composed by whoever had killed Marika. There was, of course, no immediate certainty about that. But whereas Marika's murder was so bold and savage, the aura of this letter seemed… *meek*, almost scared. Like a threat from some basement-dwelling troll on an internet message board.

"It was just sitting by the door there?" he said.

Tara nodded. "My neighbor across the hall said he saw the person walking away from my door. You could talk to him. Randolph, I mean. My neighbor."

"He say what the person looked like?"

"He said it looked as if he was—it was a man—trying to disguise himself, you know, with dark glasses and a baseball cap."

Tara related the vague physical details of her apparent visitor, strengthening Tucci's intuition, particularly from the ball cap and glasses, that this guy was an amateur incapable of anything more than bullying from afar. Of course, Marika's death had none of the evident artistry of professional work, either. And there had been no letter to Marika. No warning. This was like an addendum. Someone playing off what happened—but not the originator.

"Can I talk to him?" Tucci asked. "Your neighbor?"

Tara hesitated. "I think he'd still be up."

They stepped out and approached Randolph's door. Tara gave a timid knock.

No reply. She knocked again, slightly louder. There was a vague sound of movement inside that grew closer. The door opened—Susan, the wife, stood there, her instinct for politeness superseded by a post-midnight scowl of confused irritation.

"Hi Susie," Tara said. "I'm sorry to bother you—may I speak with Randy? Is he awake?"

Susan furrowed her brow. "Yeah, he's in the bathroom." She looked at Tucci, then back at Tara. "What's up?"

Tucci spoke. "We'd just like to speak with Randolph, ma'am."

"Hey Tara." A voice behind Susan. Randolph appeared and he and Susan briskly changed places. He looked at Tucci and his eyebrows raised. "Everything all right?"

Tucci flashed his badge. Tara noticed a reaction in virtually every muscle in Randolph's body and she felt gratified by that, almost empowered.

"Can we ask you a few questions?" Responding to the bewildered gloom in Randolph's expression, Tucci added, "This is just about who you might've seen earlier tonight."

"Oh," said Randolph, stepping out into the hall and clicking the door shut behind him. "Oh my God, Tara, did something happen?"

Quickly Tara explained the situation. Tucci prodded him further to excavate from memory anything at all that could be helpful.

"I didn't see much," Randolph said, suddenly very fidgety. "I was just taking out the trash. I saw a car parked on the street, with its engine on. It was a black SUV. I guess I noticed it, 'cause it had these cartoon angel-wing stickers on the rear-view mirrors. You don't see that every day. That's the only thing, really, that I can remember. I didn't see the driver. Didn't think to look. Then I saw the guy in the hall. He was kinda non-descript under his glasses and stuff. Pale, goatee, sort of gaunt face."

"Does that vehicle ring a bell at all?" Tucci asked Tara.

Tara rubbed her temple. "No. Not really."

"Sorry I can't be more helpful," said Randolph.

"That's fine," Tucci said.

Several moments later, both doors shut and the hallway was once again empty and silent.

"I hate to sound selfish, or silly…" Tara said as they returned to her apartment. She took a deep breath.

Tucci saw what he thought was a quick eye-roll, self-directed.

"But would you mind staying for a while?"

"Not at all."

She smiled. "Thanks. I'm not forcing an awkward call to the wife or girlfriend?"

"Well, neither exist, so I think it'll be fine."

Tara nodded, heading for the kitchen. "Somehow I figured that. But it's always nice to be polite and assume a significant other than to not."

"Thanks. You kind of compromised yourself by mentioning that, though."

"Eh, you're a detective. You would've figured me right out, anyway. Am I right?"

"I'm glad you have that much confidence in me."

"Again, just being polite." Tara brought out two mugs. "Would you like some coffee?"

"Sure."

For a quiet moment, Tucci watched her as she prepared the pot. This woman, this Dr. Tara White, had to him quickly become a unique phenomenon, someone he'd met formally, her only relevance to him based on this investigation. And yet, in so little time, she had transcended this position, as if somehow she'd long been part of his life. He reasoned all this stemmed potentially from her physical attractiveness, a thing not to be underestimated in its narcotic power. But that seemed too chintzy an explanation.

Then, he noticed something.

"Expecting more company?" he said.

Tara turned, followed his finger which was pointing to a rat trap tucked below the dishwasher door.

"Unfortunately, yes." Behind her, the coffeemaker gurgled. "I haven't seen it either. Just it's snacks and… leavings."

"Haven't caught one?"

By the restrained repulsion on her face, the implication that there could be more than one apparently had not occurred to her.

"No luck," she said. "I should probably call an exterminator, but just been too damn busy. There are days when I hope to see that mouse or rat or whatever it is just so I can smash it myself." She took out the coffee pot and poured two cups. "Very smart, Tara. Make yourself out a violent psycho in front of the cop."

Tucci smiled and took his cup.

"You want it just black?" she said.

"Yeah, thanks." He took a sip. Noticing faint surprise in her voice, he said, "That okay?"

"Of course. It's just, with all those candy-things you eat, I figured you for a sweets addict."

"They help me think, more than anything. Some people click their pens, Hemingway used to tap the E key repeatedly. I suck Jolly Ranchers."

"Better than smoking."

To that, Tucci raised his cup. He took in the artwork on the walls and the mantel. Knowing of art merely what one might pick up osmotically—the only names he knew were Picasso and Rembrandt—he nonetheless appreciated the variety: landscapes, abstracts, feminine sculptures, and some clay patterns. The paintings looked authentic, too.

"These your parents?" he said, indicating a framed, black-and-white photo on the mantel of a WASP-y couple taken in what looked like the late seventies or eighties.

"That's Ma 'n Pa all right," Tara said. "Both gone now. My dad passed of lung cancer when I was fifteen. Partly why I became what I am."

"He smoke?" Tucci did not realize the callous directness of his query until it was out.

Unaffected, Tara said, "Uh-huh."

The adjacent photo was of a horse: sandy brown with sad sage eyes and a dark-blonde mane.

"This horse from your farm?" Tucci asked, adding humorously, "Or did it come with the frame?"

"That's my horse now. Toby. I rent a stable for him in Malibu. He's my wild. Everything the hospital cuts away, he gives back. Horses in general. I love watching them at the track. Especially down in Del Mar."

"That's San Diego, right?"

"Uh huh." Tara took a seat in the living room, hands clasped for warmth about her mug, her face hovering over the dancing steam.

"Are you cold?" Tucci asked.

"A little. I'll be all right. This'll heat me up."

Right then, he pinpointed one of the strange feelings lurking in him, that of this apartment, despite his never having been here, being more *his* than hers. As if he were hosting *her*.

"So, Hemingway," she said. "You sound rather... literary, detective."

"Because I remembered a random thing from *Jeopardy*?" he quipped.

Tara smiled.

"It's better in premise than practice," he said. "I try to read. Hard for me to concentrate, though, in a completely quiet place. I need some restlessness, some background noise. So I often cave in, turn on a ball game or something. Or if I feel antsy, I go to a coffee shop, or bookstore."

"I can see that. I mean, I'm not like that, but I understand it. Usually after a day at the hospital I need solitude. Recharges my sanity."

"I think we need that kind of contrast, definitely." Tucci shifted in his seat. "And… Marika…"

Tara steeled. "What about her?"

"She was just as—solitary?"

"I know you probably find it hard to believe," she said, "but we were friends that weren't that close. We were business partners."

"You would've had no idea if she were involved with someone?"

"I don't know who she might've been involved with, no. And I'm not the type who would snoop around or gossip. Christ, if I knew anything more I would've told you. I don't think that, if she were seeing someone, she would've kept it secret. She would've bragged about it, because for her to 'see someone,' he would have to have been Mr. Right, at least in my opinion." Tara took a breath. "If she was having some kind of clandestine affair, well… that's very strange to me. It's too… sexual for her. Stupid way to say it, yes. But from the little I spoke with her about this sort of stuff, she sounded like an asexual romantic, wanting the flowers, candies, wedding ring, someday, when it was right. Not… not… well, you know."

The frog got the fly, Tucci thought. He and Tara had enjoyed all-too-brief moments of free-floating discussion, about to break the orbit of the sad reason for their acquaintanceship. Now, that reason had, like a frog-tongue, sucked them back.

"Would you like some more?" Tara said, getting up.

"I would, thanks." Tucci rose and followed her to the kitchen, handed her his mug. He stood mere feet behind her. When she turned, she halted abruptly, startled by his proximity. With trembling digits she offered his refilled coffee and he took it with both hands. Neither moved, not even to drink. Like windblown debris, incomplete thoughts swirled between them.

They stepped toward one another. Tucci fixated on her lips, moist and ripe, when movement behind her strayed his eyes.

"What?" Tara said, voice thin.

"I think we have a visitor," he said.

Tara turned, looking first at the front door until seeing Tucci's focus was on the fruit bowl, behind which jutted a small fuzzy black head, adorned with marbled eyes and nibbling furiously on some unidentified scrap.

CHAPTER FIVE
Karaj, Iran
1999

AT FIFTEEN, SHE FELT for the first time what felt like death.

For hours she remained still, her mind a pounding storm of fever-dream. Pain throughout her body, especially where the blade had struck her. In more delirious moments, she thought perhaps she had died, or was dying, and that, as punishment, she was being kept in a place between the physical and the spiritual so she might suffer the ravages of both.

But no, she was alive. It was nearly dawn, and she was still here. Alone. A wave of relief was followed by one of guilt. In thinking she was being herded toward some terrible Hereafter, she had relinquished control. Now her fate had been given back to her... not to her mother, not to her father. She even felt detached from Allah, which brought a devastating vigor. Meanwhile, her body had erupted with hunger, piercing and deep.

Slowly she rose, peered through cracks in the objects around her. The city was waking, the buzz of activity growing louder, stronger. Whisper of traffic. Disembodied voices in the twilight dark. Bicycles passing. Vendors setting up. She thought a lot of Hassan and what he might be doing. She wondered if she would ever see him again.

Where do I go?

Head down, she crawled from her hiding place. There were few people along the street—only market vendors milled about—and two of the lamps had burnt out, giving the waning night one last refuge before the sun rose. She tried to move mostly in these shadows, initially walking fast until realizing a young girl's rapid pace might draw attention. Chills tore across her flesh. They were chills of the coming winter. They were chills of the early morning. But primarily, they were chills of terror, precursors to what she thought might be a nervous breakdown. Her torso throbbed.

I should go back. It is not my place to be here. It is not right. My father loves me. He cares about me. About my family. I must plead for his forgiveness. I must amend my wrongs. I must face my death, if I must.

In her wandering, she had sensed tremors of attention but now the feeling was a steady, rattling energy focused on her. She walked faster. First she thought this person moved behind her but then he seemed to come from the side, right and left, all over. Doubtless it was male. Bizarrely, she was more certain of the gender than of whether or not this was a person—she thought maybe it could be an *Ifrit*, a cunning creature her mother used to tell her about, changing shape and direction to misguide her. But those were fictive, right?

Stop this foolishness. Stricken with fear, she realized, the rational mind became widely accommodating.

She stopped, thinking she heard her name, but again it came from all angles, momentarily pervasive in the air, alerting the world to her, *her*. She continued on, eye to the ground, paranoia her one unfortunate ally against the growing hunger.

She turned a corner and a shadow was there.

Then the shadow had a face.

Omeed Madani—her father's business partner, whom she had met several times prior. She did not know much about him and he had always intrigued her. He was a quiet man, but knew what to say and when, and in speaking he somehow gave her vicarious catharsis, because she perceived, often through tone alone, a subtle superiority, a soul fed-up with the things around him.

"What are you doing out here?" Omeed asked. "At this hour, no less?"

She stalled, unprepared to explain what had happened. The events too raw for words. But he saw her eyes and he saw her shiver and needed little else.

"Would you like some tea?" he said. "Or something to eat?"

She nodded.

He led her the block and a half to his apartment building, a short white structure with no gates that looked too open. She had to quell panic that she was being rounded up and trapped.

I must face my death. If I must.

He looked at her ragged appearance and her trembling hands. "Did you sleep on the street?" Omeed asked. Clearly she bewildered him. Or maybe he was just bewildered by all females—she remembered her mother speaking scandalously of his lack of a wife.

Again, she nodded. They entered his apartment, located atop a freshly-painted staircase in a well-lit hallway. The exterior did no justice to the interior, she determined.

"Your father is a friend of mine," he said.

She wasn't sure if this was a reminder or a subtle threat, or both.

He noticed her repeatedly tending the area above her breast.

"Are you all right?"

I cannot show him such things. Unforgivable. Unforgivable.

"Do you have bandages?" she asked.

Omeed narrowed his eyes. Without saying anything further, he went and retrieved a creased box of bandages. She took them into the washroom, where she stared at her visage in the mirror. She took a deep breath and slowly lowered her cloth and exposed the wound but she closed her eyes for fear of seeing it for the first time.

She opened her eyes. A jagged cut, not too deep. Dried blood down her breast. She ran water over tissue paper and dabbed it and it stung. Then she wiped off the blood and placed the bandage on and recovered it.

She emerged from the washroom and sat at the kitchen table. After heating a kettle he poured her a cup of tea. She took it gingerly, sipped it.

"Thank you," she said.

Omeed smiled weakly. He stared at her the way she'd seen him stare at other people. He was like a detective, absorbing, theories and opinions piling in his head. She thought of herself as some kind of human mathematics equation he was trying to solve.

He was about to say something when, without discretion, the story surged from her like an autonomous thing. In speaking, her eyes strayed from his face. She ended, ready to burst but holding the tears back, not knowing what Omeed thought of it all. At this point, she didn't even know what *she* thought of it. Why? How could this happen? What was going to happen to her now?

He is going to call your father and then you must answer to him.

When she was finished, he sighed.

"I'm not sure what I can do," he said. "Or where my responsibilities lie."

I am in safe hands. Most men would not even think about what to do next.

"Our obligation is what's right," she said. Where had that come from? Like the account itself, it had spouted from her without full approval. Never before would she have imagined being so forthright, so authoritative, to a man her senior.

After another long moment of quiet scrutiny, Omeed said, "You cannot stay here if you wish to live."

Her stomach jumped. She knew this, and nodded.

"Very likely, you cannot stay in Karaj," he said. "Or even Iran. I know your father, as I'm sure you do."

"Yes." Much as bubbles rising from depths to the surface, realizations ascended now from her murky heart to the clarity of her intellect, popping in tiny epiphany. Her family was wrong, yes, and she would have to leave not only her home, but her home country. Where she would go, she could not say.

"You are a beautiful girl," Omeed said. "No doubt you will become a beautiful woman, too."

Eyes downcast, she murmured, "Thank you."

"I remember you as a child. Your heart is pure and I cannot imagine your death would heal what I believe is a large ache in your father's soul."

Omeed's words implied a bigger, unseen reality enveloping her father, a complex history, shameful deeds or thoughts—or so she chose to interpret it. She decided not to inquire further. Given everything she'd done, she wanted to preserve some respect, for her father and for herself.

"I have two associates," said Omeed. "Or rather former partners, who are to make their way to Turkey for business." He fidgeted. "It is a business in shadow, so they travel out of the way."

She looked at him, unsure what to say. She realized with a pang that she needed to engage in morning prayer.

"I will contact them if you would like," said Omeed. "They are traveling tomorrow morning. I know their route, and can arrange a meeting. I am sure..." Omeed paused. He looked as a man would suffering indigestion, but it was more mental indigestion, as if the enormity of what he had stumbled into had just caught up with him. "I am sure they would be amenable to having you along, provided I make the proper arrangements. You may stay here today, and through the night. Then, tomorrow I will take you."

She wasn't sure what to say. A strong part of her—strengthening by the minute, it seemed—just wanted to run crying back home, to her mother's arms. To see her little brother Shaheen once more before he became a man, surely to happen quick. But she could not go back. The greater instinct told her she could not. And where else would she go? Perhaps she was right, and her soul, guided by Allah, had steered her into the waiting hands of Omeed, who would provide her escape.

"I know these men well," said Omeed. "They will get you safely beyond the border. What you do there is up to you. But I am sure they can provide some guidance as well."

She nodded.

"Shall I call them?"

Very slowly, she nodded again.

"Thank you," she said, in a small voice.

He stared at her some more, then got up. He went to the window and closed the drapes, turning the room twilight. Her chest flared.

"Are you hungry?" Omeed asked. "I can make you breakfast."

The clamor reached her well inside her sleep. She awoke to pounding. Hammering. Harsh voices.

Omeed was there in the doorway, eyes wide, teeth gritted. Was it he making the noise? No. No, it was happening beyond him. Close, however. In the other room.

The front door.

"It's your father," Omeed said.

Her face drained. Pain from her wound throbbed with her pulse, a shadow of her racing heart. Every nightmare of hers, ones she'd had, ones in the make, slithered through her flesh, coiled in her mind, crouched to ambush the next time she slept, which could be in moments and which could be for a terrible eternity.

Omeed quickly led her to a pantry between the kitchen and the living room. He opened the door and told her to crawl into the dark, compact space. Despite attempts to keep calm, he exuded helplessness. Surely he was afraid for himself, too—as a non-relative, meddling in the affairs between father and daughter brought its own substantial risks.

He cannot be helpless in front of my father.

Still dazed, and not feeling as if she were truly awake (likely to her benefit) she squeezed into the boxy crevice, legs drawn against her body, old cans and spices less than a foot from her that, save for the ones catching the vague sliver of light at the door, she could not see. It was like a tomb; blackness.

She followed the sounds. Initially violent, the pounds and knocks tapered off to more anxiousness than anger. Omeed opened the front door. A murmured exchange. She was conflicted in whether or not to listen. If she listened, tracing every word or step, she would suffer the hopeless buildup to her discovery. Shutting her ears, however, would render her ignorant, sustain hope.

And so, eyes shut, ears clamped, she waited. Her stomach clenched in preparation for the sudden light of reveal. The faint tickle of something crawling on her neck added to the tingling, shuddering chorus of her nerves, but she didn't move. She couldn't.

Time throbbed along slowly, achingly. Every squeak, gurgle or pop of her body reverberated. There was an unbroken buzzing noise, within and without, and she thought of it as her soul, mingled with the soul of the world, and they were really just one, one long and calm and wise note. She tried to meditate on this notion, on Hassan, on Allah.

She tried to pray.

Past the buzzing were the voices of the two men, fluctuating. Each time she unwittingly released pressure on her ears, the sounds rushed upon her and she was quick to cover them again. She did not move.

She heard what she thought was the door close. Then a protracted silence. Moving with slow care as if not wanting to break something, she took her hands from her ears and listened.

Nothing.

Did Omeed leave? Have they gone to get the police? Is he going to come and throw me out? Is he going to kill me himself—?

The pantry door opened and Omeed was there, illuminated—almost blasphemously—by the light behind him, which to her was blinding. He smiled, but it was not a full smile, nor a strong smile.

"In thirty minutes," he said. "We will go."

Parked in the tight alleyway by Omeed's complex was his van, an old thing stained with decades and dark country. Windowless backside and ink-black windows, it was a daytime refuge of midnight. Was she getting in this? How could she do this? Was she exchanging death for something ultimately far worse? And worse yet, what did Allah desire? Was Omeed His offer of mercy and salvation, or a torturous route to punishment?

"No one must see you," Omeed said. In one hand he held a clump of black trash bags. All throughout he smiled at her, helpful only because she allowed it to be. "We must take all precaution."

You're taking me back, she thought. Being outside, even in such a hidden spot as this, she felt very conspicuous. *You're taking me back to Father.*

Omeed opened the back doors of the van, from which wafted a very unclean stench, a miasma of things stale or burnt. Difficult and terrible to define. Arrayed there were several long, crudely-built wooden boxes, from which jutted old, rotted nails. Omeed lifted the lid of one and there was nothing inside. She understood.

"I'm to lie in there," she said.

Omeed's eyes were moist and sympathetic. "We must take all precaution," he said again proceeding to line box's interior with the trash bags. "We can leave the lid a little ajar for air."

In morbid speculation of what that box was, what it had once held, how many of such contents it had seen, never before had she so strongly desired an answer and non-answer. Much as with the exchange between Omeed and her father not an hour ago, she would not ask. He would not tell her.

I cannot turn away now.

She climbed into the noxious vehicle, crouched within the box. Lying fully horizontal, she felt she'd be entering another world.

And with deliberate gesture, as if allowing precious seconds of farewell, Omeed drew the lid over her, eclipsing all of the only place she had ever known, reducing it to a spittle of light beyond the back windows. Her entire childhood, her past, her family, Hassan, all in that light.

In minutes, the van started and began to move.

At some point, they stopped. She sensed a slight rocking motion from the front of the van, then heard the slam of the driver's side door. *Omeed is getting out.* She heard his voice, addressing other voices which spoke in dark, runny tones. Who were these people? Her pulse increased. Her tiny space became hot and moist with breath.

The van's back doors jerked violently open. The voices now close and immediate. They sounded official, very forthright and solemn. She dared not move. Even her breathing stopped. If she could have momentarily stopped her heart, she would have.

One of the men said, "The body's here?"

Hearing this, she was almost unconscious with fear. Something in her separated, and she quickly readied herself to be given over to these men, these accomplices of her father, perhaps, the people to whom Omeed was ultimately loyal.

You've betrayed me, she thought, very close to simply screaming it at Omeed.

Much shuffling and movement around her, knocking into her box. She waited. Mutterings. Men standing and bustling over her. Lifting. Hauling. She waited. They were rearranging the objects around her. Getting down at her. Any second the lid would be cast off, the terrible sun bursting in, silhouetting the terrible faces of the men that would carry her away. She waited.

But it never came. They carried out one of the other boxes, slammed the doors shut and the voices resumed their distant warble. Then the van swayed slightly with Omeed's return to the driver's seat. Slam of the door. They started again and the vehicle lurched forth, leaving her relieved, but also pondering what they might have meant by "body," and trying to abstain from thoughts of herself as a living corpse, lying boxed next to another no longer of this world.

They drove and drove. Some part of her could not relinquish the feeling that this was a dream, a feeling which in fact grew stronger, perhaps to maintain her compliance with the reality of it.

"We are almost there," Omeed said, voice raised, from far upfront. "You will not have to worry about these men. I have known them long."

You know my father, too.

Some two hours later they stopped. Omeed drew back the lid. She rose and moved cautiously forward.

"It is all right," he said. He outstretched his hand for her, but she did not take it. Behind him, the wide barren desert hummed stark and bright, the dirt road they'd taken snaking listless into oblivion.

Long gray clouds luxuriated in the sky, whispering of winter.

She emerged and followed Omeed around the van.

"Stay here," he said, and walked ahead to meet two figures on horseback, men who were irregular black prints against the whitening wasteland beyond, their faces congruous with the encompassing deadness of stone, save for the droplets of tired soul in their eyes. They wore dark, ragged clothing and carried large packs. She saw large weapons hung upon their persons. One had a rifle strapped to his back.

Her chest constricted. This could not be it, could it? These men could not be her traveling companions, her "saviors?"

Maybe this was all a devilish game, she thought. *Maybe they are going to simply shoot me and leave me to the birds and to the earth, for my dishonor…*

Resisting an urge to run (*and run where?*) she remained still. One of the horses snorted. Their coats glistened in the sun. She envied the untapped strength of those limbs. To possess such power, such speed.

Omeed spoke inaudibly with the men. He gave them what looked like money, and every so often he gestured to her and the men's eyes followed and she shrank further against the side of the van. One of them smiled her way, but she could tell he was unaccustomed to smiling at someone like her. This man knew only the smiles incurred by wartime vanquish. By death.

Omeed is not leaving me with these men. He must come with us. He must.

Omeed began waving her forward. In these seconds she hated him. How could she have fallen for this? From such unprecedented freedom, how could she in so little time have carved her destiny down to these men and this desolate place?

Allah be merciful. Allah protect me.

She approached the three men. Omeed formally introduced

them. She wondered what they did. She wondered how Omeed knew them. She wondered if her father knew—

Stop. Your father is no more.

One of the men showed her a map of where they would be going, every once in a while pointing toward the mountains on the horizon. They would be going to Turkey on horseback, a journey estimated to be twelve to thirteen days. She would ride atop one of the men's horses. Hearing all this, she recognized in her a gathering numbness.

What will come, will come, she thought, hoping to cling to that modicum of peace.

"You will be safe," Omeed assured her. Further words appeared to gather in his throat, but he forced them down.

This is Hassan's fault.

No, she thought, as she watched Omeed's vehicle recede along the way they'd come. *This is not Hassan's fault, nor Omeed's, nor Father's.*

Because I am the one standing here.

Wintry winds coursed across the hills, like a cavalcade of cold and lost spirits, spirits she imagined may have gone astray on their ascent to Heaven, nabbed by the stone teeth of this valley, caught in its dark kerfs and hollows.

Her companions did not interact with her much. They treated her as they did the equine, with food, with base acknowledgment. For this she was ultimately thankful, though ironically it was because of their deadness as men that she held mild pity towards them. Their fires had dwindled. Perhaps she would have had more to fear from younger men in the way of violent advance. Almost certainly she would have. But these men... these men were the dryness of their cloth, the world-worn fabric of their bags and pouches, the stone beneath their feet, the impervious, indifferent clouds: drifters into a long-accepted destiny.

Of course, the journey was only two days old. An estimated twelve were left. Anything could happen. To them. To her. To them all. Quietly, she prayed.

CHAPTER SIX

Present Day

TUCCI STIRRED AT THE ring of his cell phone. In the brief amnesia between sleeping and waking, he wondered where he was. His chest clenched when he didn't recognize the ceiling over his bed. But it wasn't his bed. He'd fallen asleep on the couch.

On the coffee table, his phone continued ringing. He grasped for it and opened it without looking at the caller identity.

"Tucci," he said.

"It's Tara." Her voice was low. "I may have something for you."

Whatever had taken hold of St. Vincent's, whatever had infested it, now seemed to live in her. Tara watched herself do her job, engage in tasks, and nod and smile at appropriate faces. She even spoke compassionately with patients, but it was not her doing all of this; at least not her primary self, which was trapped in a bizarrely addictive fear that to her was like a drug.

Although never admitting this supposition, in her years as a cancer surgeon, based on things she had learned regarding many of her patients, cancer increasingly seemed to her an emotional disease, an outgrowth of stress, of fear, of suppressed anger. The actual type of cancer made little difference—like a hurricane, negative emotion battered the body, leaving some parts persisting, others weakened and damaged. If one had the fortunate reinforcements of good genetics, one could remain standing much longer.

Sometime, somewhere, in some distant recess of her youth, Tara remembered trying meditation and thought now that she ought to resume it. It had been a busy time then, and many things had built up like plaque around those memories, so, unnervingly, she could recall little of how long she tried meditating, or its success rate. It seemed, like many memories, to have occurred in some dream-like wedge in her life.

A half-hour before she left for the night, there was a knock on her office door.

"Yes?"

Timidly the door clicked open. Dr. Parsons's face appeared. "Tara?"

"Hi, Janice."

"May I visit with you for a bit? I'm sorry if I'm disrupting last minute business…"

Tara waved her in. Parsons shut the door behind her, as softly as she'd opened it, and took a seat on the edge of a chair across her desk. She looked very lonely.

"Tara," said Parsons. "I want you to know I completely understand your decision."

"I'm not leaving permanently, Janice—"

"I know. I can understand why you'd be less than comfortable taking over Marika's spot. Even temporarily. I think it'd do us all good to recharge. But know what an asset you are to this hospital, Tara."

"Thank you, Janice."

Bits of small talk rose between them before Parsons excused herself and bade her a good night.

Tara watched her go, exhaled. She got the sense Dr. Parsons had, at the last thankful second, reconsidered her original intent of laying on a guilt trip for this sabbatical. Tara needed this—there was no stopping it. Whether or not it would ultimately be the springboard to leaving St. Vincent's for good, she wasn't sure. But she liked the option, a welcome perforation in what had felt as an ever-enclosing dark box.

Walking to her car, Tara kept her free hand on the mace in her pocket, though her alertness was compromised by thoughts of her sabbatical. A hopeful renewal.

Presently, she felt watched, but had ceased to differentiate real, justified worry from, well, just plain worry. These days, she always felt watched.

Snug in her car, she drove down past the vehicles aligned on either side and emerged at a stop sign. Glancing back and forth, Tara noticed to her right another car emerging from the structure's northern exit, brights ablaze. Barely heeding the stop sign, it lurched forth and sped past her. It was a larger vehicle, like an SUV, glistening black, cartoonish angel-wing stickers on the rearview mirrors.

Cartoonish angel-wing stickers.

She remembered what Randolph had said the night she and Mike Tucci had spoken to him about her... visitor. The big car idling out front.

Follow it.

Tara turned left and cautiously threaded her way through traffic, coming up behind the car. It was an Explorer, that was all she could tell. Its route appeared straight, taking her down the main boulevard, past several intersections. She took care to maintain a buffer of twenty to thirty feet, close enough for her to record the license plate number in her phone.

Follow it all the way.

But caution won out and she turned at the next light, then pulled over to a darkened curb where she dialed Mike Tucci.

"Tucci," he said, voice gravelly. He'd just woken up.

"It's Tara," she said. "I may have something for you."

The plates on the angel-winged Explorer went back to a Katherine Graham, a ten-year resident of Westchester and older sibling to none other than Carter Graham, former male nurse at St. Vincent's and makeshift leader of the protest group.

The neighborhood was flat and dull, middle-class though pushing lower. Parking about half a block away, Tucci and Bashir passed chewed lawns and crabby canines. Outside the Graham household, Tucci noticed no sign of the Explorer. Above the front door was a *No Solicitors* sign, with the rickety engraved addition: *This Means You!*

Bashir rang. They waited. A woman roughly in her mid-forties— much older than Carter, Tucci deduced—answered the door and, while trying to appear casual at the sight of their badges, it was evident something of a fragile shell had broken, spilled across her face, the raw black yolk of her pupils already hazarding guesses and frantic strategies.

"Ms. Graham," said Bashir. "Do you own a 2002 black Explorer?" He paused, gave the license number. "Angel wings on the mirrors?"

"Oh God, what?" She folded her arms, bracing for news. "What happened? My brother took it to the store. Did something happen to Cart—"

"Nothing's happened, ma'am," Tucci said. "But we'd like to ask you a few questions, if you don't mind. May we come in?"

She nodded, gestured them inside. The carpet was an archipelago of stains and toys, and the air had a foody smell either from recent cooking or neglected trash. Sitting on the far side of the couch watching TV was a boy of middle-school age in a striped collared shirt. His lap had collected crumbs. His eyes were beady, his face misshapen. He was handicapped.

"This is Garrett," said Ms. Graham. "My son. Garett, I'm just going to talk to these men for a bit."

Garrett smiled and made a groaning noise. He didn't seem to be paying much attention. Ms. Graham led the detectives toward the kitchen. She was visibly shaking.

"Did Carter do something?" she said.

"We don't know," Tucci said. "You say he uses your car?"

She nodded. "He does errands and things for me so I can stay with Garrett. I'm very thankful, really. For God's sake, he's my little brother; I've known him his whole life. He's got his troubles, like we all do, but he's been a Godsend to us here."

"He lives here too, then?"

"He moved in about a year ago. After he lost his job at the hospital. With his nursing background he's been very good. Not that he wasn't okay before. But it's nice to have him just one room over."

"I understand."

Her eyes grew overcast. "I know he's unhappy with hospital politics. He takes up crusades, that's just him. But please, just so I know—you don't think he did anything, right?"

"Like what?"

Biting her lip, she said, "Like kill that doctor?"

"We don't know," Tucci said. He brought out and unfolded the paper with the cryptic threat, left at Tara's apartment. "Have you seen this before?"

She took it, read it and hastily shook her head. "No, no, God no, I haven't." She gave it back to Tucci as if it were painful to the touch.

"It was left at Dr. White's residence. She was a colleague of the victim's. A witness described a vehicle matching yours, outside her apartment complex."

"Jesus," she said, plastering her hand over her face. "I feel sick."

"We wanted to see if you knew anything about this," Bashir said. "We'd like to speak with Carter, too."

"Well, as I said, he should be home any minute." She sighed. "I don't know. I've known him all my life. I told you, he lives here now, in a room over the garage, but there are big patches of Carter I've never seen. I'm sure of it. He's very private, always locking himself in his room. I don't know anything about any of this. Really." Her tone was on a trajectory toward panic-and-plead. Tucci expected an 'I swear' or 'Honest to God' to follow.

From the living room, Garrett made a noise and Ms. Graham excused herself to tend to him. Tucci pitied her. The house was tainted with the rot of faith, the sad acclimation to something far outside the hopes, dreams, and expectations of a younger time.

The sound of an engine drew closer, settled in the driveway and stopped. Tucci stiffened, looked at Bashir. With the speed of someone eager to prevent a conflict, Ms. Graham moved to the front door, as Carter's form shuddered past the blinds toward the porch.

The detectives bristled. Katherine greeted her brother, who handed her one of three plastic bags he toted. She thanked him dryly.

About to speak, Carter was interrupted by the very sight of Tucci and Bashir. He dropped the bags and bolted back toward the car, Katherine flailing and crying out after him. From the couch, Garrett let out one big amused guffaw.

Charging out the front door, a fierce and icy breeze struck Tucci, as if conspiring to hold him back.

Katherine caught her brother just as he reached the driver's side and the two men huddled in as close reinforcements. Trembling,

Carter seemed to hear only snippets of his sister's attempts to assuage him. Tucci noticed Carter appeared freshly shaved. Maybe he'd removed the goatee Randolph had noted.

"Carter, goddammit," Katherine said. "They just came to ask you some things."

"We won't bite," Tucci said. "We may nibble. We won't bite."

"Why don't you sit yourself down and relax," Bashir said.

Carter gave Bashir a sour look and acquiesced, and the tiny entourage returned to the living room, Katherine gathering up the dropped bags with Tucci's assistance. She then turned off the television and took Garrett to his own room, where she stayed as well.

Carter slumped into the couch, stern-faced with hazy eyes, like that of a volatile drunk. He threw furtive venomous glances at both detectives but seemed to linger on Bashir.

Tucci showed him the letter left for Tara.

"This you?"

Carter lowered his head.

"We have a witness describing your sister's car outside Dr. White's apartment, during the time this lovely little note was left. He also saw the person who left it." Tucci turned his head slightly, lifted Carter's chin with his finger. "Kinda looked like you."

"Yeah, fuck it," said Carter. "It was me. Wasn't my idea though."

"Doesn't matter. You done the deed. That's a crime. You realize that, right?"

"Writin' a note is a crime?"

"If it's a threat it is."

"So whose idea was it?"

"Well," Carter said. "Dr. Stiles told us that Dr. Javid and Dr. White were a unit. Take one down, you had to take the other."

"Told us? Who's us?" said Tucci. "You mean your ragtag group of John Bircher Juniors?"

"You know Stiles killed her," Carter said. "Or he had someone do it."

"Really? And just how do you know this?"

Carter made a move to stand. "Can I show you something?"

After a furtive exchange of glances, the detectives conceded and followed Carter toward his room and waited outside. A shuffling noise followed, the sifting of loose items and papers. The pull and push of drawers.

Carter reemerged with a manila envelope he handed to Tucci. Inside was a slew of photos, some crisply clear, others grainy and printed on an ink-jet. There were restaurant shots, car shots, shots of nice-looking hotels Tucci guessed were not local, all featuring Dr. Stiles and Dr. Javid.

"The bastard was involved with her," he said. "You know— 'doin' her."

"So we can add stalking to the list," Bashir said. "How long was this going on, Mr. Graham?"

"Me followin' them? Or him… doin' her?"

Tucci shot Bashir a look, then thumbed through the photos. Although all of the pictures showed Marika Javid, Stiles was absent from some of them. A few revealed her in what looked like an argument with someone else, a Middle-Eastern man who looked familiar to Tucci.

"Do you know how long they were seeing each other?" Bashir asked.

Carter shook his head. "I dunno exactly. Stiles was supposedly on our side, even though he was gettin' his rocks off with her. He told us he didn't like the foreigners the hospital hired; he was suspicious of them. But he never said much about her, though, Dr. Javid—not that I heard."

"Did you speak to him on a regular basis?"

"Not regular, no. I did talk to him one night he was leaving the hospital. He pulled a couple of us aside, and said that whatever he could do to help—to lend more legitimacy to our cause, he would do it. This was when we first started, y'know. Since then he's made public statements here and there, and I think he and some others tried to put stricter filters on the hospital hiring policies. But... I guess part of me didn't believe him. Especially after that Arab woman was promoted—"

"Dr. Javid."

"Yeah, yeah. Doctor Javid. I'd seen them together before, in the cafe, by the elevators, sometimes outside. I got a weird vibe from it, from him especially." Carter shifted back and forth uncomfortably. "So I started followin' them and took the pics... so I could show them to the others. Y'know, so they'd know not to trust him, necessarily. 'Cause he was like, with her, the enemy. I was disappointed. You have to smile and nod and be polite with the people you work with, even if you take issue with them. Especially the bigwigs. I mean, I know that's politics, but after she was promoted we were hoping he'd put his foot down more. Ha, right! Not gonna happen with someone you're boffing. Or used to."

Tucci held up a photo to him, "You know who this man is?"

Carter shrugged. "Nah. One afternoon I see her, that Dr. Javid, in this really intense yelling match near the parking garage. I guess it wasn't a match because he was dishing it and she was taking it, mostly. He looked Arab, like her, but older. I thought maybe it was her father. They weren't speaking English."

"So you kept following her. Even when she wasn't with Stiles."

Shrugging, Carter said, "Figured someone had to get more dirt on this woman, y'know, who's climbing the ranks. We got word that they only hired her 'cause of internal dissension. Like a 'Fuck You' to all the nurses and doctors legitimately concerned about patients, not just fifth-rate immigrants who want jobs at an American hospital."

"You do realize that Dr. Javid went to Northwestern?" said Bashir. "She's been in the States for over fifteen years. She's not exactly fresh off the boat."

"Don't matter. She wasn't born here. Didn't grow up here. You can't change that. You can't change dogma or family. Look at these terrorists that go to school here and spend years here. They aren't fresh off the boat, either. But they got an agenda. They are full of their ways and they want to inject it all into our society, drip by drip, or in one big dose. And all these… people"—he gestured, and Tucci could only guess what nastier word lurked behind that pause—"are connected. These Arabs. They come in from all sides. From Canada. From Mexico. Shit, ain't it enough, we gotta worry about Mexicans comin' in from there? Now we got Arab terrorists haulin' their asses in from there, too. And you guys aren't doin' anything to stop any of 'em."

Tucci wasn't sure whether to refute this last claim or let it slide. Given the number of issues he had, or would have, with whatever came spewing out of Graham's mouth, he had to pick his battles. The concern of border-crossing Muslim terrorists was, of course, very real, but that wasn't his problem. Marika's murder was his problem. And Carter had enough anger and hatred to make him a prime suspect. The jackass was right about one thing, though. According to various FBI dispatches over the years since 9/11, Arab terrorists not only came in from Mexico, they even posed as Mexicans, learning enough of the culture and of the Spanish language to get by.

"What about Dr. White?" Tucci said. "She was brought up here. Farmer's daughter. Americana. You threatened her."

"It's like what Stiles said. They were like this." Carter held up two intertwined fingers. "Two peas in a pod. Y'see, Americans are just as much to blame, because they let this stuff happen and they support these kinds of people. Technically, we're more mad at them than the foreigners. Foreigners wanna do what they wanna do—can't blame them too much. But these Americans let it happen. Shit, that blonde doctor hired the Arab as her partner."

"So that's why you left the note," Tucci said. "You were just talking about terrorism. You're spreading terror yourself."

Who is that man Marika is arguing with? Tucci thought in the back of his mind.

Carter looked at Bashir, then at Tucci, his gaze metallic, much colder than it'd been moments ago. Remorseless.

"It worked, right?" Carter said. "Dr. White's leaving."

"What?"

"You didn't know?" Carter smiled. "Yep, she's leaving St. Vincent's. Better catch her quick."

Finally, Carter Graham's energy waned. He began speaking only occasionally, before soon stopping altogether. As Tucci cuffed him and Bashir read him his rights, he complied silently while Katherine watched with wet eyes from the doorway of her son's bedroom. Bashir called in further units to assist in compiling relevant material from the house, primarily from Carter's room.

Tucci imagined little of whatever else they found would be as vital, or damning, as the hateful man's photo menagerie.

Despite the evidence and his confession of terrorist threats and stalking, and despite mounting temptation to make the leap, there was yet no real indication that Graham had murdered Marika Javid. The most recent photos of her had been taken two days prior to the killing, and, while uncovering several more undelivered threat letters, there emerged no bloody glove or encrusted weapon, or any clue of the sort Dickey had dubbed the "flashing neon."

At the station, Tucci scanned and copied the Graham photos. There were more unprinted pics on the smartphone found in Carter's room, which Tucci uploaded to his computer. Bashir beside him, they treated themselves to a slideshow of Carter Graham's perverse, almost twistedly admirable devotion.

From the lockers, Tucci had brought out the only photo album of Marika's, which Bashir flipped through as he sipped from a steaming cup. Tucci also had Marika's photos, some scanned, which he'd loaded onto a flashdrive and subsequently his computer. He searched them now for the face featured in only four of the Graham images: the razor-eyed Middle-Eastern man, easily her senior, with whom Marika had appeared to be arguing—yet if one went by her cold and withdrawn expression, the "argument" hardly seemed two-sided.

Liath. Aadila's husband. The first picture of him—the only one in Marika's physical album—had been small, and he'd looked different, younger, but...

Was she screwing Liath, too? And had he found out about Stiles? No, ridiculous. But they would have to check it all out. Had to knock on a few more doors.

Tucci just happened to glance at Bashir, who was staring at him with a small, knowing grin, as if he'd been waiting for Tucci to turn to him. They silently nodded to each other, grabbed their gear and headed out.

Having no luck at the hospital, they decided to try Dr. Raymond Stiles at his home in Pacific Palisades.

With the sky a searing blue, accented by picturesque palm trees, the drive for Tucci was a welcome reminder of classical Los Angeles, enjoyable more so because Bashir was driving.

"The famous Palisades," said Bashir. "My wife's already been talking about moving here, but neither of us has even been up here yet."

"Wait a little while," Tucci said. "It's either older folks or yuppie power families."

Bashir laughed. "I know those. I spent a decade in San Francisco." They continued driving, winding up to Sunset. In a clipped and quieter tone, Bashir said, "By the way, my wife wants to have you over soon."

"For what?"

"Dinner or something. She's always curious. She likes to know the people I work with. We also don't know many people here, so I think she'd like to start a kind of network."

Tucci tossed a grape Jolly Rancher into his mouth. "Sounds like a lot of pressure."

"No, no. No pressure." A pause. "And if you've got a wife or girlfriend, she's welcome too. Or a boyfriend."

Tucci looked at him.

"San Francisco, remember," said Bashir.

"Well thanks." He thought of Tara White, but tried to push her from his mind.

She's leaving. Tara's leaving.

They found the address, nestled up in the hills above the village, then walked to the door and rang. Tucci could perceive activity in the house. He motioned again to press the buzzer, when the door opened and the cosmetically-tweaked face of Charlotte Stiles appeared, her expression sour.

"He's out of town for the weekend," she said, before they could even properly display their badges. "He went fishing."

"Okay," Tucci said, trying not to sound startled. "When will he be b—"

"I don't know. Sunday, Monday. He gets lost up there. Not literally. You know what I mean."

"Sure." Tucci handed her a business card. Something about the way Mrs. Stiles took it and looked at it made him think she might crumple it up right there. "Would you have him call us? We'd like to speak with him."

She complied and they parted on a terse farewell, the door shut as fast as it had opened.

"You think 'fishing' might be some kind of euphemism?" Bashir said in gray humor, as they started down the porch steps.

Dr. Raymond Stiles remembered the stormy energy of youth, that maelstrom of passion and ambition and neuroses, when imagination constituted most of what there was, or could be, in the world. As he aged, he had been both sad and relieved to see the energy diminish, but lately it had made an incredible (and not altogether welcome) resurgence: firstly in the meet-ups with Marika, which had returned to him a juvenile tingle and a likable and familiar fear, and now in her death, which had whittled all sensations to a singular nervous dread that shaded every day.

Initially, worry had centered around Charlotte—what she would say or do when his... his actions eventually came to light. In imagining her reaction, he realized how little he actually knew of the woman with whom he'd shared thirty-two years. Long ago they had both had made peace with their mutual tendency to flirt with the opposite sex. For Stiles, it had been even more exciting to see Charlotte approach another man than it'd been for him to flirt with another woman. To the best of his knowledge, however, Charlotte had never gone as far as he had.

On his way back from the lake, she called him.

"Ray," Charlotte said.

"What?" It always irritated him when she did this, this suspenseful beat that was always a prelude to something good or something bad.

And nothing good's been happening.

"Some detectives were here today," Charlotte said. "The ones who were at the funeral. They want to talk to you."

"What about?"

Charlotte made an incredulous gasp—how could her obviously guilty husband be so damned stupid? "What else? Your colleague's death."

"All right."

The knot in his gut grew tighter. Her relative detachment spoke of some inner-held conviction that perhaps her husband was guilty of one, or more, unforgivable transgressions.

The drive back from the lake was long and lonesome. The idea of suicide, of pulling slightly left on the narrow mountain road and barreling through the guard rail and down the steep dark incline, of swallowing up whole the dread and the nerves and the politics, was tantalizing. Charlotte would forget about her anger, if she was indeed angry. No one could talk to him. No one would dare tarnish his reputation.

More than all his nervous anticipation, the sense of a greater threat, greater than that of Charlotte's cold eyes, or losing his family, pressed on him. It was a sense of bodily harm. The part of him amenable to suicide didn't care—most of the rest of him, of course, remained taut, on edge.

He had long suppressed such intuition, but it seemed all the more stronger now, perhaps because he had ignored it for so long, or perhaps because of the gravity of whatever awaited him. Stiles had listened to these… feelings before, had once outwardly, though timidly, expressed a belief in their authentic benefits, taking pains to avoid the word "psychic." In fact, his lifelong association with such sensations had informed his pursuit of neuro-studies. This tiptoe toward the edge of conventional science, however, had very nearly destroyed his career. The only way fit to recoup it: militaristic devotion to the orthodox, to the known, to the mainstream.

Slowly, the dark mountains flattened, gave way to speckles of civilization.

Stiles' thoughts turned to Marika Javid herself. Doubtless she had been a beautiful and brilliant woman. Her admiration of him, which had started afar from seeing and hearing his name in the medical community, had rather blinded her to his politics, though they rarely discussed such things. She wanted his approval, she wanted the thrill of his closeness, and he, if he were honest with himself, wanted most her exotic beauty.

As much as he tried to squelch it, to deny it, he knew he could never outrun the notion that he was responsible for Marika's death. It was hardly a coincidence that such a savage scene should occur in the midst of those protests. And he had supported them. Not some of the more fringe, racist elements—although by sheer association, no matter how broad, Stiles knew that to their detractors he could never *not* be racist—but those advancing the core message of abolishing political correctness and diversity as having any sway in the hiring process.

But had one of the fringe crazies broken loose, traded their sign for a blade? Stalked the halls for the first dark-skinned doctor he saw? Stiles could practically imagine the deed through the killer's eyes. He felt sick to his stomach.

There's also Charlotte.

Did Charlotte know about him and Marika? More and more he regretted bringing her to the funeral. Cold eyes. Clearly she had not wanted to be there. Could she have…

No, she couldn't have.

Hired someone?

Stop thinking like this.

His thoughts shifted to Marika herself. If he and Marika had a more emotional connection, he might have kept some of her inside him. Instead, the Marika he had bedded was the Marika that had died, the Marika never to return. The space in his breast that may have carried any love for her crawled instead with guilt, with self-loathing.

He pulled off at a gas station. In the adjacent stall stood an ashen-haired woman, holding the nozzle at a pick-up truck. She watched Stiles with amusement, the smacking of her gum loud in the lonely, buzzing lot.

Noticing her stare, he said, "Can I help you?"

"No," she said. "I think I know you though."

"You do?"

"Yeah. I seen you up at the lake. Oh wait." She held her finger to her mouth, either in thought or reluctance. "You… you came to mind recently. 'Cause of that woman."

The associative "click" in the woman's mind was very evident on her face. He was sure she perceived some of the color that drained from his expression. Was this how it was going to be? Even with complete strangers? The rest of them, all of them, fucking them, a Cyclopean eye honed on him, athrob with knowing? With suspicion? With accusation?

"My wife," he muttered, just to say something and hoping she wouldn't hear.

"Your wife? That woman that's been on the news? The one… the one killed? Jesus. You been up and down it. I'm so sorry. I didn't mean… I didn't…"

"It's okay. Thank you."

Stiles turned away from the woman. Toward three-quarters of a tank, he pulled the nozzle and holstered it, eager to get moving, get home, despite the certain issues with Charlotte. Stopping brought greater unease. He entertained a fantasy of being perpetually nomadic. He would buy a boat, long a retirement dream of his and Charlotte's. Except it would just be him. Him alone.

As he returned to his car the woman said, "Take care of yourself, okay?"

"Thanks."

Stiles pulled out. Soon the lights of the gas station fell to the dark horizon. For most of the journey, the blather of talk radio had accompanied him, but the droning voices became a nuisance and, with minimal improvement, switched to music.

His stomach surged. He pulled over to the side of the highway, opened the door and vomited on the asphalt. He felt hollowed out.

Marika, he thought. *I'm so sorry.*

From the thin stream of cars rushing past him, another vehicle, a red sedan, broke off and moved to the side, coming to rest about a hundred yards ahead of him, its right blinker pulsing until all lights turned off and it sat dark and inactive. He didn't see the driver.

Stiles sat for several minutes, feeling as if he were in some kind of duel. He monitored in the rearview mirrors the stream of traffic behind him, the many headlights like distant stars growing supernova in their approach, until dissipating in cold red dwarfs down the shadowed stretch.

Seeing an opening, he turned on the engine and his brights and maneuvered back onto the highway. He punched the accelerator, adrenaline rising.

Stiles looked once more in the mirror and saw the car's lights brighten. With an air of inevitability, it rejoined the traffic.

With that black-pearl eye, Toby saw her and came to her, all glorious eleven-hundred pounds of him. He snorted. Tara caressed his snout, ran her hands along the fuzzy steel of his jawbone, the Corinthian musculature of his neck.

Horses are the wilds bottled, she'd always thought. The titan-rattling thunder of their hooves, the oceans of spirit in their eyes, the economy of their shape, the stuff of a supreme, primal freedom that people constantly yearned for, and expressed, through millennia of paths forged on horseback. Horses didn't truly obey people, they obeyed the wilds, as humans unwittingly did. Why else did they say "riding" horses instead of driving them? People rode them as we rode the elements—half-blind, assuming more control than granted.

Tara hung the saddle, adjusted the muzzle, slackened the reins. There was a power in being on Toby, a partially violent power. It nourished her now, made her feel protected.

She remembered the time she'd gone riding with Marika, one of only a handful of times they had socialized outside work. Marika had rented a horse, riding it with surprising grace. As a child, she'd told Tara, she had sometimes ridden. She didn't like to anymore, though. She'd lost a loved one while riding. Tara had asked, but Marika didn't want to talk about it. That was the last time she'd joined her. Still, Tara had recognized her gift. The horse had seemed lulled, even entranced by her presence. Marika could sometimes have that effect, Tara mused, though it was usually on people, not horses.

A protestor, Tara thought, as she and Toby drifted from the stables. *Those goddamn wackos. It had to be one of them.*

Or…

Tara tried to shove such thoughts away. Detective Tucci would tell her. He would find out.

Find it all out?

She rode across the haggard trail cut in the Malibu hills, drew lower into the ragged shadow of an oak and eucalyptus forest. The afternoon was blue and still. The trail forked, and Tara took the lesser route, the overgrown, faded path darkened by a thick canopy. Toby made his diligent way over the fallen trees and rugged soil, until the path came clearer into focus and they followed it up toward a crop of boulders.

She tried also to shove away thoughts of Mike Tucci.

The rocks formed a short corridor through which Tara felt she might be entering some new realm, a dimension all her own, until it opened on a wide and undulating meadow, backdropped with distant views of peaks that recalled less of Los Angeles and more of Utah, or Montana.

The land of everything, Tara thought.

And then, with a kick, she and Toby took off galloping, Toby's hooves scraping furiously upon the dirt in great billows of dust.

What are you doing?

For his twenty-minute wait outside Maxwell's Diner, that question sat heavy on Mike Tucci's brain, invulnerable to any distraction. He felt very conspicuous out here, too, milling about on the rain-slicked cement. Even light rain was enough to scare many Los Angeles drivers off the streets, and so the roads were empty, the nearby apartment windows burning in the dark like fiery eyes set on him.

He turned and she was there at the street corner, walking toward him, a lovely human-shaped brightness. She was dressed the most informal he'd seen her: light sweater beneath a raincoat and jeans, and earth-chewed sandals on her feet. Her arms were folded across her chest, either for warmth or in subtle defense. Or both.

"Hi detective," said Tara White, lips upturned in a smirk. She looked into Maxwell's Diner. "I've passed this place for years, never been in. Good occasion for new things, though."

Tucci was about to respond when Tara abruptly turned and entered. He followed. Several male customers stared at her until Tucci looked at them and they fell once more into their late-evening meals and coffees.

They took a corner booth. The waiter, a thin, awkward

parenthesis of a person, brought them water. Tara asked for tea, Tucci for a coke.

"Thanks for meeting me," Tucci said.

"Thanks for calling," said Tara.

"Sure."

"I know you're going to ask about St. Vincent's."

"I thought I was the detective."

"Of course." She gave a tired smile and brushed hair from her forehead. Tucci mused in that moment what intriguing lips she had, and what it would be like to kiss them. Then he flipped it out of his mind.

After some hesitation, Tara said, "I couldn't take it anymore, really."

The tea and coke came. When asked about food, Tucci ordered a slice of apple pie.

"Rather ironic," Tara continued, "because I would've killed to get—oh shit." Forcefully she set down her cup, closed her eyes. "Fucking horrible word choice, Tara. Don't know what's wrong with me."

"It's fine. I didn't even think about it." A lie.

"Well anyway, I wanted the job, but was certainly happy that Marika got it. When Dr. Parsons offered it to me after the… you know, I thought it was the perfect opportunity to continue her 'legacy,' to beat these people back." Tara's gaze wandered away and her words followed. "But I think the… I don't know, I can't think of words today. I think the taint of it just caught up with me."

"We spoke with your nighttime visitor," Tucci said. "Carter Graham. He tried to run, too. Dunno what gets into their heads. But he's just like I thought he'd be. A racist jack-off. But a murderer? I don't know."

"You don't have evidence for that."

"The threat he left you… not necessarily related… just shows he was trying to create fear."

"Guess it basically worked, huh?"

"We still have to make sure it wasn't him in Dr. Javid's office that night. But I don't think he killed her."

"You don't?"

Tucci shook his head no. "He was following her, though." Tucci produced two copies, reduced in size, of Carter's photos. "It appears she was having some R & R with Dr. Stiles. That was the primary reason our charming stalker was tailing her."

"That would implicate Stiles, though. I mean, Stiles was on their side."

"Not enough, apparently."

"So strange, I swear." Tara shook her head. "People aren't dualistic. They're fragmented. And I guess I got only a fragment of Marika. I never imagined her in a million years doing something like this."

Tucci produced another photo: his own close-up of Dr. Javid's older breast scar. "I hope this isn't difficult to see," he said. "I chose one that showed the least of her."

"It's okay," Tara said. "I'm not exactly a greenhorn on this stuff."

"Sure." Tucci pointed to the mark. "Was wondering if you had any idea what that might be. Coroner thought it could be a surgical scar, which is what I thought. But we checked the records and it didn't seem like Javid underwent any procedure. But thought I'd ask."

Tara studied the photo, scratching her ear. Infinitesimal hesitation, Tucci noticed. Maybe he shouldn't have pushed that photo on her.

"I doubt that's from surgery," Tara said. "Looks too irregular."

"Really?" he said, taking back the picture. Her verdict sounded so resolute. "It's in an odd area. Usually clothed. Can't really think what would've made it."

"Trust me," Tara said. "You don't want to imagine the kinds of places people can get scars." Suddenly a lighter, more playful spirit took her. "Although I'm sure you've seen some yourself."

"Touché."

"You speak with Stiles?" Tara asked. Her blue eyes conveyed both irritation and a distant relish.

"We haven't yet, no."

"We?"

"Associate detective and I."

"Oh right, he was the one with you at the funeral?"

The waiter set the pie down in front of them. Tara, rather presumptuously, picked up a fork.

"Yes." Tucci looked at her. "Why?"

"It's nothing," Tara said, cutting off a mouthful of crust and glaze and apple. "No offense, Mike, I just pictured you more a loner. Not exactly like me, maybe, but…"

"I need all the help I can get," he said.

Chewing, Tara slowly nodded. "I know that."

The rain had started again. At one point, Tara's shoes slid on the cement, and reflexively, Tucci's hands clasped about her biceps to steady her. The contact enlivened her.

"I hope Randy's not out having one of his evening smokes," she said, suddenly realizing she had never before expressed this sentiment aloud. It had come out without thinking.

"Randy, your neighbor?"

She nodded. "He's a good guy, I suppose. But you don't need to be a detective to see he has issues. I'm sure you know the type."

"Probably less so than the average woman. Sadly."

He's a damn cop, Tara thought. *Watch yourself.*

They jaywalked across to her complex, their footsteps echoing down the vacant street.

"It's a little eerie how L.A. just retires in the rain, isn't it?" said Tara, as they entered her apartment. "It's like a watery apocalypse. We're the last two left."

Tucci smiled. "That'd be interesting."

"Red or white?"

"Whichever." Tucci draped his coat over one of the dining room chairs and sauntered, hands pocketed, into the living room. "You're the one who's celebrating."

Tara whipped a heated glance at him. "What am I 'celebrating?'"

"Your break from work. Right?"

She turned back to the counter, opened the bottle of red and poured two glasses. "I guess. I'd never thought of celebrating it, though. Not under these circumstances."

Gingerly picking up the glasses, she moved toward Tucci. He met her halfway. She was about to ask a question when he cut her off with one of his own.

"Any more visiting rodents?"

She sighed. "Thankfully, no. Though I came across some pellets I hadn't seen before. Wasn't sure if they were new or not."

She sipped her wine and looked at Tucci. What was going on in there? In his head? It both bothered and excited her that, in the time they'd been acquainted, he seemed to know more about her than she ever could have known about him. Did he know things, suspect things, see things she of her own accord would never have given or shown him? Did he keep this slight distance because of these things, or was he being the typical aloof male?

Aloof, she thought. *Look who's talking.*

"Let me ask you," she said. They stood in the middle of the living room, not more than a foot of carpet between them. "How numb are you to it all? To the things you see? You mentioned celebrating… could you really 'celebrate' after coming home from some horrible scene?"

The answer, Tara figured, was an assured yes, recalling a night she'd attended a boozy gathering not hours after losing an alcoholic patient to liver cancer.

"I don't have much to celebrate, no," said Tucci. "I suppose that's why I use the term loosely. I'll take any opportunity." He sipped his drink. "Something tells me you're not exactly that way."

"What do you mean?"

"We both see a lot of tragedy," Tucci said. "A lot of death. As if, in defense, we've more or less cut our own lives down to the point where, if death comes, it wouldn't be getting much. Make it go hungry." He smiled a dull but sage smile. "That's how I see it anyway. I've been working on seeing it otherwise."

Tara was irritated by this observation, but she wasn't sure why. Probably because it was accurate. She felt capable of any emotion now, her volatility increased by the wine. She set her glass down on the counter behind her.

"I don't have very many people to celebrate with," she said. "I work all day. I'm too busy to have a pet —"

"No family?"

Why do you want to know? she thought. *You already know. You know everything, don't you?*

"Only child," she said. "Father died fairly early on. Mother died not long after I left home."

"Didn't you say your dad used to make that chickens-in-the-fox-den analogy?" Tucci said. "But you only knew him the first four years of your life?"

"My mom used to quote him."

"I see." Tucci took another sip of wine and set his glass down on the coffee table.

"What about you?" she said.

"What?"

"You know…" Flustered, it was difficult for her to conjure words. Between surges of desire flared her more analytical side, attempting, far less admirably than usual, a definition of what she was feeling.

Then, in a heated surge, she took Tucci's collar and kissed him.

His response was instant, as if they'd met midway in chasing the same thought. A hand, tender but determined, found and cupped her breast.

Abruptly, she broke the kiss.

Head down, Tara walked briskly past him as if charting a course. Soon she slowed, stopping in the middle of the room. She rubbed her neck.

"Sorry," she said, her back to him. "I know this is weird."

Tucci said nothing. He approached her from behind, placed his hands on her shoulders and squeezed them in a light massage, then moved down her back in sensuous rubs. He slid his arms around her waist. She felt delightfully ensnared. Suddenly it was inevitable. Suddenly it was okay.

She turned and they kissed. Electric chills ricocheted between their bodies. Initially of pure drive, of sloppy instinct, the kiss took on a finer rhythm, like a symphony siphoned from a thunderstorm, and they stumbled through the bedroom door, some garments hastily and jerkily removed, lips finding newer regions of flesh. In the addictive heat they paused in their rickety path to the bed and remained against the wall, Tucci lifting Tara by the waist, her freshly-bare leg curled about him. Their bodies so close, both felt the heavy press of his breast glock against them and Tucci unclipped the pistol and tossed it on a nearby footrest.

"Hold on," he said, reaching down to his pants cuff to unclip his ankle pistol, which we laid next to the glock. "Don't want too many going off at once."

Tara chuckled and they dove into another kiss. In a burst of violent mutual agreement they wrenched from the wall and fell upon the bed, where the remnant clothes were lost. Tara mounted him, breasts full and nude, strands of hair draping listlessly about her intoxicated face. It was here Tucci registered the tattoo on her chest—a monarch butterfly, small but stylized.

Flirtatiously, Tara bit her lower lip, leaned forward and kissed him, then moved down his neck toward his chest, soft lip-presses broken by the occasional nibble. She moved further and took him slowly into her mouth. He closed his eyes.

All things drained from him as Tara gave him pleasure. A tiny reserve of reclaimed peace, long undetected or forgotten in him, was now liberated, and it filled him, spread to every hardened corner of skin.

Tara kissed up his midsection, finding his mouth once more. They shifted toward the front-center of the bed, where Tara promptly flipped them over so Tucci lay atop her. Breath and body-smoke filled the rank air between them. Her legs tightened at his sides.

"Cuff me," she said.

"What?"

Tara splayed her arms. Her eyes, meeting Tucci's from the depths of her pillow, showed calculated craziness, if that were possible. A delirious determination.

"You're a cop," she said. "You don't have cuffs?"

Tucci's eyes narrowed. "I—"

Suddenly she rolled from the bed, wrenching herself away from under him. He thought maybe he'd upset her, and so gestured for her, but could not reach her as Tara bounced toward the bathroom. In the doorway she stopped and turned back to look at him, lifting a leg against the frame. Smiling.

"What are you doing?" Tucci said. His erection throbbed, prodding the sheets.

Without a word, Tara retreated into the bathroom. Seconds later, Tucci heard a rushing blast of water. She returned to the doorway.

"I'm drawing a bath," she said. "I've got jets. It'll be ready in a second."

Tucci wasn't clear if she wanted him to join her. He almost asked, until he thought it might make him look stupid. Kill the mood. He couldn't look stupid in front of Tara White. *Dr.* Tara White. For many reasons.

Tara slunk back into the bathroom. The water rushed, crackling and splashing. Tucci stayed where he was, his erection holding.

Finally, he brought himself up from the bed. When Tucci entered the bathroom, she had already undressed and slipped into the tub, her head resting, hair-splayed, along the porcelain as if she'd been there for hours, her flesh trembling under the ripples, her knee raised above the surface like some mound of immaculate earth, an island just-risen.

Tara smiled at him. "You're gonna stand there?"

He took this as an implicit invitation to join her, even if the tub looked quite cramped already, a fact both persuasive and dissuasive.

Tucci shed the rest of his clothes and she maneuvered enough to allow him in. Heated and wet, they were instantly conjoined. Curls of water spilled over the lip of the tub as they writhed and moaned. Tucci ran his finger down her neck and across her breasts, palming one of them—supple and round and perfect—then they kissed, deeply. Tucci's fingers continued their trek across her skin, stopping at a small jagged bump on her breast. When he looked, he saw he was touching the area of her elaborate butterfly tattoo.

This woman is a goddamn butterfly herself.

He smirked. "You're not going to fly away, are you?"

She reached up and took his caressing hand in her own, their fingers twined over the water.

"No," she said, moving into him. "I'm stuck right here."

Somewhere in the stretch of timeless night, Tucci awoke, or thought he awoke. He wasn't sure of his state. He felt Tara by him, breathing softly, calmly. Having fallen asleep spooning, they had since separated. He wanted to go to her, but couldn't. The more he tried, the more his body resisted, yet the clearer were his thoughts and entailing anxiety. The room swayed.

I'm fucking paralyzed.

Someone else was in the room, too. Ahead of him. Watchful. His heart rate rose, joining in the futile effort to revive the rest of his body. He tried to think rationally. This kind of phenomenon could happen. His mother had told him about it.

At the foot of the bed he perceived the man, the fucking mutt. *Olin.* A face he hadn't seen in half a decade and it was different. Olin was still and, though obscured, appeared far paler than he ever had. His hair was falling out, too, his flesh emaciated.

Olin stared at him.

Oh God Tara wake up, wake the fuck up please —

His phone rang. Rang. He tried to move, sent the loudest command he could to his muscles. Forced them. The ringing, persistent.

Finally he was able to wrench himself awake. Freedom. Relief. The room was bare, had resumed its stoic realness.

Tara stirred and groaned at the musical cell phone. He grabbed it, answered quietly.

"Tucci here."

"Talk about a bad welcome back," said Bashir. "Dr. Stiles was just attacked near his home."

CHAPTER SEVEN

STILES' FACE WAS THE most colorful thing in the sanitized whiteness of the hospital room. The left half had sustained far more damage than the right—Tucci could barely make out the eye beneath the purple-red swelling.

Charlotte Stiles gave him a far softer look than when he and Bashir questioned her at her Palisades door. Certainly all the mistrust, suspicions and unforgiveness were there—though in Charlotte's case, maybe it was just a heap of suspicions that had, through no real reasoning, become convictions—but they existed now more as silhouettes, behind a shade of understanding.

Charlotte's expression held what Dickey had called the "shame of knowledge."

"Mrs. Stiles," he said.

"Yes," she said, sniffing.

Oh don't play the goddamn vulnerable act, Tucci thought.

"Let's talk in the hall," she said.

"Better yet, could I buy you a cup of coffee? We could go downstairs. To the cafe."

She made a strange face, a frown at the obligation. Or maybe she thought he was asking her out. Something in Charlotte Stiles inspired animosity in Tucci.

"We could do that," she said.

He held the door open. She exited with a thankless strut. He dealt one more glance at Stiles, the vivid pulp of the surgeon's fruitbowl face, the stubborn stillness of his limbs, a body terribly small without its animator. Tucci imagined that, somewhere out there, Stiles was galavanting amidst realms unseen, on a prolonged vacation from the painful bearings of the body. But it felt more like Stiles was there, watching them, debating whether or not to return.

"I won't be surprised if you tell me Ray was having affairs," Charlotte said, picking at a muffin he'd bought her. In her other hand, she held a cup of steaming coffee.

Tucci hesitated. "We only know of one."

"Marika, of course."

Lip trembling.

He nodded. "How long have you known?"

"I've long suspected, but never known for sure. Quite honestly, I'm kind of numb to it. We used to… we used to swing when we were younger. Much younger. I guess it wasn't technically swinging because we weren't married. But, um, I guess you could say we shared one another generously. Then when we married we decided to stop. Or I did, anyway. Guess it was a hard habit for him to get over. I told him it hurt me, and he said he stopped. What I don't know won't kill me, right? Except we stopped talking about it. That's how he deals with things. I'm sure that's how he deals with things at his work. All sorts of behind-the-back talk."

Charlotte sipped her coffee, which she nearly spilled. It wasn't just her lips trembling. This was not a surface tremor, either, but rooted deep within her.

Tucci sorely disliked this woman. She seemed the type to assume personas, for any possible gain. A shapeshifter. An amoeba. Personal bias aside, though, he could not rule out Charlotte Stiles' obvious motive. Maybe it had been as simple as revenge. A spouse scorned. Of course, there was a chance she had kept her hands clean. Well-endowed financially, she could have hired someone, someone who perhaps tried to mask their professional nature with a bloody, amateurish display. "Could never be a hired hit," they'd think, "too damn messy." Or she could've trolled the cheaper sections of some underground Craigslist.

Tucci showed her Graham's photo of Liath and Marika. "Do you recognize this man at all?"

Charlotte looked at it, but didn't seem to focus well. "No," she said. "I don't know who he is. Is he her father?"

"No," he said. "Mrs. Stiles, who might've wanted to hurt your husband?"

"I don't doubt there were lots of people," she said. "Ray's not the friendliest or most outgoing. But I don't know of anyone that would stoop so... so low. But you don't know it was anyone he knew, right? His wallet was taken. It was a robbery. Right?"

One too many "rights," Tucci thought. *Right?*

"We can't be sure. But it's certainly suspect that this would happen only weeks after Dr. Javid was murdered. Given their... entanglement, I'm thinking there might be a connection." He stopped short of wondering aloud why Stiles wasn't killed, until Charlotte alluded to the same thought.

"Clearly they liked Ray better than Marika," she said. "I suppose it depends on how you look at it, though."

"There were witnesses," said Tucci, "witnesses in your neighborhood that said someone confronted him in the driveway earlier tonight. I'm guessing as he was returning from his little excursion. We're still talking to them. Did you hear anything?"

Charlotte's breath came faster. "No, I actually didn't. But he told me that one of the younger doctors accosted him."

"When?"

"When he came in."

"But there was no physical altercation?"

"Not there, no. But we had words, and he left again shortly after. I don't know what happened to him after that."

"Who did he say the younger doctor was?"

"He called him Willy. Sort of derogatory. I think his name was Thomas. Dr. Will Thomas, I believe?"

The Kid. Marika dead. Stiles took his crush and the little shit went off the rails. He could see it. Problem was, three different eye-witnesses to their little driveway debate had all specifically stated no violence had occurred between them. Stiles went into the house, and Thomas, if it was Thomas, had gone the opposite way, disappearing in his own vehicle. Only one witness, a nearby dog-walker, had, not much later, seen Stiles' car being driven out again. Though it was unclear if the driver had actually been Stiles.

After a half-hour together, Charlotte said, "Thank you for the coffee, detective. May I go back to my husband?"

Dr. Willem "The Kid" Thomas readily admitted to having paid Raymond Stiles a visit at his home. He even mentioned having waited an hour for him in his car, before the senior doctor's return.

"It was stupid of me," Thomas said, sitting cross-armed and cross-legged on the corner of his hospital office desk. "But I was boiling over. I'd rehearsed what I was going to say. It's not even that I hate the guy. He's a brilliant doctor. But the brilliance is trapped in a bastard, a bastard who always gets his way. People roll over for him. I know Marika did."

"But nothing happened," Tucci said.

"No, not between us. I told him how suspicious it looked, him leaving town so soon after Marika's…" He trailed off. "Of course, if I could've I probably would have done the same. I wanted to. I screamed at him about bullshit, really. I screamed because I'm not him. Not that I want to be."

This was definitely a calmer Thomas than the one he had spoken to earlier, even if it was an odd time to show this side, a side lighter, more grounded. Like something had been exorcized.

Tucci said, "You think someone could be targeting St. Vincent doctors, for whatever reason?"

Thomas shook his head. "I don't know. We have those protestors. Some of them seem kind of nutty." His face tensed. "Do you think someone could be coming after me?"

"We don't know that, at all."

"I guess it's a good time to be overhauling the whole security system, huh?" Thomas said. "I got a notice about security pendants they plan to give out, these remotes you wear and can press for help. I mean, what is this, Fort Knox now?"

⟡

Hidden behind a tall dark-green hedge, the house from the street was virtually invisible. Tucci had in fact driven this road several times but had had no inkling of its presence. Probably a good thing, he now realized, as the rusted gate whined open on a weed-sprouted lawn, from which random items—a tricycle, and a small dry fountain, a patio chair—rose like ruins above a jungle canopy.

The house itself was tiny, more like a bungalow. Barred windows. A faded American flag hanging by the screen door.

Bashir beside him, Tucci approached the front porch knocked.

The door opened.

Indeed it was him, Liath Zuabi, that now stood before them,

looking just as he did in Graham's photo. That mildly dyspeptic scowl unchanged. As if he were constantly ready to wince, or wretch.

"Mr. Zuabi," Tucci said. "I'm Detective Tucci, this is Detective Bashir. We'd like to talk to you, if you don't mind."

"Is this about her?" Liath said. He spoke rapidly, in one blast of breath. Immediately, it seemed his English skills surpassed that of his wife's. "Marika?"

"It is, yes."

"I did nothing to that girl," he said. His face softened, and Tucci perceived remorse in there, some part that, with a head-shake, might mutter, *Although she deserved it*. But Liath remained stoic.

"We're not saying you did," said Tucci. "But can we come in?"

Liath nodded, another thing he did rapidly. A tight sack of nerves, this guy. Cats chased mice beneath his skin.

The detectives entered the house, which smelled of mildew. The upkeep of the interior was relatively nice, if rather spartan. There wasn't even a TV, though there was a TV stand, full of blooming flower pots catching sunlight by a lemon-curtained window. Admirable, Tucci thought amusedly, to be able to get entertainment from watching plants grow.

Aadila sat at the kitchen table, next to a young girl about nine. Neither of them wore a headscarf, Tucci noticed. Outside use only, maybe.

In seeing them, Aadila stiffened, mumbled something to her daughter who gathered the papers and pencils and crayons on the table and disappeared down a dark narrow hallway.

Aadila got up and drifted meekly toward them. Liath stopped her with a harsh bout of Farsi.

"No," Bashir said to him. "She can join us. We'd like to talk to her, too."

Aadila sat on the edge of the couch.

Tucci produced the photo of Liath and Marika's confrontation, held it out so Liath could see. "What was this all about?"

Liath blinked. He gestured to take the image, but Tucci held on to it.

"Who took that picture?" Liath said.

"A very angry man," said Tucci. "One of many. You look to be angry yourself. Why?"

Liath sighed hard. "Marika was a—" He said the word in Farsi.

"What was that?" Tucci asked Bashir. With his tongue he probed the side of his mouth. A canker sore was starting. In chewing the remains of a Jolly Rancher, he'd accidentally bitten the tissue.

"Contaminant," Bashir said. "Basically."

"There was goodness in her," Liath said. "But she poisoned it. Aadila was friends with her"—he looked at his wife, almost glowered at her, and she hung her head—"which I did not like. I felt our daughter Mysha was in danger, most of all. I worried what Aadila learned from Marika. What would poison us. She spat on the ways of Islam."

"What about 24:22?" said Bashir. "They should rather pardon and overlook… Allah is Ever-Forgiving. Most Merciful."

Liath blankly regarded Bashir. "Hold to forgiveness, yes, but command what is right, and turn away from the ignorant. 7:199. Marika was ignorant. Marika… she insisted on speaking to Aadila. They were friends. The others at the mosque shunned her. They saw her as I did. She was lonely. I did not understand her, why she chose the path she did. Still, I put up with her questions, her arguments, until one day Aadila told me that she was… 'close' to a man from her work. The man was married. I was disgusted."

"That's all that was said?" Tucci remarked, throwing glances at both Liath and Aadila. "That she was 'close' to him?"

Neither husband nor wife spoke. Aadila shifted, as if struck with a thought, but she hesitated and looked at Liath.

"What is it, Mrs. Zuabi?" Bashir said.

Aadila kept her eyes on Liath.

Waiting for permission, Tucci thought. *Jesus Christ.*

"We'd like her to speak, Mr. Zuabi," said Bashir.

Liath conceded, gestured. Tucci had a strong hunch that, despite any dogmatic dickishness that ran his and his family's lives, Liath Zuabi was not their guy. He was a family man. Protective of his brood. And despite the negative feelings he had toward Marika, Tucci doubted that, as a devoted husband and father, he would risk having to leave his family. In his own world, he was too much the controlling, dominant force.

In Farsi, Bashir rattled off a question to Aadila. There was a quick exchange, and he began translating what she said.

"Marika did not say directly how close she was with this man," she said. "When she approached the subject, she rather tended to ask more personal questions about me. About relationships and things. Marriage. Even sex. She avoided it, maybe she was embarrassed, but it was clear what she was talking about. I thought nothing too much of it until she asked, of all things, if I believed in 'dishonoring family.'"

"Dishonoring family," Tucci echoed.

"Muslims believe," she said, keeping an eye on Liath, "in certain familial honor codes. If someone acts in what is considered an inappropriate way—like an inappropriate relationship—it can be seen as tarnishing the entire family name. I think Marika was worried about something she did."

"But as far as we could tell, her family is in Iran," Tucci said. "Right?"

Bashir translated.

She nodded. "Yes."

"What did you tell her?"

"I told her that I believe Allah is endlessly merciful, and forgiving. Here she was helping people fight the deadliest disease we know. Whatever she did, or was doing, that she seemed so ambiguously worried about, I was sure it would not stand to much in Allah's eyes."

"What did she say about her family?"

"As I recall, they did not want her to come to America. But there was little they could do to stop her, of course. Marika was a truth-seeker, I think. She sought out the core. I think she sought answers in her practice, the scientific ones. But there were things she was totally lost on, too, mostly in cultural or social ways. She was a fragmented believer, trying to piece together ideas or traditions that had been with her a long time but not possessing, or wanting to possess, the whole picture."

"And now," Liath broke in, "we can get back to living our simple lives." He stood up, eyed the two detectives. "I think it is time for you to go."

They stood by the bed, loosely embracing one another, lips meshing. Layer by layer, clothing fell, pooling on the floor. Tara seemed to kiss harder tonight, though it probably just felt as such with the canker sore glowing neon pain on the inside of Tucci's mouth.

Damn candy.

Naked to her panties, Tara pulled back the sheets and slipped into bed. Tucci, himself in boxers, remained standing, leaned over, his lips following and pulsing upon hers. Then he withdrew, leaned back.

"Hold that thought," Tucci said. He retreated to the bathroom, leaving the bathroom door slightly ajar.

He popped open the medicine cabinet. Sometime before he had

noticed a small bottle of numbing, designed for canker sores. It didn't seem to be here and he rooted around, quietly shuffling through tubes and containers. He opened a Band-Aid container and saw in it a light blue case with two snap-on pockets.

Contacts?

Indeed, within the case sat contact lenses. Not the soft throwaways. The old kind. Hard ones, maybe gas perms. Gently, Tucci picked one up and held it up to the mirror, the light. Blue-tinted, almost turquoise. Tucci's eyes narrowed.

Were they responsible for her overly blue eyes, those perfect and penetrative aqua irises? Something about them always seemed theatrical, as if she had her own Photoshop expert following her around, for constant retouching.

He hadn't felt this way about a woman in so long. Maybe ever.

"Mike?" she called.

—she can see you she can see you—

Tucci was struck by his own apprehensiveness, his own sudden paranoia. Who didn't go through medicine cabinets, anyway? And he had a good reason, after all.

"Everything okay?" she called.

"I'm okay," he said, returning the lenses to their Band-Aid container, the container to the cabinet. Then he shut off the light and returned to bed.

Touch. That's what she had been missing. Simple touch, like water to a dry and thirsty waterbed, providing a fullness, a rounding-out of existence. So much had been hollowed out that Tara had come not to even notice the lack. But in this fulfillment she saw the person she had been, or had been becoming: tight and metallic, irritable, a machine running on fumes of humanity.

It didn't even matter if it was good sex or bad sex, though none of it for Tara was bad—it having been so long, the luxury of distinguishing was lost on her. All the better. It seemed like somehow, long ago, perhaps in some other universe, she and Tucci had been together and broken apart. Having once more found one another, they knew every connective place in which they fit.

In their lovemaking she forgot everything else. That rinse of dopamine swept away all external thoughts. Occasionally, in the midst of intimacy, she recognized this severe closeness, an anxious notion like a match struck across her brain. But while it would spark, it would never light.

Motions accelerated and the pleasure radiated through her and from her in a sensual lightshow of release, and the shuddering climax took her and they tightened against one another, as if desperate to adhere permanently. Then they relaxed, breaths heavy, their entwined bodies a smoldering bog of sex.

Tucci rolled from her. She closed her eyes, too tired to smile.

"What are you looking at?" Tucci asked.

She turned from the window, let the parted blinds snap back to place. Tucci had given no indication he'd awoken. She wondered how long he might have been watching her, eyes peeled, brain turning in the shadows.

Stop it, Tara.

"Nothing," she said. "There was someone making noise in the street. Can't see them though."

From the dark, she could feel his scrutiny. The sex was over and the cynical, paranoid thoughts had returned. She knew being with someone would have this effect, and she knew it was heightened with Tucci mainly because of his job, because of Marika. In time, she told herself, it would pass.

Not if… he shows up.

She put that out of her mind.

Tucci rolled over and, judging by the steady purr of breath, had already fallen back asleep. She was going to meet his little brother, Charlie, tomorrow—or, technically, tonight. How did this happen? How had she gotten to this point? Her relationship with Tucci did not feel real enough yet. Nor did she feel completely prepared to be surrounded by family again, at least in a non-medical setting. She dealt with families often, but always as Dr. White, not Tara. The anticipation of such closeness, such expectation, squeezed her insides a little. The pace of the relationship was at once natural and surreal; likely surreal because it was so natural.

Suddenly, a loud *thwack* in the kitchen. She turned.

Tucci awoke from his short sleep. "What was that?"

"Not sure." Eyes well adjusted to the dark, Tara moved forward, Tucci watching from the bed. She wanted to tell him that he was the damn cop, that he should go investigate and not her, but she needed to watch out for herself, to remind him, and herself, of her own capabilities.

The living room buzzed in silence. Taking several steps forward, Tara fumbled for the kitchen light switch and turned it on. Her eyes fell instantly to the rat trap tucked beneath the dishwasher, which had in its metal maw the shattered carcass of a mangy gray rodent, as dead and still as everything else in that moment.

They drove a short ways up the main eastbound road feeding into Baldwin Hills, which offered that day a hazy overview of nearby LAX and the cluttered Westside, from the Palisades to Redondo Beach.

"I've never been up here," Tara remarked. She gazed out of the passenger window.

This was the first time all day Tucci had detected enthusiasm in her tone, or even an awareness of the present.

"I thought I knew most of the area," Tara continued. "But you could've shown me a photo of this neighborhood and I'd have no clue where it was."

"There're worlds here, for sure," Tucci said, working on the last of a blue raspberry candy. "L.A.'s like Vegas in that, I guess. Subtler, though."

If you had told me days ago, thought Tucci. *That this woman, Dr. Tara White, would be sitting here about to meet Charlie...*

He noticed Tara's gaze drift down to the rearview mirror, the temporary centerpiece of which was a car following close behind, virtually tailgating. While she was trying to be casual, Tucci sensed in Tara the tautness of a predator-prey standoff. He watched the car, too—a gray early-nineties sedan, the driver a blur behind black shades.

"Don't worry," he said, trying to conceal his own nerves. That's all cop-training did—help hide the nerves, not overcome them. Not really.

Unmoving, Tara said, "Worry about what?"

"Just that," he said. "Don't worry."

The car behind them took a left, liberating Tara's full attention. She looked at Tucci with slight bewilderment in her lagoon-blue eyes.

"I'm not worried," she said. "You're the guy with the gun, aren't you?"

Tucci chuckled, weakly. "Guns."

Slowly they came to a stop in front of a white, two-story house roofed with Spanish tiles. They idled a moment. Tucci looked like he was about to say something, then stopped.

"Wait here," he said, opening his door. "I'll just run in and get Charlie."

He climbed from the car. He breathed hard. Charlie was perceptive about moods and attitudes. Tucci had to simmer down before seeing him.

The gate to the backyard was ajar and he approached the guest house. The grounds were certainly a step-up from their apartment near Compton. A gurgling waterfall feeding a koi pond. A serene pool, its periphery peppered with Hindu statues among the well-manicured foliage. There was also a vivid flower patch, each blossom a tiny universe beginning.

Then Tucci stopped, looked with a half-formed smile and narrowed eyes at the man sitting in a patio chair, face veiled by cigarette smoke. He wore a plain white shirt and oversized jeans, double-chins of denim sagging at his shins. Skinny guy. Just as he'd been when Tucci had seen him last, yet there was still that gaunt atavism to his face, a malice far stronger than any muscle. No bulk needed.

Alex Mathews—Charlie's mom's boyfriend.

"Hey Mikey," Alex said, smiling. "Haven't seen you in a while."

"No, no, you haven't," Tucci said. "Good thing, too."

Alex smiled.

"You living here now?" Tucci asked.

"I'm here," Alex said. "Gettin' on my feet. I ain't rollin' like I used to, so you don't hafta worry about me." He swung a glance back at the front door of the guest house. "I been keeping an eye on him, too. All good."

"I know."

"Hey Charlie!" Alex called. The sudden bellow startled Tucci, but he took care not to show it. "Your big bro's here!" To Tucci he said, "Been keepin' your own hands clean?"

"Don't get time to wash 'em."

Alex laughed. That serrated chuckle.

The front door opened. Charlie emerged, his dreadlocked hair hung like vegetation over his face. Even though it had only been a month or so since Tucci had last seen him, he was convinced the boy had grown significantly taller.

"Hey man," Tucci said. They clapped hands. "Like the dreads."

A faint smile, as Charlie fiddled with one. "Thanks."

"How you been? New place looks nice."

"Uh-huh. I been good."

"You hungry?"

"Yeah." He was reserved today. Unenthusiastic. Teenage syndrome. Alex's presence, too, probably. Either way it added to Tucci's nerves about the evening. For this he blamed himself. It seemed that, when he was with either of them, Tucci was either whole and lost in the moment, or he was a fragment, self-conscious, alone. This was custom—the people with whom he connected best tended also to be those with whom he could connect worst.

Hopefully, though, the stars would align tonight, give some cohesion to this funny little outing.

"Later, Charlie," said Alex.

"Bye."

"Have fun, Mikey."

As they left, Tucci closed the gate behind him.

The place wasn't exactly what he was expecting, though, in truth, he really had had no idea what to expect. Dad had talked of this *Chago* founder's previous successes in "affordable" gourmet food, more or less upper-scale eateries popularly canonized in the palettes of what Tucci assumed were New York or San Fran gasbags. That this same guy would open a little hole-in-the-wall, sandwiched in a strip mall between Third Eye Psychic & Tarot and 7-11, seemed pretty odd.

"This the place?" Charlie said.

"I think so." As there wasn't a clear sign, Tucci double-checked the address. "Yeah this is it."

"Is that a Buddha in a Sombrero?" Tara said.

"Apparently," Charlie said.

As they entered Tucci thought, *Dad what the hell?*

The odor was the first thing that struck him: a unique smell, not necessarily bad, off-putting only because of its exoticness, a potent mixture of spices and unknown ingredients.

Chago's decorative motif was that of an endearing basement, its walls lined with shelves holding treasures of yesteryear, lunchboxes and worn coloring books and peeling rubber dinosaur toys and framed posters for shows like *Howdy Doody* and *The Dukes of Hazzard.*

Behind the register stood a twenty-something man wearing a backward cap and a monocle (yes, Tucci had to confirm, a friggin' honest live *monocle*). Stacked around him were more yesteryear trinkets, this time for sale. Tucci noticed one.

"Jesus, a Rainbow sucker," he said. He picked up one of the lollipops, turned it over, then put it back. "I used to eat these all the time when I was younger."

"Get one," Tara said.

He shook his head. "Nah."

"Why not?"

Tucci turned his eyes to the blackboard menu hung above the register, all items scrawled in loopy multi-colored chalk. Specials were in graffiti style.

"You're not embarrassed, are you?" Tara said. She turned to Charlie, whispered loud, "He's embarrassed."

Charlie smiled.

"Maybe that was your dad's suggestion, to have those," Tara said.

"I doubt it," Tucci said, gaze on the menu unbroken. "My dad just cuts checks. Doesn't really care much for getting hands dirty. Funny 'cause he used to be a sewer worker." He paused. "What do you guys want?"

Just perusing the eclectic items and ingredients was a formidable task. So many weird and exotic names and combinations, with occasional spots of familiarity. While the cook in Tucci was fascinated, the patron was wary. Confessing himself a culinary chicken, Tucci got the plainest-sounding thing he could see—a prime rib sandwich. Tara got a rice bowl with kimchi, spinach, beef, and a slew of the spices responsible for the place's unique odor. Charlie got another kind of bowl, something with garlic pork.

They found a seat in the back corner, a preference for Tucci (less likely the crazed shooter will hit you, he always thought), and, after seconds of studying their meals, they plunged in. The more bites they took, the lesser the time between each mouthful, and the less they spoke.

"Charlie knows his way with chopsticks," Tucci said to Tara. He was partly proud, partly surprised.

"Just learned," Charlie said. "Friend taught me. I went to his house and his mom was making sushi."

"So Charlie," Tara said. "You're about to graduate, I hear?"

Charlie nodded.

"What're you doing afterwards? Any plans?"

"Goin' to comm college."

"Sorry?"

"Community college."

"Oh. Which one?"

"West LA, probably."

Tara glanced at Tucci, then asked, "You have an idea of what you want to study?"

Charlie made a slight dyspeptic look. "Don't really know—"

"That ain't true," said Tucci.

Charlie was a brief deer-in-headlights.

"You want to get into computer stuff," Tucci said. "Programming, you said. Right?"

"Wow," Tara said, nodding approvingly. "That's impressive. What do you want to do with that?"

With a small shrug, Charlie said, "Probably something like games. Or web design."

"This guy's a walking game encyclopedia," Tucci said.

Near the end of the meal, Tara excused herself to the bathroom. Charlie's eyes followed her briefly, then looked back at Tucci.

"You're dating that?" he said.

Unsure the direction of the question, Tucci said, "I suppose so."

"Damn. She's fine."

Tucci smiled, wanly. "Right."

For several seconds, they chewed.

"When did Alex come back?"

Charlie gave a measured exhale. "Like… I dunno… two weeks ago."

"Things working out okay?"

"Yeah."

"What's he doing?"

"Ridin' out the days I guess."

"You make it sound like he's dying." The idea was hardly far-fetched, though slow death was probably a rare experience for Alex's kind. One moment you're on one side of the bullet, the next: gone.

"He got shot," Charlie said. "In the leg. Two of his friends got shot, too. One died."

"That's what it took to get him out of there?" Tucci asked.

Charlie shrugged. Faster and faster, he shoveled food into his mouth, as if to delay reply.

"Mom's glad he's back," Charlie said.

Tucci decided not to ask about Charlie's mother, who had been in and out of psychiatric hospitals.

"And you're okay?" Tucci said.

A smirk flickered at the corner of Charlie's lips. "I'm okay," he said. "I'm busy at school. Alex does what he does."

"He still talkin' to—"

Tara's return cut him short. Grinning like she knew something, she shimmied into her seat and attacked the rest of her meal. She sniffled. "This spice-stuff packs a wallop. Really good though." She winked at Tucci. "I think your dad's going to do all right with this place."

Amidst further talk about the delectable food, Charlie's studies—queries mostly from Tara and what he was going to do after finishing school—they finished their meal and left, their bellies a notch bigger than when they'd entered, firecrackers of spice ebbing in their mouths and throats.

They pulled out of the parking lot, Tucci happy with the relative ease of the night. It had neither the dreary awkwardness he feared nor the fairy-tale family feel that some idealistic part of him, if he were honest with himself, hoped for.

He heard Bashir's words from days ago: *You think too much.*

"Can I turn on the heat?" Tara asked. "It's cold."

"Sure."

The darkness, his full belly, and the growing warmth of the car all tugged at Tucci's eyelids. He considered pulling over and asking Tara to drive, but decided to push on. Tara once again appeared preoccupied with the side-view mirror, centering her eyes on it every time headlights emerged from the darkness. While watchful as well, Tucci was more discrete—so he liked to think.

They curved up into Baldwin Hills, cruised solitary under

funereal streetlamps. They came to Charlie's home and slowed to a stop.

Tucci held up a fist and Charlie bumped it. "Great seein' ya, 'Chaaaz.'"

Charlie grinned and shook his head. "Shut up. 'Tooch!'"

The two of them laughed.

"So nice to meet you, Charlie," Tara said. "Good luck with everything."

"Thanks."

Charlie climbed out, slamming the door behind him, leaving Tucci and Tara in engine-ticking quiet as they watched the young man sprint up the driveway and punch in the code then disappear with the echoing *clang* of the gate.

"That was nice," Tara said, like they were a suburban couple fresh from a neighbor's dinner party.

He nodded. "Food grew on me, that's for sure."

"Charlie's very sweet."

"Yeah, he's a cool kid. Can be a little unpredictable in his mood. But what kid isn't, you know?"

"I must admit, I was a little confused. I thought he was your little brother," Tara said. "You did tell me that, didn't you?"

"Yeah, I did. He is, or it sure feels like it. For the past ten years."

"It's great what you've got going on together." Tara prodded, "But you want to let me in on a little more? Was he a foster kid? Did your parents adopt him?"

Tucci bit his lip. He didn't like telling the genesis of it all. But truth be told, Charlie was one of the best things that had ever happened to him. Initially, Tucci was supposed to help Charlie. From his prerspective, though, things had worked out more in reverse.

"Miranda," Tucci responded, with a pained sigh. "My ex-girlfriend, eons ago. We were together, like five years. We were living together and she got pregnant. Only she forgot to tell me. On purpose."

Tara looked at him, questions building in her eyes.

Tucci continued. "She flipped out, and got it aborted." He shook his head and laughed, but the laugh was tainted. He gave the steering wheel a playful bop. "I came home one night and she told me she'd done it the week before. Just like that. Without a word to me."

That incident, that conversation, those consecutive revelations of his child and the death of his child… in him, those moments still bled. Miranda. Goddamn Miranda. That night, it was as if all her grating quirks, her complaints, her fears, her minor faults, had suddenly turned her into a womanly Hyde—some monster replacing the person he loved, and the person with whom he thought he would share his life.

"You must have been upset… and hurt," Tara said.

"She said it was 'cause she was worried about my job. That something might happen—I could get shot, killed, whatever—and she couldn't worry about me and my kid, too. She didn't want to end up a single mother. I'm sure that was part of it. But she just didn't want any responsibility. No chains, no anchors. It's why she didn't want to get married. She said it was me who couldn't be alone. Well, fuck. I told her, you come home from seeing a teenage girl strangled with a clothes hanger or a man's brains on the wall and tell me you'd rather be alone with that shit knocking around your head." Tucci threw up his hands. "Anyway…"

After some hesitation, Tara placed her hand on his shoulder and rubbed it, caressed his arm.

"Anyway, we broke up after that. She moved out. But me, I couldn't let the whole thing go. It meant something to me. And I realized I had to do something. I figured, 'You lose a life, you got to save a life.' You lose a kid…" Tucci swallowed hard. "You have a responsibility to save a kid. Help one somehow. Some way. So I signed up to be a Big Brother."

Tara nodded, comprehending more than Tucci would ever know. About losing a part of yourself.

"Charlie's mom was an addict. His father… don't know if he ever knew him. In prison, dead, who knows? It's kind of funny—my first time with him, I was a little nervous. He was too, I think. We made quite a pair. Me and this scruffy, lonely, little six-year-old boy. I brought along a basketball and took him to the park. I didn't even think about it. Sounds bad, I know. Stereotyping. But it wasn't really like that; I just wanted a fun and casual way of hanging out, even though I've never been big on basketball. For the first few weeks we'd play, until I said something like, 'We can do something else if you want,' and he says, 'Oh, I was just playin' it 'cause I thought you wanted to.' I laughed—'I was playin 'cause I thought you wanted to,' I said. He was pretty good, but with sports he's a watcher, not a doer—kind of like me. And the rest is history."

Tucci fell silent, then started the car and pulled away. Memories flooded his brain of the things he and Charlie had done in the ten years they'd been together (*Jesus,* Tucci thought, *ten years, a decade*), which always seemed to include "that one Lakers game" the first week the Staples Center had opened, the different Christmases they'd spent buying a tree, decorating, other times, hanging out, laughing. But Charlie was almost a man now. It would all be different somehow.

Tara broke his reverie. "You've got a good heart, detective."

"I guess."

At least five minutes of silence passed between them when Tara slid a tantalizing hand onto his upper thigh. His whole lower half tingled. Her hand moved farther left and squeezed, prompting an alertness with which no food coma could possibly compete.

As he unlocked his front door, he felt the soft clamp of Tara's hands on his ass. She tightened her grip, and suddenly nothing had ever been so frustratingly sluggish as opening that fucking door.

They popped into the darkened living room, shadows into shadow, and found one another's lips, a full and rich banquet of a kiss. A kiss with calories. Tucci flailed for the light and hit it. The blackness of his closed eyelids grew marginally brighter.

They didn't need light to find the bed.

From the uncovered window, the sun pierced his eyes. His skull throbbed. He rolled over to the other side of the bed until he noticed at the edge that there was no one else there.

He sat up.

The bedroom was empty, the bathroom door still and ajar. No one. He listened for activity beyond—only the garbled whir of traffic. No clothes of Tara's he could see. No note on the nightstand. The only difference he noticed was the orderly arrangement of last night's hastily-discarded clothes. His jacket hung crisp over the back of the armchair, his shirt and tie draped with care over it, his shoes paired quaintly on the floor. There was symmetry to it all, exemplary of Tara.

He got up too fast and nearly fell back. The headache flared. He pulled on boxers and drifted toward the living room. There was an ominous familiarity to this solitude, this confusion, this growing expectation of imminent hurt.

You're not going to fly away, are you?

His brain reran a vision, tortured him with an impossible wish: Tara at the stove, moving amid steam and sizzle, making him breakfast like some romantic-comedy dreamgirl. Tucci was not one for domestic stereotypes, though did quietly admit to himself, as he got older, their increasing allure. The women he fell in with, of course, seldom had a housewife bone in their body. That was because he fell in with selfish women. Inconsiderate women. Hence the fantasy of breakfast—such a sight would break the mold, prove him wrong.

The wish was not for a foot-washing geisha, but a surprise outreach of affection. Miranda had been too worried about everything to really do anyone any good, especially him, and especially in the final corrosive end of the relationship. Tara, at least, had not dragged out this end, but apparently snapped it off clean. These women were getting more efficient, maybe. Maybe soon he would find another sophisticated Ruby Tuesday and finally discover, within hours, whatever it was he endlessly sought from these types. Maybe then he could move the fuck on.

Calm down.

He dialed her. No answer. He spent almost a half-hour deliberating whether or not the neat arrangement of his clothes was a token of affection or a subtle, guilty goodbye. But it wouldn't be goodbye. Not with the Javid case open. If she thought she could run away from him, she was fucking delusional like so many of the rest. Worse, it roused suspicion.

Goddammit, stop.

In a frenetic mental slideshow, he recapped everything he could of what he had said or done the previous night. Had Charlie scared her? Or how he revealed everything to her? Why? No. Tucci had noticed that she hadn't seemed as into the sex last night, despite doing more than he to get it going. Had she already tired of him? Was that who she was? This gorgeous girl endowed with all the blonde, blue-eyed keys to the male heart and to any experience she desired, increasingly needful of fresher fixes? She'd cut out cancer, rock-climbed... what could top these? Murder? Then sleeping with the cop investigating said murder?

As Tucci dressed, his blind bumbling for explanation took a drastic swing: what if something had happened? What if whoever had targeted Stiles—and maybe Marika—had gotten to her, too?

When the possibilities reached Olin, he stopped and made the greatest of his concerted efforts to shut down this train of thought. This made easier by the little discovery in the breast pocket of his shirt that Tara had draped over the chair: a Rainbow sucker.

Driving to her apartment, Tucci tried calling both her cell and her office number.

Both voicemail.

He pulled up alongside the complex and sat with the engine running, the radio droning. It bothered him—scared him, even—how personal impulses drove this pursuit far more than anything official or investigative. The means by which he'd met her had become distant, detached from the singular phenomenon of her.

The Rainbow sucker finished, the white stick rolled from side-to-side in his mouth. A man walking his dog returned to the complex and Tucci got out to follow him through the gate. A ball cap fixed on the man's scalp, Tucci didn't recognize him until the man looked back and they met eyes. The dog, a shuddering, yippy terrier-thing, barked twice.

"You're the cop," said the man.

Tucci nodded. "Yeah, hi. You live across from Dr. White…" He felt fraudulent in sounding so formal. "Randolph, right?"

He relished the look of surprise—and impressed fear—on the neighbor's face.

"Last I checked," Randolph said. "I don't think she's here, if you're going to see her."

"You know if she went to the hospital?"

Randolph blinked, appeared conflicted. "San Diego, I think she said the other day. She seems to go there a lot."

"Oh yeah? Would you know how often?"

Randolph shrugged. This douchebag was trying to play it casual, to exhibit indifference at Tara's doings when he probably had a stolen pair of her panties stashed somewhere. The type was not hard to spot.

"She goes like every other week, it seems," he said. "She has family down there, I think."

Family?

"What kind of family?"

"I don't know. I think she said her grandparents. Or aunt and uncle maybe. She must be close to them. Wouldn't catch me driving all that way so often to visit my folks."

"Right." Tucci chewed hard on the sucker stick until his temples ached. "You wouldn't happen to know where they live, would you?"

"I don't think she stays with them. She wouldn't want to impose."

This Randy was ready to compose a whole frickin' biography of her, Tucci mused.

"She in trouble?"

"No." He removed the stick from his mouth and flicked it into a nearby trashcan. Having done it on impulse, he was glad he made it. "Thanks."

"Sure."

Tucci waited till Randy walked down the street, then he slipped into the apartment building. Tara didn't have any family. She'd been clear with Mike about that. No doubt, she made the story up 'cause she didn't want her neighbor knowing her business. But shit, if she wasn't visiting her relatives, maybe there was someone else. A man. Another lover. Someone she went to see every other week to get her sexual fix. And what did that make Mike? The *other* man. Or maybe it wasn't just Marika who'd been seeing a married man. Maybe Tara liked that, too. Easier to keep it casual that way. Not get involved.

He jimmied the lock on her door. A nanosecond later, he was inside. He felt guilty, sure. But what the hell. He went to the kitchen. Looked at a notepad by the sink. Nothing. Pulled open a few drawers. Lots of old bills, papers. Geez, even coupons. He never figured her for a coupon clipper. In her bedroom, everything was neat and tidy.

Her night table beckoned to him. He slid the drawer open. Bingo. A notepad from the Radisson Hotel in San Diego. Actually, a couple of notepads. Maybe she always stayed there. Or is that where they met for their tryst? She and her married lover.

Stop it, Mike. Just stop it. You don't know that. You're just guessing. Imagining. Wait. Tara had once mentioned San Diego. The track at Del Mar. She loved horses.

Before heading out the door, he stopped at the framed photo of the handsome white stallion he'd noticed the first time he'd been in her apartment. He silently laughed at himself.

Tucci returned to his car and sped off. A red light stopped him. *Goddammit.* He shifted in his seat, looked both ways and ahead multiple times, like a startled feline. He checked his phone. Bashir had called twice. *Goddammit.* The light blinked green and he turned left and made his way to Wilshire, which he took to Westwood and the entrance to the southbound lane of the San Diego Freeway.

Goddammit.

CHAPTER EIGHT

THERE WAS THUNDER IN his dreams, drumming the horizon, chomping at the edge of the world. As he awoke the sound grew dimmer, smaller, until it was beside him: a fist rapping on the door.

"Juan," said a voice on the other side. It was Gomez. "*Despertarse. Vamanos.*"

Almost sunrise. He had slept late. His exhaustion had forced him to go to bed the previous night without changing clothes, and so he was more or less ready to go. Juan Delgado didn't like wearing the same things two days in a row, but he had few alternatives and little time.

"*Voy,*" he said.

He took his backpack and met Gomez outside, who stood there alone, skin almost red in the orange lamps of the motel walkway. Gomez wore a New York Mets cap. An unlit cigarette jutted from his lips. The air around them was blue and wet and crisp. Cold. Delgado shivered.

"*Estas bien?*"

Delgado nodded. "*Estoy bien. Cansado.*"

"*El trabajo nunca esta terminado.*"

Gomez was right. *Nunca esta terminado.* Work was never finished.

They had traveled together, crossed together. Gomez had known the "coyote," the one from his village, the one who had taken them over the border. Nearing thirty, Gomez was only slightly older than Delgado, yet had two sons, both very small. His wife had passed while giving birth to the youngest. Watching over them now were his aging mother and father, who also awaited the fruits of his efforts here. Delgado wondered if his own family would be proud of him.

Come eight o'clock, Delgado rode with Gomez and two other sun-creased men in the back of the rattling cargo van. The construction contractor's recent errand boy—a new one seemed to come along every two weeks—had fitful control of the wheel. Every block the kid looked at the directions the contractor had given him, as if too stupid to remember or know where he was going. The two other men across from him spoke and laughed amongst themselves, every once in a while glancing at him. He imagined killing them and the driver.

Work was never finished.

The van pulled into the parking lot of Greg's Market, a small grocery store in the flat industrial area east of Culver City. No one else said anything as Delgado got out. He trudged up the lot, head down, hands pocketed. The van receded into the dark empty streets, and he did not turn back. Then, all was quiet save the buzzing power lines.

He was five minutes late. The manager, Ms. Jonson, a curly-haired blonde lady with glasses and a dog-face, looked at him over her clipboard, as if she expected him to say something. He kept his head low, muttered a greeting, and strode to the backroom where he changed into his uniform. Then he took the mop and filled the bucket and wheeled it out onto the floor, where he would be for another three hours.

Ms. Jonson came up to him, her walk more like a forward teeter. She was fat. Or getting fat. Another overstuffed American. Her jeans so painfully tight. The badge hanging from her neck, glistening in the fluorescent light, showed a much thinner and happier woman.

"Keys," she said, holding up a set. "New keys. *Nuevas claves.*"

He nodded and, with the smallest of smiles, said, "Thank you."

Two nights ago, actually the night he was off, the market had been burglarized. Most of what had been taken was food or batteries, though they had tried to open one of the registers. Ms. Jonson wanted to install a security system but couldn't afford it. The police had assured her they would drive by a few times.

"Thank you, Juan," she said. She turned away and continued her inventory.

He watched her. What was her life like? Did she walk about her home in such spiritual desolation, too? He mused there were so many like her in this country, but not as many that showed it like she did. She was a body in aching search of spirit, as was this entire place.

Work was never finished.

Delgado was very aware that he was the only one with Ms. Jonson. This neighborhood was not very good, either, so there could be many people with whom she might have a bloody encounter. He could get away with it. He could put her out of her misery.

Like the doctor.

Thick and stubborn, the late-afternoon cloud cover haunted the entire city. In her half-year of coming almost biweekly to San Diego, Tara could count on one hand the amount of times she'd seen the famed "sunniness" of so-called Sunny San Diego. It depressed her.

Thankfully, she saw none of it within the Rock Star climbing gym in National City, in which she spent two hours, bouldering first— more difficult than she remembered, as it'd been a while—before tackling the wall. The only other climber was a young boy taking a lesson. His mother watched from below, hands tightly clasped, and he threw anxious glances down at her while the instructor, long-necked with a surfer-dude's accent, tried to right the boy's attention to the task at hand.

Tara was impressed. She had begun climbing young, but not that young. She tried to give the boy encouraging smiles. He would grin shyly and look away. When she noticed the mother giving her odd looks, Tara stopped.

People here are weird.

Hung from the apex of the wall, she felt safe. She lorded over everyone. She was queen. She did not feel like the wounded antelope in the woods, as she did outside. She did not feel vulnerable. She did not feel followed.

Hunted.

⁓

The Del Mar race track was one of those places perpetually busy, even in the most obscure hours. Weekday afternoons and mornings saw little slowdown in the flood of people that came to witness fortune in the form of thousand-pound, snorting, thundering beasts.

So many of these people—the defeated, the delighted, the delirious—were what Tara, likely because of her L.A. influence, had come to call extras. Characters to fill the scene, to contrast the stars of the show.

Right. And what show would that be?

She bustled through the crowd, headed over to the betting window, flipped over some bills. She put a hundred on Tequila Rose to win. Three to one. Tara thought the odds were generous considering the horse had been impeded in her last start, and would benefit from the additional sixteenth of a mile in today's race.

Instinctually, Tara moved fast, walking at a clipped pace like someone bustling to make an appointment. She didn't even consider her speed until forging her way through the crowd to the rail.

In the seconds before the gates opened, a tautness befell the people, a palpable anticipation. Tara enjoyed the prickly aura of this place, the dirt-smeared, unshaven religion of it, the nervous unity of these people, the power of putting fate on a singular tract.

Someone's here.

The bell clanged. The gates sprang open.

"And they're off!" boomed the announcer over the P.A. system.

The equine current flowed fast, a pounding din. Tequila Rose rode up the middle, a beautiful black horse, its jockey hunkered flat against the glossy backside. Charging, threading through, broaching the lead. The perfect symbiosis of aesthetics and athletics.

Tara grew aware of another presence. Beyond the immediate crowds, she was not alone. She had known this, too, even before knowing it—it was why she'd been walking fast.

"…and it's Tequila Rose and the Cognac Kid, neck and neck!"

People swarmed about her, cheering, pumping their arms, their beer-stained breath and bodies warming the cool shade of the overhang.

Eyes were upon her.

How do you know?

She tried to ignore the feeling. Impossible. Having begun as a prickly assurance, it had escalated moment by moment toward something very near terror. Tara felt like some demon had its lips on her soul, blowing its black breath steadily into it, filling her. The irrational tightened her.

I need to get the hell out of here.

Before the race had even ended, Tara turned and headed up the stairs, eyes meeting every face she passed. Some briefly returned her gaze, before fixating again on the thundering race. She saw no one she knew.

Following you, whispered a wordless voice. *Following you.*

"...and Tequila Rose is pulling ahead!"

The race finished, and a tremendous cloud of jubilance and disappointment filled the air. From the announcer's nasal enthusiasm, Tara gleaned she'd won—Tequila Rose was indeed the winner. Tara kept walking, unsure if she even wanted to slow her progress by collecting her winnings. She did, though, beating other victors streaming to the window. Then, money in hand, she hustled off to the car, at once wanting to constantly survey the crowd as well as keep her head down.

Driving back, Tara was in a complete haze. On arriving at the hotel, she remembered nothing since leaving the track, not that the ride was anything more remarkable than a stretch of freeway. Her mind moved unusually fast—too fast, actually, for her to catch up, thinking thoughts she couldn't even register, zipping over half-ideas and frenetic images with the uncaring hastiness of a breeze through the pages of a book. It gave her a light-headed feeling.

The sky darkened in evening, the cloud cover unbudged. Backdropping the buildings of downtown, it created a scene of metropolitan somberness, a place that might secretly invite mass destruction. She found her hotel, decidedly one of the meeker towers. She pulled into the garage, parked, then made her way toward the lobby.

"Hey there."

Tara turned and saw Mike Tucci sitting on a bench.

Oh Jesus what is he doing here what in fuck's name is he doing here—

He looked relaxed, as if he'd been sitting there for hours, though his casualness looked strained. His right cheek bulged with candy. The sight was surreal. Even as they began talking, part of Tara assumed him a mirage.

With little consideration, Tara said, "You were following me."

Yes. He was a crazy stalker, that's what it was. Already "in love" with her. He was too into her, like the Kid with Marika and he was… he was… Or maybe he knew. He knew why she was here.

Tucci looked at her, toxic wisdom in his eyes. Tara imagined her own thoughts so loud, so voluminous, that some were being transmitted to Tucci, and she wondered which ones he knew, which ones he now pieced together as he pondered her, enjoying her anxiety.

"Dammit, Mike," she said. "You scared me. What are you doing here?"

"Dr. Stiles came to last night," he said.

"Oh," she said. "That's good."

"Charlotte Stiles confessed to the beating. An hour before he woke up."

"What?"

Tucci nodded. "Yeah. She contacted an ex-lover who did the deed. Happily. Some veteran with a dishonorable discharge."

"Christ. Glad, um… glad he's okay."

"No evidence Mrs. Stiles did anything to Marika, though."

She almost said *cut the crap*, but this time withheld her tongue. "How did you know I was here?"

"Another case brought me down here," he said. "I happened to see you pull into the hotel. Thought it was you but wasn't sure. Lo and behold."

She would have contested the legitimacy of this, but his eyes restrained her. There was no way she knew for sure if it was he who'd been following her at Del Mar. But he was here, for Chrissake, a hundred and twenty miles from where she'd last seen him. Who else would it have been?

"I'm sorry if my leaving was abrupt," Tara said. Part of her chastised herself for being the one to apologize. "I like to get headstarts." She crossed her arms. "For someone on a case you seem pretty leisurely."

"I got the goods I needed."

"That was quick."

"Well, didn't get everything." He smiled at her. "Hard to get everything."

"Sure." Now that some of the irreality had subsided, Tara found herself perfectly divided in her reaction to Tucci being here. It titillated her at the same time it frightened her. Although, if she were honest with herself, the titillation came partly from the fright.

My own lap-puppy, she thought. *My own lap-puppy cop.*

"I'm headed upstairs if you want to join me," she said. "Nice ocean view."

Without another word, Tucci stood, swallowed his candy. Together they proceeded to the lobby. As the automatic glass doors parted, Tucci placed his hand at the small of her back. While so slight, the touch was momentarily very heavy; all she felt. He was subtly guiding her. He owned her. He was not her fucking puppy. She was something for his amusement. She was his chewtoy.

They entered the elevator alone, though Tara's energy crowded out the compartment. Tucci hesitated to identify this energy. He caught only fragments of a familiar Tara White, but wasn't sure now what strung it all together.

There was no mistaking the direction of the energy, though, when Tara whipped forward and hit the red stop button and the elevator shuddered still.

She charged him, violently. Attacking. He flinched, his hand going up in a defensive gesture.

"Reflex," he said. "Sorry."

She dove into a kiss. He reciprocated, though at a slower pace.

Showers of sensation went off across his body but they had no direction, and though he was aroused, the sheer suddenness of it all stunted his erection.

"You stopped a hotel elevator," Tucci said, between sweet mouthfuls of her. "They—"

"Shut up," she said. Half her shirt unbuttoned, Tara's breasts were exposed and bra-less. She grabbed his hand and placed it full on her right breast, his other hand gripping her ass. In this frenzy, this sexual spasm, no position, no touch, was enough—she seemed to desire everything, everywhere, all at once.

Tara could tell he wasn't hard, and so knelt before him and undid his belt buckle, her eyes an electrical storm. She undid his pants. She threw back a long strand of hair that had fallen over her face, looked up at Tucci with a raised eyebrow.

"Not the quickie type, detective?"

"I don't know." Tucci breathed hard, concealing the anger that now swelled him. What the hell was she thinking? And why was it suddenly so hard to accept and enjoy the stuff of many imaginings so suddenly thrust upon him? What the fuck was he thinking? What was wrong here?

Tara worked fast, but fast made her touch harsh and abrasive. In a hotel such as this, at this time of day, people on every floor would be alerted to an issue pretty damn quick. There may have even been a camera in there, though he saw none.

"It's all right," Tucci said, brushing fingers through her hair, as she grew more and more determined. He half-expected her to start slobbering. "Just screw it for now."

"What d'you think I'm trying to do?"

"You know what I mean." He looked at the doors as if they were about to open. His member had shrunk entirely—he almost felt like it was now smaller than normal. "We better keep going."

Tara rose, buttoning her shirt, looking at him like a teenager might on a strict parent. His gut tingled.

Tara released the stop button and the elevator lurched onward. They rode mostly in silence, Tucci trying to examine furtively just how disappointed or flummoxed Tara might be.

She went to slide her keycard into the door, then stopped. She took a long breath, looked at Tucci, her cheeks tinted with the remnant flush of the elevator incident.

"You didn't have to keep tabs on me," she said. "I can take care of myself."

"Thought I'd check in," he said. "Like I said, I was in the neighborhood anyway. Though you did leave pretty abruptly."

"I like to get an early start. You know that." She slid her keycard in and the light blinked green and they entered the room. "I need to shower. You're welcome to watch TV or something if you want."

Tucci felt deflated. Why wasn't she inviting him into the shower with her? Because he'd so clumsily thwarted her advance? Because he was fucking stalking her? He was a boy all of a sudden, wary of a woman greater than he in status and intellect.

This whole rendezvous was lopsided. He was entering her room. He shrank at her glance, her unvoiced opinion. And so Tucci, at the click of the door behind him, propelled himself toward her.

Coming up behind her, he cupped her ass, then wrapped his arms around her waist and pulled her snug into him. She gasped a little. His hands continued exploring, one down toward her pants, where he could feel moisture, the other cupping her breast.

She resisted initially, as he had in the elevator. Then she fell into the embrace.

He felt the tremor in her body, the fire stoked to life and they danced, conjoined, toward the desk. Their bodies meshed, their personalities, their memories, their very distinctions swapped back and forth, lost in this rapture of pure touch, this sandbox of flesh.

After climax they slowed in sweat-beaded exhaustion, segueing to the bed where Tucci lay nude, face-down, on the verge of sleep.

Outside, the moon rose sharp and radiant.

"I'm going to take that shower," Tara said, still with no invite, though he had no intention of getting up.

There were flickers of resentment at how energetic she still was. Men gave, women took. Siphoned.

He spooned her, his arm firmly hooked around her waist. She pushed lightly at his wrist. "You gonna let me up?"

"Maybe." He tightened his grip.

Tara placed a palm on his elbow. "So I'm trapped forever?"

With a dull chuckle, he released her. She stood by the bed, utterly nude herself. The way she turned—almost posing, he thought—her butterfly tattoo seemed to flutter in the play of light and shadow. She looked at him blankly.

Her gaze moved slightly past him. She frowned.

"What?" Tucci said.

Tara climbed into bed next to him, suddenly with a more nurturing air, and peered at Tucci's left shoulder blade. He knew what she was looking at. Tara ran a delicate finger over the black protrusion.

"You should get that removed," she said. There was concern in her voice but it was restrained. "Doesn't look like trouble yet, but it could be down the line."

Tucci nodded. His stomach tingled. Great way to round out great sex.

"Maybe you can do it for me," he said.

Tara smiled hesitantly, as if unsure whether or not he was being sarcastic. Then she leaned in and kissed him and the gesture nourished Tucci. He forgot earlier broodings on selfish, inconsiderate women, about wishes for loving gestures, all of it absolved by Tara's kiss.

For now.

In the predawn morning, Tara, wide awake and dressed in a white cotton shirt and khaki trousers, sat by the window, sipping one of the complimentary packets of coffee and shifting her glance from foggy downtown below to Tucci, who lay sleeping.

He has a case here, she thought. *He has a fucking case here. Sure.*

Thoughts of violence tantalized her. How cleanly could she be rid of Tucci, in case he posed a problem? Certainly, someone, somewhere, knew where he was now, but what if they didn't? What if he'd come as a lovesick puppy, upset because she'd left his apartment so abruptly, and, thus embarrassed, had not told anyone where he was going, or why?

She should've written a note, she decided. But she had left him the lollipop and thought perhaps that might suffice. She didn't want to look too emotional herself. Notes were for wives and serious girlfriends.

Listen to yourself. 'Rid of him.' What're you, some movie vixen?

In a slight revelation, Tara realized she'd come to adore this Mike Tucci. Adore? Yes, she decided, adore. He was two men, the "teddy bear" and the "tough," both sides in mutual envy, assuming that the other had more command of him, when in fact they were in perfect equilibrium.

Tara finished her coffee, retrieved her bag and, in heading out the door, stopped to look back at Tucci, who moaned softly and rolled over.

How could someone become such a welcome intruder?

A minute later she was gone. The note left by the coffee packets read: *Running errands. Back soon.—T xo*

Tucci's presence provided relief from the sensation of being followed. Of course, he had been the one following her—that she knew of, anyway. Tara didn't believe he had a case here, but would make him think she believed it. Ultimately, it was good for her if he followed her, right?

Unless it wasn't.

Tara became aware of some inner hardness having melted. Maybe as an outgrowth of tension, she felt a strange excitement. Somehow, Tucci's determination turned her on. He would never see this, though. Never know this. Or was he aware of it? No—she would know if he were.

The sensation of being followed returned not moments after walking from the elevator into the garage. Tara felt glommed on to.

The bank was only two blocks from the hotel, but she had decided to drive.

By the time she parked, the morning was fully aglow, the sky a raw blue. Streams of traffic, strengthened by the minute, then by the second. Soon, Tara regretted having driven— the openness of the sidewalk suddenly felt safer to her.

❦

He awoke ten minutes before Tara, and for each minute stared at her, wondering things, incomplete thoughts flying at her like wayward birds from his imagination.

Above all thoughts suspicious, however, above all thoughts investigative, sat one aggravatingly paranoid and stupid reality-show of a thought.

What does she think of me?

It was obvious Tara hadn't bought his story about having another case down here. He wouldn't have either, and wondered why he hadn't bothered to concoct a better one.

No time, he thought. *It doesn't fucking matter what she thinks of you. You're running out of time.* Or he already had. The first seventy-two hours of a homicide investigation were the most crucial, and they'd long since passed. The line-ups they'd assembled based on witness testimony, and the pixelated mug from St. Vincent's security cameras had only elicited furrowed brows and record use of the words "um" and "uh." Physical evidence was scant. A kind of perfect storm case, as Dickey would have called it. And here he was, chasing a blonde, fussing over his feelings.

This realization gnawed at him, filled him with guilt. Guilt toward Dr. Javid. Himself. Hell, toward every cop and every Muslim, for whatever reason. But he kept going, he kept going because superseding all sensation—just as Tara's opinion of him superseded all thought—was the deepest feeling of rightness, of being as close to the pulse of this case as one could hope to be.

Tucci pondered, of course, whether he was just telling himself this to assuage the guilt, but in his time he'd come to better distinguish notions legit and non-legit. Truth was rock, frets and fancies paper. This felt like rock.

Tara stirred and he closed his eyes, as if he were still sleeping.

She visited the bathroom, got dressed. He could feel her eyes on him and he dared not open his, though he regretted not watching her dress. His muscles clenched, he followed by ear her quiet pitter-patter about the room. His teeth gritted. She was sneaking away again. *Bitch.* Maybe he wanted her to be a suspect, wanted to see her away because of his petty resentment, not just of her, but of the others who'd left.

He listened as she fixed coffee, then sat by the window for several minutes, during which the only sound was a faint electrical hum.

Then she left.

Moments later, he was up. When he saw the note, it softened little of his resolve.

Tucci kept a few car lengths behind her, enough buffer for him to monitor at a safe distance. The initial early-morning traffic was light, but grew exponentially. He maintained a steady two to three car gap between them. He wore shades and had the sun-visor down, for obscurity as well as practicality, as the sun blazed low and blinding between the buildings.

She did not travel far. Two blocks from the hotel she pulled down a one-way street, parallel-parked at a meter and entered a West Federal Bank. Curiously, she emerged not a second later and went to the ATM next to the entrance, where, with furtive glances at the unconcerned passersby and the avenue behind her, she awaited the transaction. Though she moved with speedy precision—befitting a surgeon, Tucci mused—he was able to note the wad of cash coughed up into her hand.

Track money?

Hastily concealing it, Tara returned to the car and pulled away. Tucci waited a beat, then followed. He mused she hadn't wanted to stay in the bank, for fear of feeling boxed-in. Why?

They drifted through downtown. Her next stop was the post-office, a quaint little place on the corner of Gateway and Main. He watched as she went in, and could see through the large north-facing pane of glass that she was checking a P.O. box.

Odd.

For another ten minutes she remained there, sealing up something in a manila envelope, handing it to the clerk. Then she left. Tucci bolted from his car, hurried into the post office, flashing tin all the while.

The clerk, a young pockmarked Latina, blinked at his sudden presence.

"Excuse me," he said. "That woman that was just here. The blonde."

She nodded.

"Can you tell me how long she's had that post office box? When she set it up?"

Some hesitation. Understandable.

From the girl's soft throat squeaked, "Sure." She leaned over, checked the number on the box and went to the computer. Clicked. Clicked. Come on, thought Tucci. Every second was another foot gained by Tara.

"It was rented six months ago," she said. "By the current user."

"Thanks."

He dashed back out, climbed into his car. Sticking two cherry Jolly Ranchers into his mouth, he pulled out into traffic.

"Let me explain something to you."

In the middle of the bustling sidewalk, she turned. Gasped.

Mike Tucci. The sight of him sent an electric charge through her chest.

"Right now," he said. "We got exactly shit on who killed Dr. Javid. Dead-ends. Lame leads. What we got, what I got, is a bunch of ghost-theories floatin' around lookin for legs. That means I ain't discriminating. Someone acts funny, I'm taking notice."

Tara nodded, looked down like an ashamed child, though it was more to rub out the ache in her neck.

Tucci said, "I meet a frickin' incredible girl, woman, who worked with the victim. I'm sayin' to myself, she's brilliant, she's beautiful, all that stuff. But I'm also thinking, yeah, she's beautiful, brilliant, she can probably get away with a lot. You know? Probably has. What, I don't know. And frankly I don't care because I only want to know if you got away with one thing. I tell myself there's no way you could or would have anything to do with what happened to Marika. But when the room is clear and empty you notice the odd fly or two. You notice the funny things. Right now I feel like I'm lookin' at a funny thing, a little black buzzin' spot that shouldn't be there. Am I right?"

A sudden tide of indiscriminate, devout worship flooded Tara, desperate supplications to any deity, God, any devil that might exist if only something, right now—a stroke, a car accident, a meteor, anything—could get her away from Tucci, or him away from her.

He looked her in the eye, "You told your neighbor, Randy, you come here to visit family. But you told me you don't have family. What's a little lie between friends? Or lovers? Or neighbors?"

"I didn't lie to you. I don't have family," Tara said. "I come here to recharge. My job needs lots of recharging. It just sounds weird for a woman to be traveling alone for no real reason, so I use the family excuse. Especially to Randolph, who's so damn nosey about everything."

She was oddly regretful of what she'd just said. *Your job requires recharging. Mike's doesn't?*

"Every other week?" Tucci said. "Wish I could recharge like that." He gestured broadly at her bookbag. "And wish I had the moolah to do it with."

In a clipped tone, Tara said, "What are you doing here, Mike?"

He swallowed. Not a question he expected, it seemed. "What am I doing here," he echoed.

"What the fuck are you doing dicking around behind me like some teenaged stalker when whoever killed Marika —"

"Did you kill Marika?"

Spoken louder than intended, the question turned the heads of several passersby. Tucci took her by the arm and escorted her into an alcove slightly removed from the stream of people. Tara complied, but wrenched her arm free once they'd settled in the shade.

"Fuck you," she said. "Why would you even *say* that?"

"How do I know you're not sending that chunk of change to a pro?"

It took her a second to realize what he meant by "pro." A professional killer.

She blinked, at a loss for a reply.

"Mike," she said. "Jesus Christ." Her breath came ragged. Something like a terrible caffeine high overcame her, an urge to jump, to kick, to run, to leap thrashing and flailing from her skin. In greater quantity, it was the energy of nervous breakdowns, of school-shootings, of car chases.

"What am I supposed to say to that?" she said. "What do you want me to say to that?"

Tucci's eyes narrowed at her. His body bristled. "I want you to tell me what's going on. I want you to tell me you've really told me everything, everything you know I should know. Everything you've done I should know."

Tara felt a surge of compassion for him; wanted to throw her arms around him, hold him, hold onto him, to apologize and to run away with him. She watched Tucci. His attempt at intimidation had undermined itself. He knew this, too, which only undermined it further. She could use this to her advantage.

"You're wasting time," Tara said. "At least with Marika. I've told you everything. I'm just..."

"Visiting family?"

"No, no." Tara pinched the bridge of her nose, then ran her fingers through her hair. Already she felt like another shower. "It's all—it's all something I just need to do. It's hard to explain because people just think I'm an addict, or turning into one. But with what I do I need to be in control, always... meticulous and... I guess it's like a catharsis, doing this. It's my one hobby that's kind of out of my hands, and that's good for me."

A sardonic grin tested the corner of Tucci's lips. "Tara," he said. "What the fuck are you talking about?"

Blood rose tingling in her face. She licked her lips. "You know, don't you?" she said, trying to temper her tone. "You were following me."

Tucci blinked. "Was I?"

"Goddammit, Mike." Tara sighed. "You know I was at the track. Del Mar. I'm a horse person. It's... it's an escape for me. It's..."

You're talking too much. Rambling.

"You win?" he said. That sardonic grin had not left his face. It both agitated and attracted her.

"Um, yeah. Kind of."

"Congratulations."

Without another word, he moved. She watched him go. He didn't look back.

⌒◯

When it came to women problems, there were two species: the biting kind and the burrowing kind. Every guy experienced at least one of these two. The biters, nibbling on the outside, were easier to deal with. You could pinch them off. Flick them away. The burrowers, not so much; they broke the skin, delved deep, and squirmed in noisy and painful expedition through your stomach, your heart. Your soul.

As he drove, Tucci turned up the volume. Jagger's lyrics grew louder and louder. Music, combined with the wheel and the open road, was often an elevation, a cleansing liberation. But nothing could sway the visual strength of those last minutes with Tara. They had parted on exceedingly awkward terms and to Tucci, right now, almost nothing else mattered. Tara had burrowed, had propagated in his brain, had carved tracks in his gut.

The clouds stayed with him the whole return drive, obliterating the night sky save for pitiable peeks of a star or two. The highway, for many miles, was an isolated one, lonely between the dark waters and the dark hills of Camp Pendelton and the neighboring country.

It was obvious Tara wasn't telling him something, but, for reasons unknown, Tucci thought her concerns more benign neuroses than anything truly worth probing. His job, his presence, did have a way of unhinging the neurotic in women, especially early in the relationship. He remembered Miranda's insistence that he always drive, yet whenever he took the wheel, she became a stream of consciousness monologue of fastidious directions and rules for him to follow. Then there was her giddiness over taking two little bottles of shampoo from a hotel, in contrast to her humiliation when he once took a penny from the jar at 7-11.

But he was giving Tara the benefit of the doubt. Shampoo and pennies were, after all, totally different from detached, paranoid behavior as one of the only people close to a homicide victim.

Half an hour out of Irvine, Bashir called him. Before the associate detective could even speak, Tucci said, "On my way back."

"Kept my loins burning," Bashir said.

"That's good. What's up?"

"Noticed a strange pattern in St. Vincent's HR records," Bashir said. "When Dr. White was interviewing for partners."

Another twinge. "Yeah?"

"She only interviewed Middle-Eastern women. Mostly Muslims."

"That is… strange."

"Want me to send these over your way?"

"Sure. I can look at them tomorrow."

"All right." There was a pause. "What happened with Dr. White? Pick up anything more?"

Tucci wasn't sure how to respond. "We'll see."

Tucci popped open a beer and returned to the couch, looked at the dead woman sprawled out in photographs on his coffee table, the multiple angles on her. He picked up a closer photograph of her torso, studied it. He took it over to the desk and circled in red ink the area of her scar, the older mark removed from the horrid cuts about her breast. The coroner had thought it possibly a biopsy scar. Tara hadn't agreed. The facts seemed to favor Tara's notion, as they'd uncovered no record of any biopsy performed on Dr. Javid.

He snapped a picture of the photograph with his phone, then emailed it to Dr. Aaron Moss, a semi-retired medical examiner with whom Tucci had worked for the last three years of the man's career. Moss and his wife had moved to rural Pennsylvania, seeking closer ties with their daughter.

Tucci wrote an accompanying message: *Could be a biopsy scar, you think?*

The email went through. He finished his beer and went to bed, entering a thin and fitful sleep.

In the morning his phone rang. It was Moss.

"Mike, good to hear from you," he said. Tucci noticed a newfound lightness in his voice. "I got your photo… that could easily be a biopsy scar. It's pretty clean, as it would be for that part of the body. There's roughness to it, but the roughness almost looks artificial."

"What does that mean?"

Moss laughed. "To be honest, I'm not sure."

CHAPTER NINE
Iranian Desert
1999

BY THE SECOND DAY of travel, they had wound up far into the mountains, the cold bone-deep, pure and total in the thinning air. At night when they camped, the men would set the fire going high and she would watch the flames lapping and reaching and yearning for the distant fire-points of the stars. They slept wrapped in cocoons of hide, huddling close to the blaze. The men took shifts standing guard.

Sleep was very infrequent, more a passing daydream than protracted rest. As she had the night she'd run away, she gazed deep into the heavens, imagining the stars, those endless, endless stars, as angel eyes, peering through this shadow-veil. She imagined, too, that the moon might well be the eye of Allah, cold and radiant and wise, but dry of anything further to impart to His wayward children.

This country was alien to her. The mountains were heaped upon the earth like great mounds of clay. Dots of life moved lonely upon this barren range. She had seen little of other beasts—and thus far no other persons, despite concerns from the men—and had, in late hours, heard them shuffling the soil, or calling in primal and melancholy voice into the desolation.

Strangely, she could not think about where they were going, what was going to happen. The future would devour her, and so she ravaged her mind with thoughts of Hassan. How she wished he were with her now.

He probably does not miss me, she thought. *He has probably set his eyes on another.*

Maybe Mahsheed.

No.

She was worthless, this much was evident. A walking corpse, mercifully (or punishingly) denied rest. Dead to Hassan. Dead to her family. Dead to Allah. What of any image of her lingered or would linger in their minds? Time, the same violent artisan of these hills, would destroy her and make of her nothing.

Allah forgive me, please.

"Glorified is my Lord, the Great." Her form bowed, head upon the earth. "Praise be to Allah, the Cherisher and Sustainer of Worlds…"

Having prayed each day at proper times, she was beginning to lose connection with what it meant. Horrid to say, but praying increasingly felt unnatural in this world, this wild world which mocked such pretensions. It did not help, either, that the men she traveled with were apparently faithless.

Her relationship with the two men was very abstract. To them, she was as good as another piece of their equipment, or, at best, an animal like the horses they rode upon. She did not even know their names. What were these men? They seemed bandits, or some type of criminal. How could Omeed have been in business with them? More, how could her father have been in business with Omeed?

That was not her concern. Those were concerns for her past soul. She had a new soul, rustled awake by her passion for Hassan. Perhaps their meeting had been fated; perhaps Allah had foreseen this journey, prepared her, through him, with this strength.

But then, if it hadn't been for Hassan, this journey would not have taken place.

The third day there was snow, though it was light. The clouds had consolidated into a bright gray bog, flakes whirling down.

They avoided the roads, for reasons she did not know, and so their path took them across untamed soil. In treading the snow, she relished her footprints. Stupid as it was, they made her feel like she wasn't dead, that she wasn't nothing, that she could still mark the world, maybe even one day mark it as much as it had marked her.

But snow melts.

She may not have known the names of her companions, but, from one of their mutterings, she ascertained the name of one of the horses, actually the one she rode the most: Ghalib, an Arabic name meaning "conquerer."

In meeting Ghalib's eyes, she felt kinship, identified with the fear, uncertainty and the dumb power behind it all. Except it wasn't dumb. Only seemed so to her because she was the dumb one. Nature was God's brain, infinitely wiser than the ostracized human brain struggling to find a way back in.

Toward twilight of the fourth day they entered a long cold pass. Given her mental distractions, she had not paid significant attention to her body, partially because, beyond shivers and tolerable aches, it had not issued many complaints. Certainly her youth worked in her favor. The men were also responsible for her sustenance and water, given what they had. She had her own canteen and feasted mostly on flatbread and rice. She prayed at evening but skipped the night prayer.

Then there was the pain. It struck her thigh like a tiny ball of fire, heated and stinging up and down her leg and into her abdomen. She had endured cramps before, but this was new.

The ache so great, she buckled, stumbling among the stones.

Reaction from the men was acute, full of more humanity than they'd since betrayed. The shorter of the men rushed to her, knelt by her.

"What is wrong?" he said. "What happened?"

She explained, indicated, best she could, the origin of the pain. To her utter surprise—and mild horror, though she was too transfixed to say anything—he placed his hands gingerly on her leg. No one had touched her there. Not even Hassan.

He rubbed, gentle at first, then harder, kneading her skin, pressing, shaping. A magician of the flesh. Slowly, the pain receded, and she was left with light, doughy relief.

The man looked at her, gaze piercing. "Does it feel better?"

The wind cut low over the ridge and the fire stretched longingly with it, embers spiraling across the dark.

It had been hours since the man had rubbed away her pain. Some phantom pleasure from the touch still lingered. She dwelt on that touch. By all accounts, she imagined it terribly forbidden, even if he'd been healing her. It had been the closest male hands had ever been to that area, that area from which even her fingers had long strayed, despite mounting temptation. She had wanted Hassan to be the first to touch her there, but that was impossible now.

On the other side of the fire, the taller man slept. The shorter man, the healer, as she now privately called him, stood staunchly on guard at the outer reaches of the firelight. She watched him, then craned her eyes further on up toward the stars.

Allah is looking elsewhere.

Before she had even fully realized it, her hand had made it to her lower area, that area, and slipped quietly, cautiously, beneath her cloth. A great anticipation, a bristly pressure, filled her. An ecstatic paralysis seized her. She stopped. Enraptured. Should she keep on?

What greater heights could be achieved?

She felt as the mother of the world, swollen with mountains and skies, ready to birth it all anew. This could not be forbidden. Not this. If this was what everyone felt, men and women, it had to be a gift, a piece of paradise stored within everyone, meant to be explored, meant to be shared.

She closed her eyes.

Voices. Gunfire. Cries.

At dawn she was wrenched awake, the infant sun blotted out by the shadow of a man scrambling toward her. He threw himself upon her. Dead. He was dead—no, no he wasn't dead but rather protecting her, urging her to get up and to run—run where?—as the surrounding ridges popped with gunfire, and groaned with big-sounding engines on the distant road.

The other man had taken shelter behind a rocky wall, rising sporadically to return fire. That wall: that was why they'd camped here. A shield. A trench. A fort. The safest spot any of these wilds could pitiably offer. In case.

Between sleep and suddenly running for her life, her heart was all beast, pounding and stomping and vibrating with the rest of her vitals. Her skull was empty, all thought-making energy now in her limbs, driving her away in terrible haste. She kept low as she could, shadowed by her protector. The horses bouncing and rearing and screaming, fighting their tethers to the rock. She dared to speak.

"Are they here for me?" she asked.

Incredibly, the man's face lightened, as if he were about to laugh.

"Girl," he said. "They are here for us—"

Then he fell.

The other man fired several rounds into the gray morning and hustled to flee with them. Quick glimpses returned nothing of the attackers, only vague shapes down the mountain that moved like crazed insects.

Her protector had been shot in the leg, inky blood seeping and bubbling over his lower thigh. Most impressively, the man, with clenched teeth and harsh breaths, acted as if he'd merely skinned his knee.

But rapidly he grew worse. His skin became clammy. He said he needed something—something "to wrap," to "tighten"—about the wound. Instantly, she removed her hijab and tied it firmly around his thigh.

Gunfire simmered. Distant, rough voices. The other man, rifle strapped to his back, came to them and knelt at his partner's legs.

"Help carry," he instructed her. She took the injured man by the shoulders. Lighter than she thought. She could almost feel the soul in him shrinking, draining, beneath the creeping-cold skin. Another gun burst below. A bullet pop-whined off nearby stone. Her head was now bare, she naked to her world. In this violent trial, Allah would abandon her.

He already has.

Working fast, they sought the horses. "If they cannot strike us, they will aim for the horses," said the man with the rifle. "Then we can't get away."

She took Ghalib, whose massive equine body quaked as she led him. The man secured his partner to the other horse, behind him. She felt as if she might throw up. She had never ridden a horse alone and felt vulnerable. Fragile. How could she command this kingdom of quivering muscle all by herself?

Awkwardly they clambered, then galloped, forward. The rugged terrain presented no obstacle to Ghalib's surefooted haste, as if he were somehow protected from it. She clutched tight to his reins.

In time, the mountain winds overtook all other noise, before them, behind them.

Miles away, they settled in a bed of rock on the downslope of the mountain. They were alone again, for now. The skin of the man shot, her healer, was graying. Green-tinged, too. He drooled, and there was blood in the drool. She helped lower him to the earth, where the other man set up a makeshift place to lie, providing as a headrest an emptied saddlebag, the healer sputtered, glistened with sweat.

"We need to get the bullet out," said the other man. He knelt by his wounded companion, a flash-strip of metal in his hand.

The man coiled up a leather strap and wedged it between the healer's teeth, who bit down. She removed the hijab she had secured around the wound. So soiled now. Scarlet dots seeped out onto the stones. The ragged opening where the bullet struck the healer's pants was torn and widened. The bullet's bite pulsed red and raw. While repulsive, it also fascinated her.

From a canteen, the other man splashed water on the wound. Weakened but visceral groans from the healer. The man with the knife bent low and delicately slipped the blade into the little crater and the healer seizured in agony. It was difficult to watch even though it heartened her to see in him this swell of energy.

Every movement of the blade, subtle or not, awakened new muscles in his face. Blood gooped, poured, caught in a bundled rag held in the man's other hand. Several times he cursed. Twisting, scraping. Finally the thing emerged, a metal accent in the tissue. In a few more delicate strokes of the blade, it popped out. The man poured more water on it and told her to fetch another towel. It was the first time in thirty minutes she broke her trance.

"Tomorrow," said the man, crouched and poking at the flailing fire. "In the morning, we cross the border."

"What will happen then?" she asked.

The man explained. They were to take her to the home of a man named Kadir Mehmet, in Yuksekova. Another business partner, she wondered, but didn't ask. Beyond that, the man did not know. The rest of the story was in the hands of this Kadir Mehmet.

So many people know of me, know of this, she thought. *This was a mistake.* If she had succumbed to—obeyed—her father, she would now be at peace. She would have nothing more to do with the coldness and the darkness of life. Her father would not have protracted the pain of her death, as she was doing now.

Omeed is your savior. You are indebted to him.

On this last night in the wilds, she distracted herself by tending to the wounded man. She protected him now. They had stemmed the bleeding, but he had lost much. A massive, dark stain stiffened his pantleg. A long, red-soaked towel covered the wound. He coughed often, and lay close in the glow of the fire, which he watched like a stage act. He requested the contents of one of several seldom-opened sacks hanging from the saddles. They were tiny black pellets, or seeds. Handfuls of them. She cupped some under his chin and like a dog he licked them out of her palm.

Afterward, he closed his eyes, exhaled long as if releasing all pain. Some ghost of a smile haunted his lips. As the fire shrank in the enclosing dark, she watched as his eyes opened once more and looked toward the stars. A streak across the sky.

"Did you see that?" he asked her.

She nodded.

"Those are the souls of horses."

She watched the sky. When she turned back to him, he was asleep, his breast a gentle pulse.

A nudge. A stronger nudge.

She awoke bleary-eyed. Stretching up toward the sun-cleansed sky was the figure of the other man, his face in dawn-shadow, his foot nestled at her side.

"Come," he said. "We must go."

He handed her the canteen and she sat up and drank. She shivered, terribly aware of her head-to-toe dirtiness.

Then she saw it.

Yards off from the campsite stood a small mound of loosely-piled stones. She glanced around. The healer was nowhere else. Her chest clenched.

"Come," repeated the man, his back to her as he readied the horse. "We need to make our destination today."

For the remainder of the journey, her now-lone companion did not speak much. She dwelled often on the healer, where he might be now, what truths he might be uncovering. If Allah had granted him redemption. Non-belief was perhaps an evil, but it was the easiest evil, the most forgivable.

Maybe, she thought, *he is riding the stars.*

CHAPTER TEN
Present Day

AFTER ONLY AN HOUR out on the trail, she'd brought Toby back to the stables. He didn't seem to have as much energy today. It concerned her, but she chalked it up to a normal low ebb, simple tiredness. We all got tired. And Tara had been tired for weeks, maybe even months. She felt her youth, her vitality, were being taxed away at a faster and faster rate. Only when she thought about it did she remember, on a daily diminishing scale, the gusto she used to have.

Five years to forty. What then?

She spent the next hour grooming Toby, filling his hay corner. He snorted often, his head lowered, moist eyes mellow. Malibu's hills and fields and clustered wood were cast in the homey sheen of the mid-afternoon sun.

"How's he doing?"

A voice from the stable entrance. A figure stood there against the glow and its thousand shadows littering the tree-lined path.

Mike Tucci.

"Hey there," she said, staying where she was.

He approached, his eyes on Toby but his mind clearly occupied with heavy, solemn things. "How's he doing?"

"He's fine," Tara said. "How's—"

Promptly Tucci handed her a ziploc bag with a small newspaper clipping in it. "Sorry," he said, "didn't have time to frame it."

She took it. "What's this?"

He shrugged, with mercurial humor. Tara looked at it through the bag. It was a classified posting.

Wanted: Information Concerning Iranian Doctor. Reward.

"I'm… not following," she said.

"That came from an editor at the Times. Printed six months ago. He recently came across it again and thought of the Javid case and brought it in. Didn't know if it was something to consider. Is it?"

"I don't know."

"Six months ago, you opened a P.O. box in San Diego. You're drawing money from an account in a city you don't live in. The balls are knocking around, Tara. Can't get 'em into the net but you mind helping me out some with these little coincidences?"

"There's nothing coincidental about it—"

"Six months."

"So?"

"So we got HR records showing you interviewed only Middle-Eastern women for Dr. Javid's position with you. What's that about?"

"I was… I was under pressure to… diversify the faculty. And a lot of those that looked the best were Indian or Middle-Eastern or Asian. What can I say?"

Again, Tucci shrugged. "I'm trying to throw you a rope."

"Tell me, please," Tara stammered. "Just tell me what you think this all is. What are these 'balls' and where are they going? Give me your quarterback of this 'plan.'"

Tara was lightheaded. Muscles flexed in Toby's statuesque bulk and he stuttered a foot or two back, flicked his head, mane drooping like gold tinsel.

Tucci glanced at the horse, then returned quickly to Tara, who gathered her composure, clasped her hands piously and stepped in close to him. She placed her hands on either side of his head. He tried to be casual, but she discerned in him an impulse to withdraw, until her touch sunk in, and that cute softness rose in his eyes—the eyes into which she now stared.

"Mike," she said. "Look at me. Tell me I had anything to do with… with Marika. Does it make any sense? You look in the right places you're going to find circumstantial curiosities everywhere, in everything. You think I could kill someone? Do you? I save people. I kill the killers. Sounds stupid I know, but I do. You know this. How could I… how could I do what you're thinking? With what you know of me?"

Keeping deadpan, Tucci said, "I hope I know enough."

People were fucking slippery. Trite as it was, there was permanent truth in saying "no one really knows anyone." Fathoms beneath fathoms, certainly, in all moms and dads, sons and daughters, best friends, brothers and sisters and cousins and wives and husbands. We used little of our brains and weren't sure how to fill the rest, too free were we to roam in there. Too free to think, to imagine, to crave. To obsess.

What the fuck is wrong with people? he'd thought, driving back from Tara's stable. *What goes on up there?*

In this case, Tucci reasoned, he would find out.

Tucci called a third time, but still his father didn't pick up.

Extra long shower, he thought. Or bath. Or old-man dump. All these things were plausible. All these things had previously accounted for Dan Tucci's phone delinquency. And, given Tucci was at the store and wanted his father's preference for dinner, he had made all such calls within half an hour.

As the outgoing message replayed, though, the calls became concerned check-ups.

Droned the outgoing message, "Hello… this is Dan, Mr. Tucci, or Dad, depending. As you can see, I'm out. You know the drill."

The calm and the rational theories were, for whatever reason, not clicking. His gut knotted.

Something was wrong.

Tucci tried a fourth time while in transit. No luck. Ten minutes later, he pulled into the driveway, behind his father's pick-up. He wanted to get out, charge on in, but instead he sat for several long seconds staring at the two shuttered windows facing the street, waiting for one to open, to reveal his father's lopsided grin, his beckoning hand.

One last time, Tucci called. On the third ring there was a sudden click and brief dead noise. Fumbling. Then a timid, "Hello?"

"Dad?"

"Mike."

"Is everything okay?"

"Are you on your way?"

"I'm outside in the driveway. I'm about to come in."

"Don't."

"What?"

"Just please. I don't think I can talk long."

"Dad, I'm here with dinner." Even as he said this, he climbed from the car and walked, sans groceries, toward the back entrance. "What's wrong?"

"Jesus Christ, don't come in."

Tucci stopped, lightheaded with bewilderment. His father's behavior was almost too bizarre to be real.

Then his father appeared behind the back screen door. Tucci hung up, remained still.

"Dad, are you okay?"

Dan Tucci looked completely ashen and frightened. Tucci felt a jolt in his chest. The color had drained from his father's face, his eyes wide. His stutter-footing on the other side of the screen door recalled movies about aimless zombies.

Casually, Tucci slid his hand beneath his coat, felt the butt of his pistol. He started toward the back porch, but stopped at his father's outstretched palm.

"Please don't come in, Mike," Dan said, voice wavering. "I'm sorry I didn't answer the phone, but he said not to, and I wasn't about to screw around with what he said."

"Dad." Tucci's throat constricted. "Are you alone? Who?"

You know.

"I'm alone."

Tucci rapidly blinked twice and said, "If no."

"I swear I'm alone," Dan said. He glanced about the porch. "He said he rigged the goddamn house. That if anyone came in it would…"

"What?"

"It would blow up."

Tears misted Dan Tucci's eyes. "I didn't know what to do. What the hell is going on?"

Tucci stepped forward, cautiously. He recalled similar "compassionate approaches" on patrol, when they would try and talk down or negotiate with a harried victim, or suspect, usually on a domestic dispute. And here, just as it had in those instances, the business of it overtook him, and he was able to mercifully suspend constant reminders that this time the harried victim was the man who'd once, in grand showmanship, chased the monsters out of *his* room.

"I don't see anything, Dad. No wires, nothing bad." From where he stood, Tucci surveyed the house, as much of it as he could see. "Who… who told you this?"

You know.

The effect of Dan Tucci's encounter, whatever had happened to him, frothed in the old man's eyes. He seemed to want to move to Tucci (for protection, Tucci thought, ironically and sadly), but he was frozen, like one very knowingly in the crosshairs of a sniper.

Tucci put a few cautious steps forward. His gut wrenched tighter as his father stumbled back into the kitchen and looked at him like he was diseased.

"Dad," he said. "The place isn't going to blow up."

Tucci cautiously opened the screen door. Looked, listened. He followed his father into the kitchen.

Dan was still too shaken for any relief, his attention half in, half out. Tucci sensed a kind of disappointed shame in his father, too, perhaps at his own gullibility, and the terror that had allowed it.

Tucci continued with his father into the dining room. Dan took a seat.

"I know it isn't, I know," Dan said, hands covering his face, looking out on the room through the quivering jail-bars of his fingers. "He definitely knew you. He's one of yours."

Tucci was both irritated and hurt by this comment but said nothing.

"He was dressed up," said Dan. "N-nice suit, it looked like. Shiny skin, almost didn't look real. Bald head. Totally. Shaved I think."

That didn't mesh with old descriptions of Olin, with his long graying hair and salt-and-pepper goatee that Tucci remembered so vividly. He'd had the eyes of some soul-dead Soviet hitman, set in the visage of an aging rocker. Still, it had been years. He easily could have changed his look.

"He told me to sit down here," Dan continued, turning and pointing, "in the living room. He sat at the couch and we faced each other and he had his briefcase in his lap and just stared at me over it. Smiling. Looked like he was daydreamin' like a little kid. Thinkin' about something but nothing. I get to thinking this guy's high as a kite, that there's something wrong here. I ask him how can I help him and you know what he says to me?"

"What?" Tucci said with a narrowed, unbroken expression.

"'I'm sorry about your wife passing.' That's what he said."

Tucci blinked.

"I didn't know whether to say thanks or to punch the guy," Dan said. Moisture accumulated in his eyes. "Fucking talking about Ellen. Your mom. But that was three years ago. This guy wasn't from the restaurant or anywhere, but he knew about that, too."

Tucci told himself to stay calm for his father. "You want a glass of water, Dad? Or some juice?"

Dan shook his head, then took a long breath. "He started off on some kind of philosophizing. Something about death making people gods."

Sounds like Olin.

"Something," Dan said, choking up, "I don't know, it was something about death making people pure, making people role models and heroes and martyrs. Said death gets rid of us before we get sick of each other, that if we lived forever we'd just find out the real ugliness in everyone we love. Some crap. I remember one specific thing. He said, 'Death keeps hope alive.'" Dan shook his head, sniffed hard. "Guy was fucked up."

Tucci tried to keep his breathing measured. "What else did he say, Dad?"

"Said he'd gotten all heady after where he'd been. I asked where he was. 'Jail,' he says. I froze. He saw my eyes and laughed. Then he said, 'Guess how I got there.'"

Tucci remained expressionless. His father stared into his eyes, as if coaxing Tucci to fill in the answer.

"'Your boy Mikey,' he said," Dan continued, wincing. "'Your boy just about bent over backward to get me in there. Did some things he wasn't supposed to, I think."

Tucci thought his father on the verge of throwing up so he leaned forward a little, ready to tend to him.

"Then what?"

"He said how weird it felt to be back out again. I'm guessing he meant out of prison. He said the world was endless again, but that it made him crazy. Then he asked me if I had that phobia of going outside. I said no." Dan's fingers drummed rapidly on the table. "He told me to prove it. If I did, he'd leave. So… I stand up and go to the door, when he tells me he's rigged the whole house to fucking blow up. And the phone."

"The phone."

"If I answered the phone. Or called someone."

"Jesus." Tucci slammed the table, feeling silly the second after he did so. His hands throbbed.

"I don't… I don't know why I believed him, Mike," Dan said, tears coming prodigiously now. "Goddammit, I'm stupid. He got up and walked out the door. He even stepped a funny way so he wouldn't set off the bomb or whatever it was he told me about. He walked away and was gone. I just sat down and couldn't move."

"Charlie ain't here, Mikey."

"Not here for him."

They regarded each other, Tucci deadpan, Alex with that small playful smile. Somewhere in the shadowy yard, the fountain gurgled.

Beyond them, Baldwin Hills rose toward the cloud cover, hued purple by the airport lights.

"Ain't here for an arrest, right?" Alex said. "I don't do that shit no more."

"No."

"What then?"

Tucci reached in his pocket, brought out two mugshot prints and handed them to Alex, who took them hesitantly in his spidery hand.

"More info written on the back," Tucci said. "He's shaved his head since. No goat either."

"What'm I s'posed to do with these?"

"Shake him up, maybe?"

"Done?"

Dammit, yes please. But Tucci shook his head. "No. Just put the fear of God into him. Bring him down a notch. I don't care how. Be creative."

"Mikey," said Alex. "'Sup with this guy?"

"You don't need to know anything else."

"I told you, I don't do this no more."

"Not you. Pass it along. Anton. Chris. One of them. They owe me."

"Whatever, man."

"You gonna do it? Or am I gonna have to dust off a few files?"

"Calm down, Mikey, I got this."

Tucci turned.

"Hey Mikey."

He looked back.

"You going to Charlie's graduation next week?" Alex asked.

"I'll be there," said Tucci, eyes lowered. "And this is just between us."

"Men," Tara quipped. "Last minute on everything."

"Yeah, yeah."

Pulled well into the red, Tucci switched on the emergency blinkers and dashed from the car into the card shop. *Tara's right,* he thought. Pretty pathetic. The graduation ceremony was in just three hours and just now he was running to get something for it.

Charlie would understand.

He surveyed the vast wall of options, narrowed his search to the graduation section. Was it too hokey for him to get an actual graduation card, though, especially for Charlie? Didn't seem like enough. All he'd be doing was signing his name. But what else to write? Good job? Idiot. How to distill into a few sentences their time together? Maybe it didn't need distilling. The memories were enough, the result, was enough.

Something funny, but not overly so. Something sentimental, but not overly so. Something maybe with computers, videogames…

He narrowed it down to two choices, then went with the decidedly cornier one: the picture of an astronaut receiving a diploma from an alien and featuring a glib line about *Going High Places!* He brought it, and the envelope, to the cheery cashier.

"This all for you?" she said.

"Yep," he said, laying a fiver on the counter.

Tucci's eyes strayed to a glass display case next to the register, where he noticed frames for sale. One of them, four-by-six and silver, had as its default photograph a strikingly familiar couple. Elegantly middle-aged, the man stood behind the woman, his hands clutching her upper arms. The woman, in profile, looked back at him. Giant, wide, Disneyland grins.

Black-and-white. WASP-y.

I've seen them before.

"And here you are," said the cashier.

"Thanks."

He stopped and looked closer at the frame.

Was it… that photo? Tara's parents on the mantel. No. It was a slightly different position. But the faces—

Glancing out the storefront windowpane, he saw Tara in the passenger seat. She saw him too and waved. There was, as there'd been of late, a forlornness in her smile.

He hurried out, climbed into the car.

"Find a good one?" Tara asked.

"I think so. Need to think of something to write."

"That shouldn't be too hard," she said.

Idling in her car by the parking lot, Tara glimpsed her third-floor bedroom window, mysteriously aglow.

I didn't turn that lamp on before I left.

She thought hard. No, she hadn't, she was sure of it. Seldom when she left during the day did she turn on the lights, even when anticipating a nighttime return. It was not a second-nature habit she would forget having done.

Engine grumbling, her fingers tightened on the steering wheel. In between glances to ensure there was no one behind her, she watched for any movement in her apartment: a rustling of curtains, a shadow flitting on the wall. Or the stark vision of the intruder himself.

Nothing.

She continued on down into the garage toward her space, the only moving car, the only moving thing through the oil-stained stone and metal.

There was the pepper spray in her purse, of course. Or she could go straight to the lobby. Or call someone on her cell.

Mike.

No. She wanted to, but no. Right now she wouldn't have been half-surprised if it was Mike Tucci and Co. in her apartment, overturning her belongings, dissecting her life with messy doggedness.

For several moments, Tara sat in her car, staring at the Non-Resident Tow-Away warning nailed on the wall before her. She bit her tongue absentmindedly, stopped only when it felt like she might draw blood. Anger foamed fast in her, corroding her reason, and she partially relished it. Fucking Mike. He had *used* her. He had known things all along, had played the cheap lover card to shortcut his way in. Now he was privy to everything, entitled to all she kept, she knew—so he thought. How could she let this happen? She had lost somehow. In what had either been an egregious misstep on her part, or a rebellious stroke of fate, she had managed to lose to a man who'd cut his teeth not in classrooms, but in cars. On street corners.

She brought out her pepper spray, then deliberated at the elevator. This was one time when she might be happy to have Randolph out here, smoking his butt, ready to do just about anything. She could have him go inside first.

This is my home. My home.

She stepped into the elevator. It hummed up to her floor and, with a spastic halt, the doors parted and the long spartan hallway glared at her. She trod the carpet delicately, went to her door and listened. Nothing. Didn't seem like Mike or the police were here. Good. She stood back and used her cell phone to dial her landline. Faintly from within she could hear the succession of rings, milliseconds ahead of the rings in her phone. Then it went to voicemail. Normal.

Maybe I did leave the light on.

Pepper spray still ready, she went to unlock the door but found the deed had already been done.

Shit. Shit.

Someone was here.

Tara backed away again and rapped on Randolph's door. Waited. No response.

Call the police. Call Mike.

Yet there was that tendency, that impulse, long with her, of needing to take things head on.

Tara leaned forward and thrust the door open and instantly withdrew, as if the knob were coal-hot. She stood still, waiting for noises, voices, movement. An overture of sensation throughout her body, blood running thunderous in her veins.

"Hello?" she called.

The living room light was still off, though it was paled by the shining lamp from the bedroom. Maybe it had been on an automatic timer? She had never fiddled with that feature before, but maybe by accident she'd set it to turn on.

Who unlocked the door?

Tara turned on the living room and kitchen light.

"Someone here?" she said, hand poised on the light switch, ready to throw it off again should anyone emerge. "I'm calling the police."

Curiosity joining her fear, she stepped further in, her attention focused across the room. She stopped.

A noise. A person. It sounded like it was coming through the walls or the ceiling, and grew unmistakably louder the closer she got to the bedroom doorway. A hiccuping, wet sound. Rhythmic. Crying? Wait. Laughing. It was laughing—giggling. Subdued. It was male.

What's funny, asshole?

She stopped, looked behind her. Still no one. The laughing seemed to come from one direction and then everywhere. But there was only one place it could have come from because she now heard other things there, too: a subtle scraping, spurts of running water, the clearing of a throat.

On the carpet between the bed and the bathroom was a single sneaker, on its side. Gray and worn. Not hers.

Tara stopped at the frame—one sprint and she was at the kitchen knives—and peered toward the bathroom, the door of which was ajar. She could make out a bobbing elbow, flashes of skin reflected in the mirror. The water on and off. The rapid palpitation of a razor tapping porcelain.

Someone's fucking shaving *in there.*

She yelled, "Hey!"

The person flinched. The door pulled open. Against the harsh bulbs of the bathroom he stood there in askew, manchild glee, a dumb-drunk smile displacing the shaving cream smeared on his face. He was lopsided—only one foot had a shoe. Recognizing her neighbor's utter intoxication—probably beyond alcohol—Tara imagined he'd be lopsided no matter the footwear.

"Randolph," she said. "What the hell are you doing here?"

He blinked. A dollop of cream fell from the razor in his right hand. "This isn't my place, is it?"

"No… it's not. What are you doing here?"

"Tara… shit, I'm so sorry. I came here by mistake. By mistake."

"Okay. Please leave then. And I'd like my spare keys back."

"Sorry, sorry." He staggered back, turned on the water and messily rinsed off his face, drying it with a washrag. He missed the smudges of cream by his sideburns, and in his ear.

"What's going on?" Tara said. "Where's Susan?"

He laughed, that careless giggle she'd heard coming in. With every step he advanced, she drew back, until he fumbled for his stranded shoe and knelt down to clumsily strap it back on. She could see the redness of his eyes.

"Susan's gone—I mean, not gone. Not gone like your stuff—"

My stuff?

"—but gone for the week, I mean. With the kids. I guess I got confused. Sorry Tara, again… so sorry."

"The keys, please."

"Tara, I'm sorry."

"I'm sure."

"Please don't tell Susie about this."

"I won't, as long as it doesn't happen again." Tara glared at him. "That means never."

Randolph nodded overzealously, which Tara took as sarcastic. Probably everything to him was sarcastic.

Tara could smell him, a musty mist of toxins, the ripe sweetness of weed, pungent hints of liquor.

"Randy," she said. "The keys."

"I didn't open the door," he said. "It was already open."

"What?

"Yeah, already unlocked. I swear, I swear."

"Just give me the keys. Please."

He dug in his pockets, took out the keys and threw them on the bed.

"Thanks," Tara muttered.

She moved well aside to make room for his passage toward the front door. At the kitchen counter, he stopped.

"Susie's gonna ask why you took them back, the keys," he said. "What're you—you gonna say?"

"More like what are *you* going to say?"

"Look, don't screw around with me," he said. "Come on. You've been doing that too long. You're the biggest cocktease ever. What is it you do but screw and screw with me?"

"Please go, Randolph."

"I know you're all creeped out, but you're not gonna find a guy more honest than me. I cut out the fat, Tara. The guy who gives you wine and roses and shit is going 'round the long way. I'm the shortcut. We both want the same thing. I cut to the chase. We all want it and you do, too."

With every word, his resoluteness grew. A mock sobriety in his face. He stepped toward her. She tightened her grip on the pepper spray.

"Don't have to spray me," he said.

"I hope not. But if you don't get out, I'm calling the police."

She pressed nine on her phone and he came at her, moving low like an offensive lineman, or some hunchbacked beast. Instinctually, Tara turned away. She tried to evade him, but his arms enveloped her in a bear hug, nearly squeezing the wind from her. He hoisted her up off her feet and started carrying her.

"Get *off* of me!" Arms free, Tara tried elbowing him but missed, tried kicking, tried prying loose the arms that were like hairy mandibles clasping her midsection. None of it worked and he heaved her clumsily onto the couch. Spots danced over her vision, and then his face blotted everything as he collapsed upon her, struggling to shift her into better position.

Muscles aflame, Tara kneed him in the side, pounded and elbowed his back and his neck, but his wet sloppy weight held.

Finally, Tara, welling all strength, shoved him away from her. Randolph stumbled back, clawed for balance, then collapsed on his backside. A sort of euphoric violence roared up in Tara. She dashed to the kitchen, drew a knife and charged toward him.

For some of those few seconds, or so she would later realize, there wasn't a doubt in her mind that she would kill him. Randolph must have seen this, too, for in minutes he was gone, clambering to his feet, rasping broken apologies on his way to the door.

"Sorry, sorry," said Randolph. "I'm so fucked up right now. Sorry. Don't tell Susie. Don't."

Tara followed him out, blade out the whole way, then closed the door and locked both bolts and stood there still facing the entrance, breathing, breathing, the knife raised, ready. She, herself, ready.

Ready.

Then, the phone rang.

Tucci stood there on the sidewalk, the crackling recorder in one hand, gun in the other. He hadn't locked the door behind him. *Goddammit. Stupid fucking idiot.* Spend that time getting in and setting it all up in a heartpounding fever only to get so sloppy at the end.

But maybe he had locked the door, and Randolph was just bullshitting.

From his seat half a block away, he'd heard the entire altercation, crackled out from the voice-activated recorder. He'd bolted from his car, ready to bust in, ready to give that heavy-breathing waste-of-skin neighbor of hers an unforgettable lesson in deep-throating a Glock. But now he stopped. The douchebag seemed to have left. Tara seemed to be okay.

He stood there looking at her complex, blood running heated in his ears. Then, steadily, he turned and climbed back into his car, lowered further into the driver's seat. The recorder once more riding shotgun.

The two microphoned bugs, while crude, worked well enough. And crude was fine now. Crude was appropriate because it was just him, doing nothing fancy; ideally, he would rig the landline, so he could hear both sides of a conversation, but Tara, like a third of the world's population, used primarily her cell, and bugging that wouldn't be practical. And unfortunately, because neither bug was attached to a phone, and because of their limited range, he didn't get the best reception. He considered moving closer, but couldn't risk it.

Occasional static was more preferable than fucking himself over by being spotted.

Tara, and her apartment, had quieted down. In the darkness of his vehicle, the orange bead of light on the recorder held firm, like an isolated star, ready to flip green the moment a bug floated over a transmission.

He sat low, skull cap drawn over his scalp like a criminal. Who else, after all, would wear a skull cap in fucking Los Angeles, when even winter evenings rarely dipped below sixty? But he sometimes envied the psychological freedom of criminals to move as desired, to break violently through any obstruction. No bullshit paperwork, no rules.

Tucci was moving now, and moving forward.

Olin had fucking visited Dad. Had visited his fucking father. Where had he been? At the motherfucking store. And meanwhile, Marika Javid's killer continued to elude. And right now, hearing Tara confront that cocksucker across the hall… it was another tease, a funhouse reflection of some slippery and evil force popping up all around him, about which he could do nothing.

Not anymore.

He waited.

Then—a crackle. Faint voice. Female. The orange light turned green.

He listened.

"Oh, hi," said Tara, faintly, then louder: "How are you feeling?"

A pause.

"…I'm going back this week…"

This week? Where?

Her voice seemed to go in and out. Pacing around the apartment, probably.

"…I told Janice, yes…"

Maybe back to work. That's what it is.

"…Thanks, I'd love that… I miss her, too…"

Despite genial words, her tone was flat and on guard. She did not like this person.

"…Take care of yourself, Ray…"

Ray, Ray… how are you feeling… work… Ray… missing her… Raymond… Raymond Stiles… Yes…

The conversation ended. For a few hopeful seconds, the recorder's light kept green before once more clicking off.

He waited. Waited. Hunger prodded him. Simultaneously, he popped two lemon Jolly Ranchers and winced. He craved a cheeseburger. There was also another part of him too knotted-up to eat.

More time passed. In a nearby yard, a dog barked. Furiously.

Then, the slow-rushing tide of a new transmission. The light turning green. Tara—

Wait.

Tucci scrutinized the recorder, certain at first that it was picking up other signals, even though that was impossible, since it could only read dispatches from the bugs near Tara. But this woman speaking was not Tara. It was a voice vaguely hers but distorted, because she was not speaking English.

She was speaking Farsi.

May The Creator strike them down, Delgado thought.

But that was not the way He worked. He worked through Delgado. Despite divine assurance, however, Delgado could still make mistakes. He was an imperfect vessel, after all.

He did not think the old man had noticed him. The man was vigilant, but Delgado had remained low, disguised against the dark sullen people between them on the bus. They had exited at the same time, through opposite doors.

He had followed the old man to the warehouse, a large and grimy thing. He wasn't sure if it was still in use. What a garbage dump this whole place was, inside and out. Americans spoke piously, but what was truly in their hearts was what he could now see, smell, hear all around him. Immodesty, sin, gushing from every pore. The true products of their souls.

What is this old man doing? he thought, until he saw her, the blonde-haired woman. She had her arms crossed, she looked nervous, and did not stray far from her vehicle, which she kept running. They spoke in low tones to one another. He listened, could barely hear it, but heard one thing and that was enough.

No. No no no—

Delgado remained in hiding, drowned in shadow. Attack them. Destroy them both right now. No. That would not work. Despite the urge of his every limb, ambushing them right there would threaten his duty. It was a woman and an old man, sure, but there were still two of them. And with this new revelation, he had to be extra careful now, to ensure this time that he was correct.

He strained to listen further.

You were fooled.

The blonde whore climbed back into her car, backed out of the little alleyway. From the sheeted entrance of the warehouse, the old man watched her go. So did Delgado. He noted her car, the make, the license plate. He knew how to find her.

Silently, he asked The Maker for forgiveness.

"Mike, you look sick."

Tucci leaned forward and slid the recorder and headphones toward Bashir as he lowered himself into the other booth. Tucci nursed a cup of coffee, something he now regretted as the caffeine turned his queasy antsiness into violent urges.

"Thanks for coming, man," Tucci said.

"Sure. What's up?"

"Listen to that. Need it translated."

Bashir eyed him, hesitant.

"Please."

"Mike —

"Please."

Bashir strapped on the earphones, played the audio. Listened. Abruptly, he stopped.

"This is just one side of a conversation."

"I know." Tucci sighed. "I mic'd Tara White's place."

Bashir shook his head. "Jesus, without a warrant? Mike—" He stopped, looked at the recorder. "Dr. White speaks Farsi?"

Tucci shrugged. "You tell me. I don't need a line by line. Anything important."

"Audio could use some cleaning."

"I know."

They fell quiet as Bashir listened further. When the tape finished, he removed the ear pieces, digesting what he'd heard.

"She seemed surprised to hear from this guy—"

"Who is he?"

"She called him Omeed. It sounded like he was warning her about something."

"Threatening her?"

"I don't know. One half of the conversation, remember? There was something she said about the 'stain of dishonor not yet lifted, even with Marika's death,' but she said it in a tired, almost incredulous way." Bashir sighed. "Remember what Aadila Zuabi said about family dishonor."

A picture was coming together in Tucci's head. The newspaper ad. The interviews. Tara's apparent entanglement with these people. "You think she could have been involved?"

"Obviously you do," Bashir said. "She said something about meeting him, too. At a warehouse. In East Hollywood."

"Where?"

"Didn't get it exactly." Bashir looked frustrated. "Doesn't sound too good, does it?"

"No, it doesn't." Tucci closed his eyes. "Fuck."

The Metro bus roared and rattled, its windows scratched up as if by the nails of animals desperate for escape, filled with the wrought faces of the late hour. Most eyes were trained on the floor, or on a cell phone, or lost in some tired daze. Some were wide and alert.

Like the old man's.

I failed, thought Delgado. *I have failed but this will be set right. The All-Powerful will see it so.*

Hood drawn over his scalp, Delgado sank lower into his seat, kept his glances furtive, minimal. He had followed the old man from the warehouse, from his meeting with the whore. The *whore*. For the entire pursuit Delgado had made sure not to make direct eye contact with the old man. Not that there was anything short of God that could alter his fate. Not now. For Delgado was his fate. The man was alone and frail. Delgado was also pretty certain the police were not following him.

He looks so lost, thought Delgado. *He is a tired and useless creature. It will be to his favor that he will be gone, given to the Creator's judgment.*

The bus pulled to a stop somewhere in East Hollywood. Outside were closed shops and bordered windows and homeless persons shambling across the sidewalk. Delgado sat up as the old man rose and hurried as quick as his limbs would permit toward the front door. When he was sure he wouldn't see him, Delgado bolted from his seat and exited the side door, which closed instantly behind him as the bus screeched back to the hollow streets.

He is too meddlesome, thought Delgado. When one man's will contested the will of the Creator, and all created, what did he think was coming to him?

Hood still drawn, Delgado kept close to the shadow of a streetside tree. He watched the old man make his way over a crosswalk, gazes furtive, as if tracing the path of a bothersome insect. When he was well on the other side of the road, Delgado mobilized. He had to make sure the man didn't have a cell phone, didn't contact someone out of his obvious fear.

He knows he is to die.

There was comfort in knowing this. In knowing that, at some level, the old man would accept it. Yes. It would not be too difficult.

Delgado followed him to a small decrepit building called the Starlight Motel. He waited while the man climbed the stairs to the second story, then ascended fast after him, his footsteps trembling the rail, echoing across the gutted lot.

The old man stopped. Turned.

Less than ten feet separated them now. Delgado stood still, stared at the old man whose face began to break in emotion. His eyes moistening. But there was nothing he could do, and the man realized this quickly. Futility overwhelmed him, and his whole aged body shook, tears flowing as he fell to his knees and began to supplicate. Began to pray.

In a nearby window, a curtain parted, a curious face appeared. This was drawing unwanted attention. With what any third-party might have construed as compassion, Delgado gently approached the old man and placed his hand on his shoulder. The man flinched. Through cloth, Delgado could feel stark bone. He guided the man up from the cement, accompanied him to his room door. Tears continued to fall, clear mucus collected in the man's nose, but the original frenzy of his reaction had lessened with Delgado's reassuring touch.

"Look at me, old man," said Delgado.

The old man obeyed. Delgado studied him, peered into his eyes. There was no mistaking it—this was the man he was looking for.

They entered the room. The bed was crisp and made, the luggage sparse. Delgado closed the door softly behind him, then drew the blade and drove it swiftly into the old man's stomach. Twisted it. Withdrew it. That jolt, that holy elevation, lifted him to ecstatic realms. Blood ran dark and prodigious.

The man coughed, issued sad, child-like whimpers, his shame caught in his throat, his many years draining from him. He doubled over, but Delgado held him up, unleashed a rain of steel into his back, cutting deep through the soft, aged flesh. Diseased flesh. Occasionally he struck bone, and thought he heard the dull crack of a rib.

The force of the blows sent the ravaged body teetering in multiple directions, but Delgado held onto him. He took the man's collar and leaned in toward his whitening face, where the eyes rolled limp with life, the eyelids fluttering, twitching like the wings of a wounded bird. Blood drooled over his shriveled lip.

"Allah awaits you," said Delgado, in Farsi.

He pulled back the man's head. Against the blade, the throat was like softened fruit.

He was late again, Juan Delgado. He was so quiet tonight, too, looking at her with scorn. Increasingly, Melissa Jonson was growing more and more uncomfortable with this man who cleaned her store's floor. Incredibly, she sensed haughtiness in him, a pretension of superiority. He was above her, and he knew it.

That's blood on his shirt.

Spots, she noticed. A line of darkened liquid at the bottom of his shirt. Could be grease, could be oil. He did have another job, in a garage or in construction or something. Why did she think blood? Could be anything. Maybe he was in a gang? Who knew what these young "hombres" did in their spare time. That one housecleaner her mother used—her son had been shot in a donut shop parking lot in East LA. They'd said it was likely a gang initiation.

As a precaution, Melissa wanted to fire Juan, ever since she saw on the news the hospital security footage taken after that young doctor's terrible murder. They'd blown up the black-and-white face, cleaned the pixels and shadows as best they could. Certainly there was doubt, but the build, the walk, the blurred arrangement of the face had struck her as being that of Juan's. That was even before the reporter had mentioned witness descriptions of the culprit possibly being Latino.

It frightened her. She wanted to let Juan go, but had been suddenly seized by the thought of his retaliation. Maybe he tolerated her because he needed this job? If she were to get rid of him, maybe he'd be like one of those wacko disgruntled employees and come back and kill her. Or, if she'd contacted the police, maybe one of his cronies would come by, trash the place, do a drive-by. Who knew what went through such people's minds.

At the time she heard tonight's report, Juan was working in the back, she at the front, closing out the register. The radio at low volume.

"…breaking news, an elderly man has been found dead, stabbed to death, in a Hollywood motel. Witnesses describe someone with the victim moments before they entered his room together. They say he was a man in his twenties or thirties, wearing a hooded jacket and jeans, with a dark complexion…"

Juan had been wearing a hooded jacket, hadn't he? Definitely jeans—

"…authorities say the crime took place between 8:30 and 8:45, at the Starlight Motel…"

That would make sense. He could've been there. What do you truly know about this man? That's why he was late? But he's usually a little late, right? But that was blood. That was definitely blood.

She lowered the volume. Mop in hand, Juan appeared around the canned food aisle, head down, eyes both heavy and vacant. He looked at her, wooden, lingered for a second, then continued cleaning.

Pathetic and sad, is what it was. This old man here. Omeed Madani. Omeed. No, he had not heard the last name on the transmission, but how many Omeeds were running around East Hollywood? Curled up, bloodied in a fetal position, like some oversized abortion.

There were virtually no signs of a struggle, and why would there be? The man was defenseless. Tucci could see in his moist open eyes the shrinking stain of his humanity.

And who could easily take an old man? Anyone younger and stronger. Someone who rock-climbed, worked out—

No. The female witness had said a man had done it. A hooded man. Like Dr. Javid's killer.

Tucci hustled fast from the scene, stomach surging. Eyes of colleagues burned on him, questions and statements on their lips, but he pushed past them all like a frantic lost child. The ambulance and squad cars flashed red, epileptic. Finally he found a spot—a dumpster area, dark and removed—and he bent and hurled up that day's intake, which was slim, so slim he could taste bile at the back of his throat.

Tara fucking Tara oh goddammit TARA—

What would happen if he just left, right now, drove quietly and quickly back home, and shut the door and never spoke to anyone? Divorced all this? Funny. From his mind's melodramatic ruptures, his adolescence could emerge intact. Spurred again by a fucking girl.

Though Tucci never had a cigarette before, he wanted one now, craved one, in fact. In desperate times, the rhythm of smoking attracted him.

There is no doubt about it. Not any longer. Tara is fucking involved.

Chills broke out over his body. His stomach clenched, throat scorched, his brain pounding.

I have to talk to her. Before anyone else.

Returning dazed to the scene, Bashir was the first to greet him.

"Dr. White," Bashir said, in a done-deal voice that grated on Tucci.

"I know."

That pity in his face? Sympathy? Something? Young bastard knows about us. Maybe suspicion. Fuck. "Young"—he's only five years younger than me.

"Listen," said Tucci. "I know her. I mean, she seems to trust me. Besides—there's no evidence…"

He stopped. Bewilderment crinkled Bashir's expression.

"We know she's got something to do with this, Mike," he said. "We got the tapes of their conversation. We know she knows why Dr. Javid was killed."

Tucci stared at the pavement.

"Mike?"

"Yeah. Yeah, I know. But we have to be careful with her. She might be slippery. And we don't know how many others are involved.

Or what the hell's going on now. She could be expecting us. I can talk to her. Soften her up."

Bashir hesitated. Tucci, boiling in impatience, limbs hungry for grand, vicious movement, didn't wait for a reply as he headed for his car, muttering, "Be back."

She made her way into Santa Monica—quite a leap from where she'd seen Omeed—toward another rendezvous. Everything contaminated. People looked at her and they were not people, but creatures of wild lands. Scavengers. Predators. Pile them on. *Just leave me the fuck alone,* Tara thought.

She did not want to go see Stiles, but he'd said it was about Marika. Everything was about Marika. And truthfully—though maybe this was just giving him the benefit of the doubt—on the phone, he sounded softened, less Raymond Stiles-y. Less authoritative and knowing. More humbled.

Traumatic comas will do that.

Tara parked along a well-lit stretch of road, then bustled into the corner coffee joint where she saw a window seat available. She waited, though, until someone toward the center got up and left. She sat down, gaze darting about.

"Dr. White."

She looked up. Somehow, in her quick glances, she'd missed him coming through the door. He wore all denim, his shirt a lighter shade than the jeans. He reminded her of some proud southwestern grandfather. Stiles' nose was crooked, one eye was smaller than the other, and some of the minor cuts still glared on his face. In his left hand he held a hickory cane. In his right, a totebag.

He sat down. "Thank you for coming. I know it was probably an inconvenience."

Tara fidgeted. "Don't worry about it."

"How've you been?"

She felt fleeting embarrassment that he was the first to ask that question, but she was too distracted for much social etiquette.

"I've been better," she said. "How about you?"

"Getting there. Undergoing physical therapy for my knee, which actually isn't related to what happened. I don't like being alone, for sure. It's a little silly, but I do miss Charlotte. Living in an apartment, I feel like I've regressed thirty years, but got robbed on the accompanying youth."

Miss Charlotte. *Ironic, considering you're here to talk about the woman you cheated on her with.*

"You said you're coming back," Stiles remarked.

Tara nodded. "This week. Who knows if I'll end up staying. I'd like to go somewhere else. But I need it now. A month off was good, but part of me's been somewhat stir crazy."

"Understood." He smiled at her with nothing of his former creepiness, even though, for a few awkward, quiet seconds, the smile overstayed its welcome. "I think I'll be officially retiring, myself. I may move to the lake. That's really my favorite place."

"You have some things for me?"

"Ah, yes. Just a few things. They were Marika's."

"I'm surprised."

"What? Why?"

"You had an affair with Marika." Tara said. "Why would you…"

"I couldn't give them to her family or friends… but maybe you could." Stiles chuckled, but there was a sigh amid the laugh. "I know. I screwed up. I did bad things. I want to start atoning for them, however silly that may sound. It's out, anyway. I can't hide from it."

Tara kept nodding, her arms and legs crossed.

"I'm trying to lighten the load," he said. "Now that I have less space. And maybe someone would want them. Or you? Just thought I'd ask."

"Okay. I'll see what I can do."

He brought the bag onto his lap, took out two cashmere sweaters, neatly folded. Tara blinked. It sickened her, the thought of Marika having worn these with Stiles during a rendezvous, but she took them thoughtfully.

"I'll just give you the bag to look through and you can decide what you want to do with them all," Stiles said. Tara started look through it. There was a jeweled bracelet—*Doesn't seem like Marika would have that,* she thought—three books—two fiction, one medical—several more articles of clothes and, what struck Tara most, a sleek blue fountain pen with a Farsi phrase engraved on it.

"'Fly Free,'" Tara said.

"You can read that?" Stiles said.

"Picked up a little from Marika."

For another fifteen minutes they spoke smatteringly. Tara sensed confliction in Stiles, a vague eagerness. There was definitely a grander debate playing out behind the man's aged and battered tissue. Some people, in their later years, segued naturally into humbled introspection. Stiles had been shoved into it.

As she made body-language to leave, Stiles closed his eyes and, stammering as if trying to recall something, said, "Did—did I tell you about how, as a kid, I looked for arrowheads in the backwoods?"

She shook her head. What?

"Did you never do that? You said you grew up in rural Illinois, right?"

"Yes. Never did that, though."

"I used to love to do that. My brother and I would scour all over the place for them, after a classmate at school told us he'd found one down by the creek. But we never found any. Then, one day, we're out doing something. I can't remember what. Football maybe. We were in a field, I know. But at some point I fell, and lo and behold, my face is inches from hitting the business end of an arrowhead sticking up from the ground. Right under my nose. But… I didn't pick it up."

"Why?"

"Because it was too easy. I almost didn't believe it."

"All right." Tara made motions to go, and Stiles watched her, confused. "Thank you for bringing her things. I'll figure out something to do with them."

"The world teases, so don't fall for it," Stiles said. "Leave the arrowhead alone."

❧

Having grown up in Los Angeles, the loneliness of the city, often mentioned by tourists or transplants, had been a thing Tucci understood conceptually but not experientially. Until now. Smeared across the desert, it seemed not a body but a collection of limbs seeking connection.

Fuck you, Tara.

He had to calm down. Parked in the street outside her complex, not far from where he'd heard her crackled conversation with Omeed, he placed his hand on the steering wheel and took deep breaths. Then, he went into the building, took the stairs to her floor. *Swear to Christ,* he thought, *if that stupid prick Randolph comes bumbling into my face…*

She wasn't home. Of course. Calling her would do no good. It would just give her forewarning, allow her a head start.

He went down to the parking lot. Her spot was empty. He would wait. Wait out of sight until she got back.

His phone rang. Bashir. He ignored it. Set it on silent.

He watched her pull into her spot. She was so expressionless. Who was she? *What* was she? Did she at all have any sort of affection for him? Or was it all just one big Hollywood-Movie-Dame game, giving the detective the runaround, for caution, for kicks?

You did this, you did this, you did this—

Tucci remained on the outskirts of the garage lights, waited until she'd moved into the semi-illumined courtyard before he emerged, stood in her path. Her head down, legs pumping, she didn't see him until he spoke her name.

"Tara."

She jumped, exhaled heavily. "Dammit, Mike, you gotta stop popping up like a jack-in-the-box—"

"He's dead, Tara." She was about to mouth *Who?* but he kept on. "Omeed Madani. Gone. Stabbed like Marika Javid."

There was nausea in her eyes. Color left her face. Whether due to the news of the death, or her looming conviction, he wasn't sure. She kept walking. He followed. She wasn't going to strut away, if that's what she was thinking. She wasn't going to ignore this. Ignore him.

"You don't mind if I go up with you, do you?" he said. "I'm the one standing between you and a fucking cell."

He thought he heard her grumble, as if she didn't believe him. But she seemed to acquiesce to his company. They climbed the stairway in silence, and in minutes had entered her apartment, where she tossed her bag on the couch and stood to face him, lips stern, eyes hard.

"We have a recording of you two, talking," Tucci said. "In Farsi." He shook his head, unhappily. "Geez, Tara, you never cease to amaze me... but in the strangest ways."

Tara stared at him. "You don't understand, Mike. You don't know, you just don't know."

"I'll tell you what I *do* know. I know Marika was murdered in an honor killing, by a family member. For something she did that got their caftans all twisted up. But where are you in all this? And then I think—the ad. In the newspaper. Your secret P.O. box. And I put it together. You see the ad, you contact the family, tell them where their long-lost dishonorable daughter is. Not only do you get a nice payoff, you also eradicate your competition at the hospital."

As he spoke, she bit her lip, stood there with her arms crossed, eyes glazed but fierce. Admittedly, this first-draft theory did not click in Tucci's mind the way he would have liked—or not liked; its holes were Tara White's saving-fucking-grace. He could not account for the HR records of her mostly Middle-Eastern interviewees, for instance. Unless that had been a way to draw Marika out, perhaps, to reel her in. He needed only to feel around, press certain places, squeeze out the right stuff eventually.

"Mike," Tara said. She closed her eyes. Twitches and trembles in her expression; her face was a surface weakening, caving, under the piling weight of emotion. Tears leaked down her cheek.

Tucci had an impulse to touch her. There was a Tara he adored, never wanted to upset, and he wanted to embrace that one, to hold that one, but that Tara was now cast in the one he wanted to dismantle, even destroy.

"You're right. I am responsible for Marika's death. But… not like that. Not in the way you think."

He crossed his arms. "Like what, then?"

CHAPTER ELEVEN
Garsbon, Illinois
2001

ANOTHER ONE WAS COMING. Would be there by the time she got home from school, they'd said. A girl about her age, they'd said. Tara could see them now, Mom and Dad seated at the kitchen table next to this new person who, at present, was nothing but a shadow in her imagination. This new girl was also a teenager, apparently, and had come from one of the Arab countries, which Tara knew pretty much nothing about.

This could all be either really cool, or really lame.

The day's final bell rang. Tara strapped on her backpack and joined the raucous laughing, teasing, running, stumbling crowd. Winter still held firm in the air, but the days had definitely grown warmer, at least hinting at spring. Milky clouds stretched across the sky, faintly tinted by a promising blue.

Nothing but sun, she thought, *when I make it to California. Only one more year.*

Well, a year and a half. Things looked good, grade-wise. Decent extracurriculars, too. There was still the SAT, but if she didn't screw around, it wouldn't be too big a deal. Dad could help her with the verbal stuff.

She made her way across the rolling front of the school, down the road curving out toward the rest of Garsbon. The wind picked up, cold slicing through the pines. She walked faster, heating her blood, brain thinking, wondering.

A new addition to their life. Even as she sometimes resented her parents for their openness, she ultimately had to admire it. And it did help keep things exciting around here.

The food was definitely bland. That was one of the few things she'd heard about America that appeared true. She hadn't heard much else, or had ignored and forgotten most of what she'd heard because of how far away it had always been, even if its distance, and its power, did give the country a warped romanticism.

Her father had sometimes grumbled about America, even though he loved their films. Particularly films with that one toothy actress whose name she couldn't remember.

But America was now here, unfolded around her, the apex of this terribly surreal journey, which in hindsight was more like a fever-dream. Somehow she had made it. Somehow, through Omeed's deftness, she had made it as far away as possible from her father's hand, to this country, to this state, this house, this kitchen, this turkey-mayonnaise sandwich in front of her, and the genteel woman serving it.

"Our daughter Tara should be home from school any minute," said the mother, whose name was Allison. "She's about your age. I'm sure you two can learn a lot from each other."

"Thank you," she said, smiling.

The father, a stout, thin-haired man named Robert, sat next to her at the kitchen table, which stood in the silver light of a window looking out upon wintry trees, clustered in white fields. At their feet was the family dog Thumper, stringy-haired and reddish-brown, head resting on his paws.

"When Tara gets home she'll have to show you her horse," Robert said. "We got a couple horses on the farm. Tara used to ride in competitions when she was younger." He said this with a tint of regretful nostalgia, which roused Allison.

"She got busy with school, Rob," Allison said. "She got into other things."

They showed her to her room, which shared a bathroom with Tara's. Once belonging to a nephew of theirs who'd since moved out, they had since converted it into a guest room, which they told her she could "decorate to however she saw fit."

Mid-afternoon, their daughter Tara arrived. A beautiful girl, Tara fit a kind of exotic mold of American, her chest-length hair a wheaty blonde, her eyes a soft blue contrast to creamy pale skin. More than anything, she sensed kindness in Tara, and felt an instant affinity toward her.

Tara hugged her in their introduction, unexpected though very pleasant, even if the gesture felt forced.

"My parents didn't scare you away?" Tara said, with a smirk.

"No," she said. "They've been showing me the house. It's beautiful."

"That's a new one," Tara said, pouring a glass of orange juice. "Do you want some?"

"No, thank you."

"Tara," said her father. "I told her you'd introduce the horses."

"Can I ask you something?" Tara asked.

She looked at the blonde girl expectantly, inviting her to continue. They were sitting in Tara's room, Tara on the bed, while she sat straight-postured on the edge of the desk chair.

"Why don't you wear that scarf? Don't Muslims and stuff wear those things around their head?"

"Not anymore."

"You mean, you don't?"

She shook her head. "No. It's called a hijab. And I don't wear it. Anymore."

"Why?" Tara asked, then said, "Nevermind. It's none of my business. To be honest, though, I always thought those were weird. Why do they cover themselves?"

Despite recognizing the innocuous curiosity, she felt that she—as well as her family, her life—were suddenly under attack.

"The Prophet Mohammed's wives," she said. "They used to wear them. For modesty."

"Huh," Tara sad. "I hope I don't offend you. It just sounds kinda depressing to me."

She said nothing.

The phone rang. Tara went to get it. The blonde girl had her own phone line! She hadn't even had to ask for it—Tara's father installed the line to prevent any arguments over who was using it. She could never imagine her own father doing such a thing. Envy could not be denied, but Tara was a good soul, not to be resented.

A flush came over Tara as she spoke. The name "Pete" peppered the conversation. Her legs crossed. Her feet moved in circles. She fiddled with her hair.

"I can't talk too long," Tara said into the phone. "I'm hanging with the new foreign girl."

New foreign girl, her mind echoed neutrally.

Tara said goodbye, gently hung up. She bit her lower lip. "Sorry," she said. "That was my friend Jackie. She likes to blabber on. Especially about her boyfriend."

With a boldness that even startled her, she said, "You like him, too?"

Tara blinked, seeming to take it as an accusation. "I dunno." She paused, picked at her red fingernails. "I actually think he likes me."

"Oh, I see."

"What are they like where you're from?" Tara said. "Boys, I mean. Where is it you're from again? Iraq?"

"Iran," she said. "And boys are boys."

Tara chuckled. "Boys are boys. Did you have a boyfriend? Are you sending him letters?"

She swallowed. Was Hassan a boyfriend? Had he ever been a boyfriend? Boyfriends were non-existent. You were either by yourself or married, or about to be married.

"I very much liked a boy," she said.

Frowning, Tara said, "Liked? You don't anymore? What happened?"

She is rather intrusive.

"We weren't to be together," she said. "Our families forbid it."

"Wow, that sucks. Why? Was it like *Romeo and Juliet* or something?" Tara splayed a hand over her face. "Sorry if I'm being too nosey."

"It's okay," she said. She didn't know what *Romeo and Juliet* meant, but continued anyway. "He's... he's the reason I'm here."

Tara sat up. "That's weird. Why?"

She hesitated.

"I won't tell anyone," Tara said. "I swear."

"I'm sorry," she said. "I just can't."

Tara pouted a moment, this girl who always got whatever she wanted. Then suddenly, she broke out in an ebullient smile. "Maybe you need a diary! To write it all down."

The blonde teen hopped to a bureau and pulled something from a drawer—a book with a red floral cover, the pages of which were blank. "I have an extra one. You put all your most secret thoughts in it. And no one ever sees it but you."

That night, when she was alone in her new bedroom that had been decorated with fresh flowers and balloons and a welcome sign, she looked at the journal Tara had given her. She opened it, fanning the blank white pages within. She stared at them, as they beckoned her to tell her story. To empty her heart and soul.

She began writing.

She recounted all she'd been through—her long and painful journey here, her feelings, her fears, her anguish. It was cathartic, unleashing it on the page. It was no longer only sensations. In writing, the experience seemed to take on the aspect of a bedtime fairy tale, one of the stories with which her own mother might have once regaled her, those sprinkled with magic or djinns.

How do you know the spirits weren't there with you? You're here, after all.

Safe.

She drew quiet pleasure as she lay across the beautiful bed, writing of everything: sleeping in the streets, wounded and desperate; the divine intervention of Omeed; his taking her to the two men; the hills, the gunfire, the horses; those terrible wilds and the cold and the death of the healer and the meeting in Turkey with the man called Mahmet, to whom Omeed had sent her for his affiliation with an international adoption agency specializing in war orphans. She had gone to London after that, where she solidified a little more of her English.

Then, in a whirlwind, they had set her up to be sent across the world.

When thinking about how little she knew of the details, whether or not any laws had been broken, or how traceable they'd made her journey, it unsettled her, brought back a sense of vulnerability.

But I'm here now. I'm okay.

For now.

She fell asleep, clutching the diary to her breast, inches from her scar which, alongside these pages, was now the only evidence that her father ever existed.

In the morning, Tara softly rustled her awake. She sat up, put the diary down beside her.

"Did you write in it?" Tara asked.

"I did," she answered.

Yet Tara did not know, could never know, that she'd woken up in the middle of the night and gone to the bathroom, still clutching the diary. That she had read what she'd written and cried for what felt like an hour. That she'd torn out every page she'd scrawled upon and she'd ripped up all those pages, every tattered memory, and flushed the pieces down the toilet. And that only whiteness now filled the diary-book, just as when she'd received it.

"Maybe one day you'll let me read it," Tara said. "Do you think so?"

"Maybe," she said. "I don't think it would have happened if Allah had intended otherwise."

Tara nodded. "I kinda feel that way, too, I guess. Of course, not everything that happens is God's intention. But He probably goes to extra effort for special people."

A flutter in her chest. Special people? Was she a special person? Why was she special? She had deserted her family, dishonored her father. Abandoned her home country. Was that the specialness of it?

"It's so awesome that you're here," said Tara. A daze came over the girl's aqua-blue eyes. "Can I be totally honest? I know this sounds crazy, but... part of me is almost jealous of you."

She blinked. "Why?"

"It sounds dumb, I know. But you've come from another world.

Had an adventure. So secret that you can't even tell anyone. It sounds so exciting. But me? Ugh. Garsbon is so freaking boring, you have no idea. We're totally whitewashed here."

She was confused about the term.

"Whitewashed. Just means dull, bland. One color. One big sweep across it all. I dunno… sorry, I just can't wait to bust out of here. Two more years."

Why on Earth would Tara be jealous of her, with all she had? Why couldn't people like this girl appreciate every day, the things and people around them? Why couldn't that be the thrill, that rush of knowing one is loved, and loved forever?

Their conversation was interrupted by the call to breakfast.

It was a warm day for winter, bluer than normal, though the snow still claimed the land, the roads littered with slush. Tara rode up in the passenger's seat, she in the back. The mother, Allison, was driving.

"I think Garsbon is probably much quieter than what you're used to," Allison said to her. "Or than what you might have thought of America. We're not New York or Chicago or Los Angeles, that's for sure. But what we lack in size, we've got in heart."

She watched Tara who, slumped against the headrest and lost in the passing fields outside, added nothing to her mother's words.

They rolled down Main Street, which was arrayed with only a few cars and even fewer people, all walking about or sitting in front of stone and brick buildings. The orbed lampposts looked like perfectly-formed snowballs. She had seen these kinds of places in movies and on television, and now felt like she herself was the star of some movie, playing all around her.

At one point, Allison drifted over to the curb, stopped. She turned to her daughter. "Want to drive the rest of the way?" No response. "Tara?"

"Sorry, what?" Tara said, wrenched from daydream.

"Do you want to drive?"

"Oh," she said. "Yeah, sure."

She watched this exchange between mother and daughter, wondered why Tara was so unenthusiastic about driving. Wasn't she itching to drive to California? Within two years, was it? Maybe that was the problem. Driving with limited freedom was too much of a tease.

Mother and daughter switched positions, Tara sitting rigid and small behind the wheel. The car lurched forward.

"Remember the signal," Allison said. Tara clicked it on. *Tick—tack—tick—tack—*

They rolled back onto the road, Allison offering comments and compliments. At stop signs, Tara broke sharply.

"Ease up on the brake," said Allison. "Remember."

As they continued, Allison divided her attention between driving tutor and tour guide.

"There's the high school," Allison said.

They passed a long green field—*For American football?*—and several stark white buildings rather bereft of soul. At the entrance stood a crooked marquee with *Garsbon High School* written in bulky red letters.

"That's where you'll be going in a little while," Allison added.

She dwelled on this idea. Going to school in America. Never before had awe and terror been so seamlessly conjoined in her breast. Doubtless she would learn many, many new things.

As if heeding this resolve, when they returned, Robert took her aside and, in a quieter tone—perhaps unsure she would want Tara and his wife to know—said, "This came for you today." He presented a letter addressed to her in scratchy handwriting. She thought she recognized it. Her breath stopped.

"I thought maybe you'd like to open it in private," he said.

She thanked him and adjourned to her room, closed the door. Even locked it.

They know where I am.

No, she realized. The letter was from Omeed. Unfortunately, that still did little to comfort her. That anyone on that side of the world knew where she was bothered her, though it was inevitable.

I pray this finds you well, Omeed had written. *You are in no debt to me for my efforts. Your only responsibility now is to follow the path Allah has forged for you, the path almost thwarted by your father. You must figure out what that is. I cannot help much more beyond what I have already done. I believe your father suspects me of something, but is uncertain as to what. Rumors have circulated about you here. Neither your mother or father wish to speak much about it, but I believe they are saying you traveled elsewhere for schooling. Your father and I have ceased to work together. In separating our business affairs, he does not visit me or speak to me himself. From time to time I see your younger brother nearby, and I wonder if he might be watching me.*

Tears misted in her eyes. Shaheen. Seven years old. Watching behind the kitchen wall—the last she had seen of him. He was once sneaky because of pure and wonderful curiosity. She hoped her father was not exploiting that tendency of his, twisting him into a wind-up toy to do his bidding. Spoiling his innocence.

You should know, the letter said, *that I believe I have always seen in you something your father or mother never did. There is a light in you. It must avoid darkness, and run from it. I have done what I could. I did not do it to avenge your father for any perceived wrong, or even to appease what I believe to have been Allah's will. I did it because I believe in your strength and your spirit.*

Come the start of the spring semester, she enrolled in Garsbon High, her curriculum determined by specious placement tests in reading and arithmetic. While they put her in a standard mathematics class—geometry, in fact, which she shared with Tara—for English they placed her in a remedial course. There was some back-and-forth about her taking an English as Second Language class.

She felt her motivation at school came primarily from the newness of her environment, and the will to conquer it, to know its every side, to make the best of it. Had she grown up in Garsbon, she probably would be just as dulled as her classmates seemed to be.

Her presence on campus did not create as much of a ripple as she'd feared. The school had seen several foreign exchange students come through, and, according to Tara, was probably one of the more diverse "in the sticks"—"with all two of our black people," which she had added with a cynical smirk.

Tara's friendship, of course, was an invaluable part of her social acclimation. Over lunch breaks, she got to know Tara's friend Jackie, as well as Jackie's boyfriend, Pete.

"So we doing Aaron's party Friday?" Pete asked them one day as they sat in the cafeteria.

"Sure," Tara said, munching on chips, then turned to her. "That cool?"

She hadn't yet been to a "party," and was more interested in it academically. There was probably going to be drinking. She'd never had a drink. And dancing. She'd never done that, either. What was she going to do? She felt a mixture of excitement and dread.

"I could swing by and pick you all up," Pete said.

"Tara's getting her license this week, right?" Jackie said, bright-faced.

"Yeah," Tara said, "but I can't take passengers for a while."

She watched Jackie and Pete hold one another, noticed especially

Jackie's contented smile. And, despite the hundreds of kids around her, she felt a sudden, striking loneliness.

The party was not nearly as large as expected, which was fine with her. At Tara's side, she cautiously surveyed the plates of junk food and bottles of soda. Liquor made the rounds, too. Several people offered her a drink, but she declined.

She wasn't happy to see Tara pouring liquid from a flask into her party cup, but she kept silent.

Tara sipped, then turned to her and giggled. "This makes Garsbon a whole lot more fun." Her eyebrows lowered. "Don't tell my parents, though."

Music blasted from a boom box in the corner, and some of the boys played videogames in fits and starts and yelps on the couch. Others, including Pete, took their drinks outside, and were standing in a wide circle of laughter and smoke.

She asked Tara where her friend Jackie was.

"I think she and Pete had a fight," Tara whispered, dramatically. "Don't say anything."

Watching all these couples dancing—and kissing—she thought of Hassan. She'd only had one kiss with him. But Americans were different. If a boy and a girl liked each other, there was no hesitation. Maybe they didn't even have to like each other. It seemed as if they just kissed and kissed over and over, maybe did even more, just because it was the thing to do.

She decided to stay put on a lounge chair in the family room, watching the glazed guys pound and scream away at the videogame. Tara moved about, went outside for a while. When she came back her eyes were a little red. She looked excited, too.

"Pete is gonna take me for a quick drive," Tara said. "If that's okay."

"That's okay."

Tara smiled. "I won't be gone long. Promise."

This was not cool. What about Jackie? But never had Tara felt such excitement. And who was she to obey? Her boring moral side, or the one that craved adventure, some soap opera-spice (yeah, yeah, *shoot me*) in her life?

"Want to go for a drive?" Pete had asked.

That aggressive cuteness in his face, such a perfect mixture. It tickled her. Sure it was probably heightened by the drinks, but did that make it less authentic? Maybe she was just feeling her real self now.

Tara climbed into the passenger seat. The world floated, she and Pete no longer part of this flat country. They'd risen above it. Alone. Together.

This is not cool.

"I'm glad we'll get some time together," Pete said, starting the engine. "I've been wanting to talk to you for a while, but never got the chance."

The noise of the party receded, the dark country infinite around them, pimpled by town-light and starlight. The car sped from the streets into the more rural roads, passing clumps of forest. Tara shifted.

"I'm gonna be honest, Tara," Pete said. "I think you're fucking gorgeous."

Holy crap holy crap holy crap yes you are too yes I'll say yes yes I do yes—

Somewhere on the outskirts of town, Pete drifted over to the side of the road. Nothingness in all directions. They were truly alone now, but, instead of the heavenly tickle, Tara felt a twinge in her stomach and a desire to bolt from the car, to race across the fields and into the woods, because anything she might find there suddenly seemed far more preferential to what was now coming through Pete's words.

He shut off the engine. Crickets sang. "How do you feel about me?" he said. "Be honest."

Flushed, Tara stammered out a reply. "Pete, um…" She chuckled. "You know I think you're awesome."

"No, really, come on," he said, staring at her, arm draped over the steering wheel. He sounded increasingly belligerent. "Do you like me?"

Tara started to reply when Pete lunged and kissed her. A rush of contact like never before. Instantly Tara was sober, though knew another intoxication.

Wrong this was all wrong—

"Pete—"

No reply, just his liquored breath, a heated fog of food-smell, liquor and something else sickly-sweet. He kissed her again, harder and more persistent, his tongue angrily probing her mouth.

"Pete."

She wasn't ready for this and he wasn't listening. But what could she do? *Weakling,* she thought. *You know. And what is this? What are you? Spoiled little white-bread girl who can't even go against one stupid guy—*

"Pete, fucking stop, *please!*"

She shoved him back. He fell into his seat, struck his head against the window. He looked stunned. She wanted to apologize, but was too embarrassed. For too long Pete sat there and stared at her. She didn't meet his gaze, just glanced out the window.

Pete adjusted himself and started the engine. The car drifted back onto the highway, increasing speed. Tara was too ashamed to ask where they were going now, but she hoped, prayed, they were going to head back into town.

"Hey," Pete said. "I'm sorry, okay?"

Tara was quiet. They were approaching a curve.

"Tara?"

Pete reached over and put a hand on her thigh. The car swerved and she jumped, cried out. He looked at her, stupid and detached, and the car jerked again and suddenly there was no road but only the woods, and then there were no woods but the one tree in front of them, so plain in the headlights, and then there was a terrible rattling and shattering.

Then there was nothing.

Two Years Later

Sure this country was flat, but the flatness appealed to her. It reminded her of her liberation, that all directions beckoned.

She, however, had chosen west. Where the flatness actually stopped, apparently, where the earth rose in monumental twists, where some of the highest mountains challenged the sky.

Two years, Tara had said. Getting to California.

"Go," they'd said. She had to think about herself, her future. Of course that was the case. But two years removed from the accident, and Robert and Allison were still grieving. She imagined that, in some form, they would be grieving the rest of their lives.

They nurtured her the rest of the way toward womanhood, adulthood, and she tried not to burden them. But like Omeed, they knew she had a path to forge, and, she sensed, they hoped Tara might be forging it with her, helping her in any way she could, from wherever she might be.

Bent over the motel sink, she applied the first layer of bleach to her hair, combed through it and put in the second and final layer.

She ran the shower and gently flowed shampoo and cold water over her scalp, then tussled it dry with a towel and applied the blonde toner. Let it soak. Rinsed again. She looked into the mirror, not yet accustomed to her colored contacts, her eyes sky-blue portals in her face.

She went to the window, peered out over the Kansas darkness. Her rental car sat in the parking lot, awaiting the morning ride. How far would she go tomorrow? Certainly she wanted to get past the Rockies. But she wanted to see them, too. This whole trip, this whole transformation, was one big push-pull between the journey and the destination.

Enough journey, she thought. *I need destination.*

The journey, of course, would never stop. But there were at least smaller destinations that could satisfy her.

Like choosing a name.

The first name had been easy, but the surname? More difficult. She belonged truly to no family, no lineage. Not any longer. She'd started over. Reset herself. What was the term? Blanked over? Wiped over? Whited out?

Whitewashed, that was it. White. The color of erasure, of a clean slate. Yes.

Tara White.

CHAPTER TWELVE
Present Day

ROCKING SOFTLY ON THE edge of the couch cushion, arms and legs tightly twined, Tara looked almost like an autistic patient, lost in some mental maze.

From his seat on the arm of a lounge chair, Tucci studied her. It took effort to suppress the emotions now whipping through him.

"I'm the one he was looking for." Tears amassed in Tara's eyes. "He wanted to find *me*. To kill me. I am the daughter who dishonored her family. It wasn't Marika. It should have been me."

Tucci tried to maintain a stoic expression. In light of these revelations, he felt simultaneously closer to and estranged from her.

"I came to Los Angeles," Tara continued. "It was different from anywhere I'd ever known, and it may as well have been another planet." Tears trickled down her cheek. "I altered the name on my high school transcripts, and got into college and med school. Then, when I began making money as a doctor, I started sending some of it back to Omeed, to thank him. Repay him. For all he'd done for me. To this day, I'm not even entirely sure why he did it."

She paused, looked at the carpet. "Omeed was my savior. I can't believe he's dead now… because of me."

One thing of which Tucci was pretty confident: her honesty about this. She had the pale, self-aware demeanor—tinged with relief—of someone spilling the truth.

"The San Diego mailbox was a security buffer," she continued. "I was nervous about my address falling into my family's hands, which is… which is I guess what happened. Omeed came to warn me. He told me my father died recently. Upon his death, the task of restoring honor to the family would have passed to his son. To Shaheen, my brother. Shaheen didn't come for Marika. He came for me. To carry out the task that eluded my father. All those years." Tucci perceived in her distant gratification. "To clear the outstanding blemish on the family name."

For the first time during his visit, Tara looked directly at him, eyes red, face tear-stained.

"And now, you know," she said.

Tucci peered at her.

"Take out your contacts," he said, face hard.

Tara blinked, recoiled a little. "What?"

"Tara…"

Then, moving slowly, she lowered her head, dabbed her eyes and removed two blue-tinted contact lenses to reveal deep, earthen irises now glistening before Tucci.

His gut tightened.

"It's so fucked up when you think about it, right?" Tara said. "It's worse to know your daughter held hands with a boy than to fucking *murder* her. Somehow, killing your own daughter is not the dishonorable thing. 'How's your little girl?' 'Oh we caught her kissing a boy, so we had to stone her, stab her, bury her,' 'Oh, I see, too bad—anyhow, what's for dinner, my darling wife?' My father—the whole custom—knows no fucking logic. It's just…"

Tara's whole body hiccuped, convulsed. She sniffled, sniffled harder, as the tears traced rickety paths down either side of her nose, reddened now with the rest of her complexion.

Quickly, Tucci checked his silenced phone. A voicemail awaited him. Bashir, probably. No, wait. Unknown number. He put it away. Later.

"I was supposed to die that night," Tara said. "Shaheen wanted me. Marika was caught in the crossfire. It's a weird feeling, a terrible fucking feeling. You're in the crosshairs your whole life, then… when the trigger is pulled, the bullet misses."

"Jesus. He was after you…" Tucci regretted having mistrusted her so. Even if she had lied to him. She could have been the limp body he and Bashir presided over that early morning at St. Vincent's. Their living flesh never would have touched.

Tucci went and sat by her, warming back up to the idea of touching her. Instead she initiated contact, placing her hands on his knee, resting her head on his shoulder. He reached over to the end table and plucked a tissue for her.

For long moments they were silent. Tara spoke again.

"Everything I've done, I've done because of those crosshairs. As a means of security, as a way of, I don't know, proving myself. We all know we're going to die, but not many outside the woods and the battlefields have a form of death they know has eyes on them. It was my death. I had to outrun it. I had to do the most with my life that I could. Too many days it was overwhelming, what to do. What to cram in, in case I opened my eyes or the front door and he was there. What to leave behind. Who to leave behind."

"Almost make it sound like a good thing," said Tucci.

"I don't know," Tara said, wiping her nose. "That's what you have to do. Embrace the whole life-death paradigm, I guess. Always know it's there. I don't think you're truly happy if you willingly ignore or try to forget about death. I think you're most happy if you're always aware of it and it becomes as close and real a thing as the air you breathe. And so you're constantly facing this natural tension, constantly you're understanding and knowing you're in fact still able to draw breath, that you haven't shut off. Sorry, I'm rambling."

Tucci crossed his arms.

"What I need to do," she said, "is let it happen."

"What?"

"I need to face my brother," she said. "I need to face the idea of my brother."

Tucci's own words came back to him: …*you don't spend healthy days waitin' on the flu. Flu's gonna come, it's gonna come.*

"I'm going back to work soon," she said.

He didn't reply.

Tara's hold on him tightened. A fresh wave of tears moved through her, breaking her voice. "Marika," she uttered, then, less audibly, "Marika."

❧

This man, this man he knew only through two photos and a few golfing anecdotes, seemed to anticipate his arrival. When Tucci entered the hospital room, the man rushed from his bedside seat to greet him, as if hastening to buffer him against the sight of the patient now lying only feet away, motionless head propped by two pillows.

"Mike," said the man, shaking his hand. "You're Mike, right? Danny's boy? I'm Rich. Rich Cosgrove. Not sure if your dad ever mentioned me, but like I said in my message, we're Eagles golfin' buddies—"

"I know… I know of you," Tucci said.

Ill-postured with sagging skin and heavy eyes, Rich was markedly older than his father.

"Thanks for calling, Rich," said Tucci. "Were you the one who called 911?"

"Actually, it was my wife. She'd just made this casserole your dad loves. We invited him to eat at our place, but he said no. So she decided to take him some leftovers." Rich slowly shook his head. "I don't know if you've noticed, but with us he's been… not himself. Been about a week or so now. Didn't feel like playing our last round. Didn't return calls. I know he gets bees in his bonnet, things he plays with or whatnot, but when I talked to him last, he was real sullen, like he knew something bad would happen. You know anything about that? You see that?"

Olin—

Tucci gave a long, gutteral sigh. "Yeah… um, I've been up to my neck myself—"

"You're a cop, right?"

"Detective, yeah."

"Wow." Rich looked at the comatose form of Dan Tucci, hoses running in and out of him, machines at his side keeping cold electric vigils. "Well anyway, like I said, after dinner we thought we'd bring him leftovers. We know he loves to eat, that guy. Not gonna turn that down, even if he turns us down. But my wife Jean—she's in the ladies room right now—and I go over there. Knock a few times. Call him on our cell phone. Jean goes around back and peeks in the kitchen window, sees him lying there in the doorway. She bellows out to me, gets on the horn to 911. It was a stroke, they said. Not the bleeding kind, so I guess, I don't know… I guess that's sort of good." Rich lowered his head. "Sure sent him down for the count."

Cautiously, Tucci knelt by his father, stared at the closed, unknowing face.

"Will he be okay?"

"Doctor'll be back around," said Rich.

Tucci couldn't tell if the man's hesitation came from true ignorance or his unwillingness to be the full bearer of bad news.

For another hour, Tucci sat there. He met Jean, Rich's wife, who gave him a hug, half-heartedly reciprocated. She related her own abridged version of Rich's account. The doctor came in, a sharp-faced Asian man named Dr. Bao, who shook Tucci's hand and told him about the immediate surgery, the benefit of which, he explained with forced emotion, might be marginal, given how long his father might've gone before Jean spotted him.

"I'm sorry, but there's a good chance he's sustained a significant amount of brain damage," said Bao. "With any kind of stroke, the longer you go without treatment, the greater the chance of permanent injury. Then again, there are patients who do recover."

These faces, these words, these consolations, the hugs, the shakes… none of it reached Tucci. His exterior was that of a dull mannequin. His shell left to auto-pilot, as he shut himself deep, reran the same image, over and over. The image of the man. The image, slightly modified, that his father had seen that afternoon, not two weeks ago.

He decided he was going to blame Olin for this, whatever the actual circumstances. The cocksucker's little visit had sent Dan Tucci on his downward spiral. Tucci knew this was an instinctual reaction, but son of a bitch, it was the right one and no amount of internal back and forth would change his mind. The stroke could have been destined. It could have been twenty years of cheeseburgers and food like Chago. It could have been financial stress. It could have been a scary movie. It could have been God. It could have been all such things, but it was really just Olin. The fucking mouse.

Donned in gym wear and a basketball under one arm, he crossed the front yard, much of him detached from the present moment, even uncertain as to whether or not he was really living this moment. The world had become slippery, uncontainable, out of control. Even the anticipation of seeing Charlie, something that normally made for an escape, was now tainted.

Because of you.

Alex wasn't out on the porch. Tucci approached the house and rang the doorbell. A fumbling, shuffling inside, a distant "Coming!" from Charlie's thickening vocal cords.

The door opened. Charlie wore a Clippers jersey and long black shorts. "Hey, Mike."

"Hey man." Tucci tried to smile as wide as he could, regardless of how forced and fake it felt.

They walked the two blocks to the neighborhood park, Tucci occasionally dribbling the ball en route as they spoke sparingly about sports or school or the kinds of courses Charlie planned to take in college.

Approaching the park, they spotted an empty half court. Charlie snatched the ball from Tucci and bounded toward the open basket and, with exaggerated flips and kicks of his limbs, missed the layup. He shot it again from within the faded key and made it.

"Bit rusty?" Tucci said, as Charlie passed him the ball.

"Yeah, whatever," he said. "Just worried about mom. Ever since Alex left, she's been in a mood."

"He left?"

"No calls, nothin'. She's bummed. But she'll be okay."

Tucci suppressed a gut reaction. This was *his* fault. He knew. "I hope so."

"Yeah, her and men. You know."

From the three-point line, Tucci launched a wayward arc that went nearly a foot wide.

"Talk about rusty," Tucci said.

They played for a little over an hour. Then, with sweat-soaked shirts and heaving breaths, they walked back to the house. At the gate

Tucci was just about to ask if he should say hi to Charlie's mother, when the kid snapped his fingers and pointed at him.

"Crap," he said. "I forgot. You know a guy gave me something this morning at the bus stop. Something for you."

A thin layer of frost spread instantly through Tucci's breast.

"What is that?" Tucci said. "Who was this?"

"Hold up," Charlie said. He trotted toward the house, entered the front door where, within sight, he took his backpack from the coat hanger and riffled through it. Tucci walked forth, trying to quell the ominous sensation brewing in him.

Charlie trotted back with an envelope in his hand and held it out for him. "Here."

Tucci took it. No postage, no return address, not even a proper recipient address, just *Mikey Tucci* it read, in rickety handwriting.

A lump formed in Tucci's throat.

"I dunno who the guy was," Charlie said. "He was big and white and bald. He said he was a friend of yours."

He recalled his father's description of the man who'd visited him. The man who'd frightened him so. The man who, who —

"Everything okay?" Charlie said. Though Charlie's naturally moist eyes always made him appear more emotional than he was, visible and genuine worry haunted the boy's demeanor.

"It'll be okay," Tucci said, half-aware he'd not properly answered Charlie.

The boy studied him with a mixture of childhood trust and burgeoning young adult cynicism. "I hope so," he said.

Tucci slipped the envelope into his gym shorts pocket and didn't bring it out until he'd returned to his car and driven two blocks out of sight of Charlie's house, where he pulled over and opened it. Inside was a blank tri-folded paper in the center of which, written in the same familiar scrawl, was a singular phrase: *Nice try.*

Tucci closed his eyes, gritted his teeth. He craved desperately to inflict more violence on this single sheet than just balling it up or shredding it. With one hand he crinkled it, then pounded it repeatedly against his thigh, over and over, creating a gratifying pain in his leg that was also frustrating because it wasn't painful enough.

Losing control, whispered a voice in him. *You're fucking losing control.*

He sat for a moment, collecting himself.

So take it the fuck back.

⁂

It was likely the first time he'd ever felt warm in an exam room. Shirt stripped, Tucci sat hunched on the edge of the padded table, Tara behind him, her hand placed on his shoulders as she scrutinized his odd skin protrusion.

"It doesn't look like it's grown," she said. "That's good. But you can never be too careful."

"For sure."

She slid her arms diagonally around his torso, embraced him. Held him. He laid a trembling hand on hers and for a short while they remained like that as the late hour ticked on.

"I'm sorry, again," she said. "About your dad. I hope he pulls through."

"Me too."

Soon Tara resumed the business at hand. "I'm going to swab the area," she said. A dip-glunk from the alcohol bottle. Then a dab, light rubbing. "Then the epinephrine."

She prepared the syringe. There was a weird glee in her as she worked. Tucci imagined it having dwindled over the years, maybe even to the point where she didn't know it was there.

"You don't have to let me know every step," he said.

"I know," she said. "Force of habit." Needle full and ready, she hovered over Tucci's shoulders. "Sting coming."

She stuck him. Heat, fierce and localized, grew.

"It burns a little," he said.

"Yeah. That's the pH of your skin reacting to the solution."

"Thanks for telling me."

The numbness set in.

"Can you feel that?" she said.

"What?"

"I'm poking the area with the syringe," she said. "Checking for numbness."

She could just slit my throat right now.

He took in a fast, heavy breath. Hopefully, that was one of the last of these paranoid thoughts.

Hopefully.

Suddenly, he thought of Marika Javid and the scar on her breast, the possible biopsy, for which no record had been left. He realized that Tara wasn't making this particular appointment official: no forms signed, no paper trail left.

"Do you do this often?" Tucci asked.

Tara's brow furrowed. "What's that?"

"Behind-the-scenes medical treatment?"

Tara gave an odd smile. "Only for VIPs."

"I see." He felt a hard press against his shoulder. "What's that?"

"I thought you said not to explain every step!"

Tucci chuckled. For another minute, she worked in silence. Tucci tapped his fingertips against one another. There was a simmering in his gut. Stupid nerves. Probably it was some holdover childhood fear of the doctor, simple. He always registered higher blood pressure in his physicals.

Strange—he had shouted down, lorded over, beaten up those

who took lives, but twinged in the presence of those who saved them.

Tara showed him a scalpel.

"We're ready to cut the sucker," she said.

"Tara, thanks so much for coming."

Coming? Or coming back?

Tara took a seat on the other side of Dr. Parsons' marbled desk. She moved the chair around so it was parallel to the wall, the entrance now visible with a flick of her head.

Dr. Parsons smiled at her but the smile, lonely on her lips, had little effect on the rest of her face, which was tight and dazed. She now wore greenish eye-shadow, and a red streak divided her bob cut. Fashion advice from an interplanetary magazine.

"It's so nice to see you," Parsons said. "I hope you were able to recuperate some."

"Some," Tara said. "Got quite a backlog."

Parsons snorted. Mocking sympathy, if such a thing existed.

"I wanted to bring you up to speed on something," Parsons said. She reached into a drawer, brought out an item resembling a garage door opener on a lanyard and handed it to Tara. "As part of the new system, Mr. Stanton commissioned the implementation of these security pendants. You wear them around your neck. They send out a signal every three minutes to update your position to a central source." She pointed towards it. "You'll notice the black button. Any trouble, you press that and it'll summon security. If need be, God forbid."

"Sounds like you've spruced things up."

"Well, it's been a long time coming. Sprucing. I guess you can now say we're officially spruced. We can't be prepared for everything. Obviously someone like you ought to know that. But we can take as many preventative and precautionary measures as possible."

There was sales-pitch desperation in Parsons' voice. Trying to convince her to stay for good? Tara wasn't sure. Probably the sales-pitch was directed inward. *Why was it that speaking to someone else made our bullshit far more legitimate to us?*

"It's not the greatest welcome back gift, I know," said Parsons, "but hopefully it'll make St. Vincent a safer place than the papers have recently speculated."

What about outside *St. Vincent's?*

Undeniably, there was gratification in returning. Despite being the site of bigoted protests and petty politics, despite all of what was happening having started here—*No,* Tara thought, *it started when you kissed Hassan*—coming back to St. Vincent's was a little like returning to the island on which one had just been stranded, after weeks futilely braving the open ocean. There was a sense of custom here. A sense of duty. A twisted sense of home.

Her second day back, Tara spent several hours in the OR with a prostate cancer patient, a Wayne Reynolds. One of Marika's.

In the Iranian borderlands, Tara had watched the man remove a bullet from the other's leg. Since then, the interior of the body held quasi-religious fascination for her. It was another world, taking cues from some schematic beyond (daresay another intelligence?) working in removal from the chaos of the external world—until a bullet, or something else, disrupted the harmony.

Tucci peered up from his desk. Bashir was there, beside a forty-ish, overweight woman. Her eyes twinkled, nervous relics of bygone beauty.

"This is Melissa Jonson," Bashir said. "She wanted to see you about the Javid case."

"Hello," he said. She smiled wanly, shook his hand and sat across from him.

Bashir pulled up another chair, elbows rested on his knees, and leaned in.

"What can I do for you, Ms. Jonson?" Tucci said. "Do you work at St. Vincent's?"

"No," she said. "No, I own a small store, Greg's Market, just east of Culver City, toward Adams. I wanted to talk to you about my night cleaner. His name is Juan Delgado. He, uh… he isn't legal. I think he may have had a hand in killing that doctor. The woman doctor." She paused. "Then there was the other one, too. The old man? The other night. I saw it on the news."

"Yes," Tucci said. "What makes you suspect your employee?"

"Well, he looks like the man in the footage. I know it's hard to tell, but he does. They said he might be Mexican, the killer, right?"

Tucci nodded. "Go on," he prompted her.

"Juan lives in a motel near Hollywood, where they said that man was killed. And… well… I think I saw blood on his shirt the night of the man's death. Juan was late that night, too. But I don't understand, why would he be killing Arab people?"

Tucci's body sprang from his desk, even before his brain had digested the possibility of what this woman was telling him. Arabs posing as Mexicans. *Shit.* How could he have missed this? He'd mused on it when Carter Graham ranted about all the illegal immigrants and Muslim terrorists coming in through Mexico. But he hadn't given it another thought. How could he have let it go? The post-9/11 FBI dispatch had centered on members of al-Qaeda and other terrorist groups, of course, crossing the border, pretending to be Mexicans. Perhaps Tucci had subconsciously separated this phenomenon from the case at hand. After all, if groups of people had done it, why not just one person? And why would that person have to be a terrorist? They could have a far more focused agenda.

A personal agenda.

"Are you sure he's Mexican?" Tucci said.

"I—I assume so. His name… he speaks Spanish…"

He and Bashir took down all the relevant information, thanked Ms. Jonson, who appeared to not want to leave the station, then hustled to the car. They were hardly ten minutes on the road when a dispatch came in about St. Vincent's Memorial Hospital: shots fired.

Tara had not seen the sun all day and, by the time it had already gone down, she felt the lack of it. For the past couple days of her return, she'd been walled up in the concrete crate of her office, or the artificial sterility of the operating room.

Eight o'clock. The day passed and she remained at her desk, poring over endless forms and figures. Duty at hand. Good distraction even though it did not distance her enough. Not even surgery distracted her enough, which was dangerous to the patient.

Get the fuck out already.

A quarter of nine, Dr. Tara White collected her things to go, clutching in her hand her bottle of mace.

Eight minutes shy of nine, she boarded her elevator alone, closing her eyes, breathing hard, in, out, in, out, as it made its rumbling descent.

Three times during the elevator ride, she touched the security pendant, ensuring it was there. She nodded to several more faces, went out the lobby, trickled solitary toward the parking garage, feet a steady pulse on the cement. Eyes surveying the night, she noticed petty details—napkins strewn on the cement, a burned out lamp. She didn't know why these stupid things bothered her, but they did.

A car pulled out, lights splashing across the landscaping.

Tara ascended the incline toward her car. An empty plastic water bottle lay just under her bumper. *Lazy pricks.* There was a trashcan by the elevator not fifty yards away. Tara bent toward the bottle. Arrowhead Spring Water.

She stopped. Stared at it.

Leave the arrowhead alone, Raymond Stiles so cryptically told her.

Wrongness thickened the air.

She turned toward her car and he was there. Her heart contracted, her gut aflame. Peeking out from behind her sedan, half his face visible, just as when he'd tried to hide himself behind the kitchen wall all those years ago, when he was merely a nosey sneak, a curious child-eye wishing to see and to hear her confrontation with her father. His fingers curled. Nostrils flared.

Except there was no curiosity now. Only certainty.

Only duty.

"Shaheen—"

Hearing his name galvanized him. Without remorse, without thought, he charged. Flash of metal. Wild grimace. Primal eyes. Tara screamed for help, her voice careening across the garage. She unleashed a spew of pepper spray, but her brother anticipated it, jerked to avoid it as he sent the blade on a wild arc toward her, catching her arm which erupted in pain.

She dropped her attache case and she fumbled for the security pendant but he followed her gesture and ripped it from her, hurling it down the concrete. The blade found her again, ramming into her side, she feeling the potential fatality of it. Tara screamed.

Shaheen grabbed her by the waist and pressed the blade firm on her throat. Faces inches apart. Acrid breath mingling. She saw all the years accumulated in his eyes. Perversely, some distant part of her wanted to know about that time, his whole life, what he had done, had seen, in her long absence.

"Please, Shaheen!" she cried in Farsi. "No. You don't have to do this!"

"*Shut up*," he hissed.

Shaheen tore at her coat, revealing her butterfly tattoo. His eyes narrowed, but as he ran a harsh thumb over the colored scar, he smiled a tainted smile. Tara could feel the wetness of her blood beginning to seep out over the blade pressing deeper. Second by second her exhaustion grew, life dripping down her arm and down her side.

Over Shaheen's shoulder, a figure appeared. A security guard. One she recognized.

The guard shouted.

Shaheen flinched, looked furtively back. Tara, fending off pain and weakness, brought the spray to face-level and dispersed more. She caught some of the backspray and recoiled, coughing. Shaheen cried out, cursed her. After some hesitation, the guard ran toward them.

Tears down his cheeks, Shaheen flailed madly with the blade, maintaining a frantic buffer against attack. He cursed her again, fast, gruff.

The guard stopped, pulled his gun and looked at Shaheen. "Stop!" He fired a warning shot into the ceiling. "Don't make me do this!"

Disoriented, Tara stepped in and sprayed more, mostly missing again. The security guard trembled as he aimed the pistol. Shaheen whipped around, waving his blade wildly. He charged the guard, tackling him. The gun flew and struck a cement column and discharged a second explosive shot, shattering a car window. It skittered across the ground and was lost under another vehicle.

When Shaheen rose, the guard was on the ground, glossy-red hands covering a gut now blooming with blood. Shaheen's blade had found flesh.

"Do you see what you have made me?" Shaheen cried to Tara. "Do you see? You have made me a murderer! You killed this man!"

Tara grabbed her attache case and thrust it at his head. It popped open in transit, exploding in papers and files. He staggered, iron-hold still on the knife.

No.

Tara approached Shaheen from the back, clasped his throat in the crook of her arm, though she would not have the strength to keep herself there and her exact strategy remained unclear. Shaheen's thrusting weight was metallic, fastly loosening from her grasp. The blade slashed her thigh. *Fuck Oh Fuck Oh God it hurts.* She cried out.

Then, an even greater thunderbolt of pain as the blade plunged between her breast and shoulder, not far from her heart. She screamed and, wrenching away, aimed as best she could to send another spray directly into his face.

She needed more, though. She needed more and so took to her pockets… coins, papers… keys, could use keys… a shaft, what was this… a pen. Yes, a fountain pen. The one Stiles had given her…

Fly Free.

Her hand scrambled, blind, feeling for the right end. She popped off the cap and drew the pen from her coat and plunged it into Shaheen's left eye, penetrating the soft retinal tissue. Blood foamed up over the rim of the socket.

The scream, shrill and high, coincided with the approaching cry of police sirens. She pressed further, meeting tangled, goopy resistance, then stood back, leaving the pen hanging from the red mush. Shaheen dropped the knife. The sirens grew louder.

He fell to the floor, writhing, shrieking. In gut-wrenching moans that were half-sobs, half-screams, he yanked the pen from his mutilated socket and dropped it on the reddened cement. A rill of blood streamed down his cheek, dripping and pooling everywhere.

Torn and pushed in, his eye threw a dead askew glare at the underside of his skull. With his other, he regarded her. Tara grew limp.

"Sister," he muttered. "My sister."

Across the way, on the eastside of the garage, a car rounded the bend, drove up. Familiar. She'd seen it before but did not, could not, register the driver. Tailing them was a squad car, lights ablaze.

Then she knew. Tucci.

Shaheen extended a blood-dripping hand toward her. Part of Tara wanted to take it, to squeeze it, to hold it reassuringly like an older sister would to a brother in pain. She stood there, face wet, nose running. Bleeding. Bleeding. Breathing. Dizzy. Delirious. Nauseated.

Tucci and his partner bolted from their seats, standing guns-drawn behind their car doors. The accompanying officers did the same.

"Stop right there!" Tucci shouted.

And they screamed for him. Screamed for Shaheen. But he didn't acknowledge them, going once more for the blade, burning with duty to Allah and his dying father. They shouted again and Shaheen went for her and then a gunshot roared, Tucci grimacing, and then another gunshot, fireworks from all angles. Shaheen's abdomen burst forth in strings of blood and gore, and he fell for the final time.

"Tara!"

The detectives and officers scurried toward her as she slumped to the floor. The coldness of it felt right. Tara dry-heaved, her vitals shuddering, shifting.

Releasing.

The shaking would not stop. Pain had shuddered awake unknown or forgotten sections of her body. Head propped on his leg, Tara found it difficult to look directly at Tucci. Increasingly she imagined herself as a shell, that most of her, whoever "she" really was, had since left this realm.

All this is my doing, Tara thought.

"The security guard?" Tara asked weakly. "Is he… is he…?"

"He's stable," Tucci said. "I think he'll be okay."

In short, panting breaths, she said, "He tried to help me… Marcus… I think his name is Marc—"

Tucci tried to quiet her, "Shh, save your energy." He turned and bellowed, "Help over here! Quick! Now!"

Paramedics hustled over and loaded Tara onto a gurney. Accompanied by nurses, they wheeled her into the hospital, through the corridors. Tucci jogged alongside it. He grabbed Tara's hand. Her eyes met his. She tried to talk. Only a rasp of a breath remained in her.

"My family… they are all gone now." Faintly, she smiled. "Guess I'll"—she swallowed, welled up breath—"be leaving, too."

"No!" Tucci said. "You'll be fine. Gonna heal you right up. And I'll be here. I'll be your family."

No, she thought, eyes fluttering, closing. *Not that simple.*

Her body twitched, then lay still.

CHAPTER THIRTEEN

THE MINISTER SPOKE. SPURTS of God-shaped air, hollow as the comfort they were designed to bring. Tucci ostensibly watched the man speaking at the podium, but peered past him, as if into some other reality accessed only by his thoughts. In the corner of his eye swelled the enlarged, wrenching photo, framed by a wreath.

Can't be gone, he thought. *Can't be gone.*

He barely listened as the minister droned on. He couldn't help himself. Going over the crazed events of the last few weeks that had led to this. Could he have done more? Could he have prevented it? Could his actions have caused it? Or was it his inaction that had allowed it, this death, this death that was way too soon? His brain signaled him to just stop—no more second guessing.

What's done is done. Pay attention to the service. To the minister. Celebrate the time you had together, not what's lost.

From beside him, a hand reached over, took his own. Tara looked at him with understanding. She squeezed his palm. Here she was, just out of the hospital, bearing multiple bruises, recovering physically and mentally from that fucked-up, horrific ordeal, yet she now comforted him. He gripped her hand tighter.

Fittingly, the service was set up in a secluded area of the Cloverdale Golf Course, where every week for nearly twenty years Dan Tucci and his "Eagles" had played a brisk nine-hole round.

An array of pine trees stood between the crowd and a quiet residential road. Past the podium, the ground swayed down toward the ninth hole, where breezes slanted the pin, thwapping the crimson flag.

Where is Dad now? Tucci thought. Probably hanging out here, a ghost-golfer, chipping ghost golf-balls. Now part of that spectral spectatorship Dickey ruminated about. *Hope it's a good time up there, Dad. Hope you're laughing. Hope all this stuff really is, in the end, a practical joke.*

The people from Chago—Dad's business partners—had spoken with Tucci. He would pick up his father's stake, but it was a hollow consolation prize.

"…we'll now hear from Daniel's son, Michael," the minister concluded.

The man gestured him up. Tucci nodded, rose, walked forth mechanically. He was going to have to speak. *Son of a bitch.* Somehow, he was going to have to keep his smarts, keep his cool.

You're all here because of a fucker named Olin, he wanted to shout, as so many eyes blinked back at him. But he didn't.

"Hello all." He cleared his throat, swallowed. "My dad crammed a lot into his years, for sure"—*You didn't thank them for coming, asshole*—"used to drive Mom crazy sometimes."

There's Tara, there's Bashir, their watching faces and there's a million more. "Dad used to say…" *What did he used to say? I'm forgetting.* "…'Lots of things in this world to do, so if you're going to do them, get them done fast, but make sure they're done and done well…'"

Yeah that's how he died, get it? Get it —?

"Thank you."

When he finished, Tucci returned hastily to his seat. An out-of-body experience, was what it was. His father split into those hundreds of eyes, many of whom Tucci didn't even know or remember.

Tara returned her hand to his, where it stayed for the rest of the service. Afterward, when crowds dispersed and engaged in gloomy talk, Bashir and his wife Najat approached him.

"I'm so sorry, man," Bashir said, offering a strong handshake, and a cursory greeting to Tara. Najat hugged him.

"Thanks for coming," Tucci said.

"Would you like to have dinner with us sometime next week?" Bashir asked. With some obvious cajoling from Najat, he added, "Both of you."

"I think I can do that," Tucci said.

"Sure," said Tara, with minor hesitation.

Tucci looked at her. She was rigid, a little uncomfortable. He didn't necessarily blame her.

"Everything okay?" Tucci said to her.

"Yes." Tara nodded, slowly. "Next week's just going to be busy, I think. But I'll make time."

Beneath her, all of Toby rippled, mane splashing, hooves pounding back at the hard elements that made them. They passed a hiker, but from there on out the coastal woods were their own, and the trotting turned to a methodical stroll.

Tara purposefully deviated from the trails she knew, following one she had always neglected because of its rusticness.

What if you never come back?

She turned Toby accordingly and they descended toward a whispering grove of eucalyptus trees. The canopy swayed in the wind. Toby snorted, pressed on.

Tara fell into meditation. She sniffed. Tears welled.

The trail led upward on another, familiar path, which ended in a waterfall she'd been to before. She noticed she could keep going, and the trail culminated in an even greater waterfall she had never known was there.

Tara gasped, feeling faintly like Magellan or Columbus here. First eyes on the New World. As attested by the spotty trail, she was obviously not the place's discoverer, but it was enough, in this day and age, after so many surgeries on the world's wonders, to *feel* as Magellan, or Cook.

She strode Toby toward the shrubs, dismounted and, on youthful impulse, threw off her clothes and slipped into the sharp, cold water. Shivers exploded over her skin, but it was a wonderful feeling.

She was *alive*. It was over. Finally. No more. She was alive and could be alive. She. Herself. Whoever "she herself" really was.

Head above the surface, hair fanned out like moss behind her, Tara swam, ecstatic with the thrill of the coldness. Red salamanders and tadpoles glided beneath her.

Getting out, she realized she didn't have a towel, and so stood in a patch of sunlight to warm up. She stroked Toby, hugged his neck, cried. When she was dry enough, she donned her clothes, then rode for another hour before returning, one last time, to the stable.

A strange evening, for sure. Sitting across from Bashir and his wife in their home. Eating Najat's homecooked Middle-Eastern delicacies, one of which included *tahchin*, the first meal she'd shared with Hassan. Najat's version did not taste as good, though Tara knew her memory was probably informed by titillating context.

They all knew now, Mike Tucci, Bashir—they all knew that such food, the culture around it, the lives and the histories around it, were also her heritage. She was as much Tara White as she was not. Paradox? Maybe. She could be both—for between names and labels stretched an ultimate, primordial freedom. Others knew these dual sides of her, but had come to see, as she had realized, that neither side defined her, only the person behind it all, the surface on which these identities were printed.

Back at Tucci's apartment, she was quiet and pensive. Words had exhausted themselves. Sheer thought and concern and all other attendants to language had exhausted themselves. She wanted only to sense, to feel. To be.

Tara took his hand and led him into the bathroom, his bathroom, as if she owned the place. She started undressing him. Tucci imagined his smile was goofy, but that was okay because Tara had a goofy smile too, and it was still fucking sexy.

His eyes strayed from hers to her butterfly tattoo, but zipped right back up, as if in shame. Her smile grew, and she lifted a hand to lamely cover the tattoo. Then she brought her other hand to her eyes and removed her two contact lenses. Her vivid blue eyes were now a rich, earthy brown.

Steam filled the bathroom. Tara parted the shower curtain. She rested one well-toned leg on the rim of the tub, then slipped inside, seldom breaking eye contact with him. Part of Tucci stubbornly believed he was watching something with which he couldn't interact, a movie or a lucid fantasy. Easy to dispel such a notion, though, by placing his hands on the elegant curve of her waist, then sliding them up to her breasts.

Tara gripped the metal bar overhead, and, to his surprise, indicated the handcuffs—his own—hanging there, which initially Tucci hadn't noticed.

"That was sneaky," he said. "How'd you get those from me?"

Tara didn't reply. Tucci joined her in the shower, slinking behind her. He ran delicate hands over her silken, wet form. He grazed the pinkish streak of the wound on her thigh, kissed the smaller one on her arm, then moved his lips to hers. Their tongues touched. He wasn't quite sure how to make a smooth transition to the cuffs—she liked that stuff far more than he—but he did it slyly enough, clasping her hands to the bar. She stood there, arms raised and bound like some sacrificial maiden.

She can't go anywhere.

He wrapped his arms around her firm belly, carefully entered her. She moaned, fake-struggled with her restraints. Though fully aroused, stand-up sex was exhausting for him. This was going to be a saga, an odyssey toward climax. But he couldn't be too concerned about himself. Now was all about her. All about her.

He uncuffed her and they moved to the edge of the sink, where Tucci's legs flared with cramps. The pain was okay, though, because of her immersive pleasure, which sustained him.

There was something transcendent of other times he'd been with her—a freshness, a release from the ravenous questions, a sense of something truly beginning, with all that went before an awkward prologue.

He picked her up off the sink and carried her toward the bed. They set upon the edge of the mattress, a writhing twine of damp flesh. He motioned faster. Faster. Her legs tightened around him. Drove him further. She moaned. Rising, a great upswell of imminent climax and then finally he came and they slowed to moderate rhythm, his body one big, gratifying ache.

They climbed further onto the mattress, lying close atop the sheets, breathing hard, the ripe, sweet smell of their bodies thick in the air.

They lay quiet, breathing, stroking gently, engines cooling. Tara was lost in the ceiling. Tucci, nuzzled against her shoulder, stared off toward the buzzing light of the bathroom, his touch running delicate over her skin, which was partially ravaged by Shaheen. His fingers were cartographers of her fine, hard form, tracing dips and curves, the perfect mounds of her breasts, smooth neck…

He came to her butterfly tattoo, in the middle of which was a bump, almost as if the body of the image were three-dimensional. Curious, Tucci dwelled there, until Tara removed his hand. She leaned forward, closer to his ear.

"It's your turn," she said, most of her words breath.

"My turn?"

She hopped off the bed, sprinted to the bathroom. He heard the *clatter-snap* of his cuffs. Inexplicable fear cut through him. He was aware of a portentous feeling coming over him, a prickly intuition.

Tara returned with the cuffs. She stood by the bed, lips fixed in a sultry grin. She was waiting.

"C'mon, put 'em up," she said.

"You'll have to force me," he said, trying to maintain his previous enthusiasm.

"Oh, detective," she said with relish, mounting him.

Meeting no resistance, Tara took his right wrist and clasped it to the bedpost behind his pillow. He flittered about with his other hand, challenging her to catch it, her hand the net to the butterfly. While mostly playful, when she did finally grasp his left wrist, Tucci felt a brief urge for violence.

Quietly, he acquiesced as she shackled him to the post.

"I like control, too," Tara said, straddling him once more. She leaned down and kissed him, sending a tickling heat through his insides. "But you know that, right?"

Admittedly, it was somewhat intoxicating, this helplessness before the beautiful woman now looming over him. She could do anything to him and he would have no choice but to succumb. He was a feather blown by her breath.

Yes, he thought. *She can do anything.*

As if in counter to this pleasant intoxication, that earlier intuition was now creeping into his intellect, finding logic. With it he grew more desperate.

Shimmying her body across his, Tara didn't seem to notice his preoccupation, even as his erection softened.

I like control, too.

She moved further up on him, angled her breast toward his mouth. He received it with his tongue, though his eyes probed the butterfly tattoo now hovering inches above his eyes.

"Oh my God," he cried, when she leaned back, her nipple wet and erect.

"You like that?" Tara said playfully.

"No," said Tucci. "It wasn't a fucking mistake. It was *you*."

She stopped, her brow furrowed in what seemed like genuine confusion.

"You did it," Tucci said.

Tara frowned. "What?"

"You…" Thoughts battered his skull. Tucci could feel the click of every synapse as they connected, forming this picture as much reviled as revelatory, both horrific and beautiful in its symmetry.

"You put Marika there," Tucci said. "Made it so she'd catch the knife and not you. You hired her… you searched for the perfect candidate to put in front of Shaheen, throw him off the track…"

Tara slid off of him. The zest of the last few moments retreated from her. Her face hardened.

"Marika had no family," Tucci said. "No real close connections. She was your shield."

His words hung between them, congealing.

Moving with cold determination, Tara began to withdraw from the bed. Tucci whipped out his legs and scissored her around the middle. Squeezed. She pushed on his thighs, her face calm, assured of his futility.

"Really?" she said, prying at his knees.

He squeezed tighter, squeezed with all his fury at her betrayal. *Crack a rib or two.* Tara struggled, her calm giving way to frustration, impatience.

"Let me go," she said. "Now."

Vice grip. Wind her. Crush her into oblivion.

In one snap gesture, she raked her nails deep across his inner thigh. Tucci cried out. His legs loosened and Tara freed herself, hurrying away from his reach.

She stood and looked at him. Her eyes were distant. Tucci's gut hollowed at the sensation that, even with him in the room, she'd already begun the process of forgetting him, that she might suddenly look at him the way she had the day he'd first approached her: as some strange, unwelcome intrusion.

"Tara," he said, pulling on his cuffs. How could two small wooden posts and a few metal links restrain 180 pounds of coarsened, primed flesh and muscle? It didn't seem right, more a typo in the laws of physics. "Tara, goddammit."

Still naked, she stood with her hands on her hips, her expression afloat in something like a daydream. That was too optimistic, though. More, she appeared neutral, the veil of her humanity crumpling down.

Finally, Tara met his gaze. Moisture built in her eyes. "You don't understand," she said. "You can't understand."

I was right. It was irrevocable—Tara had spoken, had confirmed his accusation. Tucci's chest twinged with the actual finality of it all. As nauseating as those seconds of detached silence were, he could at least delude himself that, maybe, Tara simply felt ill, or utterly appalled at his assertion. There'd still been room for doubt.

No longer.

"They would never stop," she said. "I'd been sending Omeed

money for years. To thank him for saving me. Not that he wanted it, I just needed to do it. But it would always go to him from some anonymous place. Some random destination I would go to just to mail it to him. But then I got a letter… about a year ago. Omeed wrote to me. He'd found me, and told me how they could find me, too. He wanted to warn me. He told me that my father had died, still feeling that onerous shame. And that in his last breath, he'd asked Shaheen to carry out his failure—his duty to restore the family's honor. I realized then they would never give up. Never." Tara closed her eyes. Swallowed hard. Then continued.

"I had to do something. To protect myself." She looked away. "I couldn't live like that the rest of my life. Waiting. Wondering. Always fearing they would come."

"So you hired Marika. So she could 'be' you."

"That was the start." Tara flinched. "It was just a precaution."

"Right. Of course. I get it."

Tucci's throat constricted.

"Detective," Tara said, her voice melancholic though dully edged with ironic humor. "You think too damn much."

Gingerly, she placed her hand over her butterfly tattoo and scar.

Tucci closed his eyes. He needed some kind of respite from seeing her. Deeper and deeper, her image bored a smoldering hole in him. "How did you get her to along with the biopsy?"

"I switched mammograms," Tara said.

Hesitantly, Tucci opened his eyes. Tara was scouring the room, setting sights on her clothes.

Don't you fucking leave, Tucci thought.

"I showed Marika someone else's," Tara continued. "Someone else's DCIS, *ductal carcinoma in situ*. Beginning stages. But it had to be in the right place. So the scar would be right. She wanted none of it to be known, of course. She was in line for a big promotion. So, as you might say, I gave her the 'behind-the-scenes VIP treatment.'"

He breathed, hard. "You… you saw your chance. You found a mammogram that would match your scar…"

"I looked at hundreds until I found the right one. I knew I would never be free until they thought I was gone. They would never stop, *never* stop, until they'd cleansed the stain on the family. My family, my brother, hadn't seen me in decades. Where else would he look for confirmation that it was me?"

Tucci thought, *What's to stop her from going into the kitchen or bathroom and pulling out scissors or blades and just finishing me right now? End this at me?*

"Tara, my God—"

"It takes a lot to fool death," she said. "Don't think I don't feel anything for Marika. Of course I did. Still do. We were friends. But sacrifices needed to be made. And I had to end it. Living my life in fear. I had to gain control. But you know that. I always need to have control." She looked at him, a distant smile drowning in her eyes. "Except maybe when I'm with you."

"So then you told them where you were," Tucci said. "You 'accidentally' put letters into their hands."

"I couldn't go through my whole life waiting. I'm not that strong."

"Jesus Christ."

Yes. Yes. He got it. Her trips to San Diego, the P.O. Box. Reward for Iranian Doctor. She'd communicated with her family in Iran, sprinkled the breadcrumbs. She had carefully lured them out here, lit the long fuse that would travel across the ocean and across the country, eventually culminating—exploding—at St. Vincent's.

To make them think they'd succeeded.

That they had secured her father's honor.

"Control, Mike." Tara shook her head, as if incredulous. "I had to." Then, softer, "I had to."

Officiously, Tara began collecting her clothes off the floor and dressing. The moisture had left her eyes. In her mechanical movement, she resembled less a creature of complex nerves and chemistry and more one powered by gears and machine code. Tucci watched her, partially stunned. This was a movie he was watching. An act. A dream. The unbearable reality of this whole situation had yet to fully sink its weight into him.

"Tara," he said. "Let me out of these."

She didn't reply, didn't look at him. Fully dressed, she left the bedroom. He tugged again at his restraints, putting all he could into it, but to what felt like mounting madness, nothing gave. He had visions of himself two weeks from then, a shriveled corpse, naked and bound like some abandoned dog. What if, like in Tara's apartment, a rat showed up? And then it returned with all its friends to gnaw at his skin and eat away at his face? Eat everything so no one would know it was he, Michael Tucci, who had allowed himself such a pathetic fate.

But was it not altogether fitting? Tara had used someone else as a buffer, a shield to protect herself. Had he not done the same goddamn thing with Olin and Alex? How much better was he? Marika was innocent. Yes, she'd been completely, helplessly innocent. In Tucci's circles no one was innocent, including himself. Sure, Alex wasn't in the same category as Marika, but still, because of Tucci, the man was dead. And Olin was still out there. But Tucci couldn't worry about him now. Now he had to worry about Tara. She'd tricked him. Maneuvered him. *How could he be so...*

Tara returned with a small medical bag from which she extracted an object of which Tucci, in his limited vantage, caught only glimpses—until such glimpses cohered in a numbing realization.

A syringe. Full of clear liquid. Whole areas of his body seemed to shut down. He couldn't swallow. A motherfucking needle.

"Tara," he said. "What the fuck is that?"

She ignored him. *Not even looking at me.* She popped off the cap, and the needle glistened in the lamplight like a tiny rapier. When Tara finally again turned and faced him, he knew no longer "Tara," but an empty human container, a mobile mannequin lacking any trace of compassion or memory.

Yet as she approached closer, needle raised, and as Tucci wrestled vainly with his restraints and as more light traced her looming features, Tucci saw—or desperately thought he saw—the Tara he'd known, quivering against its own restraints beneath this soulless, plastic shell.

Tucci started kicking, yanking, pulling. Tara recoiled, watched him with the annoyed patience of a schoolteacher waiting out a child's tantrum. The bed lurched a little from his weight, *scrape-squealing* across the wood floor. Too fixed and too strong, however; his restraints never gave. Tara rushed toward him and he brought his knees up and struck her elbow and hip. She cried out, though she didn't drop the syringe. *Goddamn bitch.* Yet more humanity evaporated from Tara's expression, a fleshly likeness of dry earth. Moving fast and forcefully, she bent over him. He spat at her and she whipped back, the saliva grazing her cheek. It didn't faze her much.

"C'mon, Mike," Tara said, tone edged in cold grave humor, "who's really going to win here?" She waited, still watching his fidgeting. In a flash of limb, she plowed a fist into his solar plexus and pressed, pressed, and in the shock and the ache Tucci's breath evacuated him like fleeing spirits. He groaned, stalling enough that Tara was able to swing herself onto the bed and straddle his stomach, clamping him to the mattress.

"You're worse than a child when it comes to needles, aren't you?" After a breath, she added, "I'm sorry, Mike. Please know I cared for you." She leaned closer, stared her gaze into his as if to emphasize her genuineness. "I still do."

In one snap of movement, Tara clasped her hand against Tucci's right bicep. She was forceful, both surprising and unsurprising, and she held him down. He looked away, not out of fear of needles, but out of refusal to see Tara doing this to him.

The prick of the syringe. The spreading tingling warmth of the drug through him, seeping, an encroaching eclipse of him.

What are you doing to me?

What—what —?

"Tara," he said, head rolling back toward her.

She was turned away from him, clasping her bag. The texture of the room became wavy, dreamlike. He could poke a finger in it, and the walls and the mattress might ripple like the surface of a pond.

"Tar—" he started.

Wavier. Hazier.

Where's Tara? She was no longer here. Fleeting shapes from the darker corners of memory and imagination flittered across his consciousness. Where am I?

Then—darkness.

He blinked. Blinked again. As with each swipe of a windshield wiper, every blink clarified the world, crystallized the images that, while fleetingly alien, were now becoming familiar.

A strange grogginess filled him, one that made him feel both heavy and light. He glanced over and saw his hands still cuffed to the bedpost.

Tara. Tara yes Christ Tara she—she—

She had drugged him. Yes. He breathed heavy and hard. His abdomen throbbed. *I'm fucking naked.* The key. He glanced over at the dresser, where the cuff key lay. Shifting his body so that his feet touched the floor, he began what felt as a nearly mythic effort to haul the bed across the room. Slowly he pulled it, wincing, groaning, the bed legs a squealing, gouging symphony across the wood.

He struck the lamp shining on the nightstand, and it fell and cracked and the room became dark. *Fuck.* Yet he was able to position himself within a leg's reach of the key, and with his left foot he scoured the top surface of the dresser until, touching small, cold metal, he swiped it onto the sheets.

Tucci felt almost simian as he pinched the key between his toes and the balls of his foot and tossed it toward his chest, where it slid down by his armpit. He had enough leverage to pick it up in his mouth and, turning, he drove it into the lock and turned and one cuff popped open. Quickly, he undid the other.

He rose from the bed and very nearly collapsed against a sudden onset of dizziness. He sat for a moment. Drug still wearing off.

Slowly, he stood up. How long had he been out? It was hard to tell, but the sun appeared to be out. A whole goddamn day? He couldn't be sure. He wanted a stiff drink, but was concerned it might upset some tenuous chemical balance in his system.

With mindful haste, he got dressed. He couldn't compromise himself any more than Tara had.

For the hell of it, he called her name.

Tingling silence.

She's gone. He moaned. *Forever this time.*

But...

But no matter Tara's head start, and no matter what stood in his way, Tucci would find her again. Somehow.

Somehow.

But for today, fuck it. He'd get dressed, then get the hell out of here.

EPILOGUE

THE SUNGLASSES. HOW TO properly utilize those. Without them, she felt too exposed, but she also knew that wearing them indoors sometimes drew unintended attention, like the shades-donned celebrities in Los Angeles. Who are you and why are you important enough to be wearing sunglasses inside? Maybe for her, the tight-wound hijab neutralized this oddness. Maybe, somehow, the two went together, reinforcing a vibe of Don't Talk To Me.

Concerns about airport security proved in vain. With only a single light carry-on, she trundled seamlessly through. Head cast down, she managed just as seamlessly to scurry through the current of people toward her gate. At any moment, she expected a clasping hand on her bicep. Any moment, the cry of her old, newly-abandoned name, the name no longer hers. Any moment. But it never came, and so suddenly she knew the finality of this change. It was real and willed. Something happening, something happened.

She visited the restroom. In approaching the sink, she stared at herself in the mirror as if her gaze might burn through the glass, peel away her reflection toward some other realm. The hijab—she'd not donned one in about twenty years, and this would be the last time she would ever wear one.

After leaving the restroom, she found the gate and sat by the wide window. Cold and gray outside, though miles away, toward the horizon, a silver ribbon of sun traced the clouds. A plane took off, another taxiing behind it, across the runway.

As she boarded her flight, she thought of Mike Tucci. She thought also of Hassan. He was a man now, somewhere, living a man's life. What was she doing? This was not a woman's life. Not even a proper person's life.

You're a murderer.

For close to half an hour they sat on the tarmac, lights bonging on, crisp-suited flight attendants charging up and down the aisle, contrasting the tired passengers scouting their seats. Some looked at her. One—an older Asian woman—sat next to her, but they shared no acknowledgment.

Let's go, she thought. Trapped. She was trapped. Not free. This was a prison, hundreds of judging brains surrounding her.

She wondered if she might be evil.

Tears came but she suppressed them. She fidgeted in her seat. Opened a book. Finally, the plane began to move, shifting toward the runway. Rolling. Sitting. Sitting. Rolling faster and then it was speeding forward, whisking to the wind all things on either side, and then it upturned and those things below—those people, those cars, those houses—were diminishing, becoming, she thought, like bugs she could playfully flick off the map.

She returned her eyes to the window.

Then the clouds whistled in, frosted over, and by the time it cleared again, she could see the crinkled blue of the Pacific. On the horizon lay the thin strip of the receding country, a country that, like her first, she would never see again.

There was something very affirming about walking barefoot in sand, which she realized she'd not done in years, despite living so long in

Southern California. It was a subtle sensation of groundedness, of being attached to and even wanted by the Earth, as opposed to some flimsy, windblown piece of debris.

She walked far enough down the coastline where she could no longer see people, where the hush of the waves overtook their voices and all other sounds. Her scalp remained in the cloth embrace of the hijab, fitted far tighter than the blouse and ankle-length skirt covering the rest of her body. In the village she noticed she'd drawn an eye or two; whether because of the scarcity of Muslims here, or that it was odd to see a Muslim woman walking alone down the narrow path, she could not be sure. But it didn't matter, especially not now.

She turned and climbed upon a small peninsula of slick, tide-lashed rocks. The water was clear enough to glimpse even the trembling silhouettes of smaller fish mobbing the corral.

Carefully, she navigated the peninsula until she reached the endpoint, as far as she could go without setting foot in the ocean, where she sat down and gazed upon the flat infinity of sky and sea. She felt the salty spray, tiny sprinkled kisses to her pores. She glanced back over her shoulders, where only the slanted palms stood nodding at the slight wind.

Then, with one swift gesture, she removed the hijab, unleashing to the breezes a firework of red hair that whipped about her shoulders.

Softly, almost tenderly, she threaded the hijab through her fingers. She would need it no more. It had dominated her first life, haunted her second. But this was her third life, stirring in its womb.

She considered also it was her first *true* life. This thought simultaneously brought ecstasy, dread and regret. She had much to compensate for; she'd had two long dreams and was just now beginning to wake, even as another aspect of her argued how much life she'd indeed lived compared to others, how many experiences she had tasted, how much good she'd done as a doctor. All valid, of course. Still, all of it felt like a fever-dream.

Almost on reflex, she held up the hijab between her thumb and forefinger and released it like a haggard bird upon the wind, where it fluttered before coming to rest on the swells of the sea.

The authors would like to thank you, the reader, for taking this journey with us. Creative artists and writers depend on their fans to help spread the word about their projects. If you enjoyed DISHONOR THY FATHER, we would appreciate your posting an online review.

ABOUT THE AUTHORS

MIKE ROBINSON is a novelist, screenwriter, and literary editor, based in Los Angeles. His novels include *The Enigma of Twilight Falls* trilogy, *The Prince of Earth*, *Skunk Ape Semester*, and *The Atheist*. More of his work can be found at www.mike-robinsonauthor.com.

M.J. RICHARDS is the pen name for the screenwriting team of M.J. Anderson & Richard Rossner. They are writer-producers of film and television with several movies and TV Series to their credit. M.J. wrote multiple episodes of *Friday the 13th – the Series* and is also an award-winning author, speaker, and playwright. Richard co-hosts several podcasts, including *The Dark Side Of* and *Unexplained Mysteries*.

Additional information about the authors can be found at www.DishonorThyFather.com